Holly Martin is the bestsell... ... ...
lives in a little whi... ... ...
at university, which led to a very glitzy care... a hotel
receptionist, followed by two even more glamorous years
working in a bank. She then taught for four years but escaped
the classroom to teach histor... ...
Viking one day and an Egyptia... ...
long journeys travelling aroun... ...
to plan out her stories and sh... ...
what she loves.

Follow her on Twitter @HollyMAuthor

ALSO BY HOLLY MARTIN

The Holiday Cottage by the Sea

HOLLY MARTIN

sphere

SPHERE

First published in 2018 by Bookouture, an imprint of StoryFire Ltd.
This paperback edition published in 2019 by Sphere

13 5 7 9 10 8 6 4 2

Copyright © Holly Martin 2018

A CIP catalogue record for this book
is available from the British Library.

ISBN 978-0-7515-7720-4

Printed and bound in Great Britain by
Clays Ltd, Elcograf S.p.A.

Papers used by Sphere are from well-managed forests
and other responsible sources.

Sphere
An imprint of
Little, Brown Book Group
Carmelite House
50 Victoria Embankment
London EC4Y 0DZ

An Hachette UK Company

www.hachette.co.uk
www.littlebrown.co.uk

To the lovely, supportive, inspirational authors at Book Camp.
You guys are amazing.

CHAPTER 1

As Tori Graham navigated her way down the tight country, cliff-top lanes, she caught her first glimpse of the indigo sea, glittering and twinkling through the trees, and she felt some of the tension in the back of her neck seep away.

She needed this break. Having been locked away in a darkened studio almost every day for the past year and a half, she needed to feel the sun on her face, the wind in her hair and talk to people other than plasticine models or her colleagues who she had worked with on the latest stop-motion animation film. By the time shooting had finished, they'd all had tiny squinty mole eyes from the lack of seeing daylight for months on end. The studio had almost become her home with the amount of time she had spent there, which had been much more preferable to spending the evening alone in her flat every night.

She needed a break from that too. Even with the TV and radio playing, the flat had been way too quiet. She had never considered her best friend to be the loud and noisy type, but since Melody Rosewood had moved out of the flat they shared in London, she had missed the laughter, the silly conversations, just the sound of her clattering around in the kitchen.

Melody had suggested a long overdue visit to Sandcastle Bay and it couldn't have come at a better time. Tori had missed her friend so much and she was looking forward to catching up with Melody, her sister Isla and their adorable nephew Elliot while she stayed here.

Melody had put Tori in touch with Emily Breakwater, whose family owned a fruit farm, and in return for help with some fruit-picking she was going to stay in Blossom Cottage for free. It was an idyllic-looking dusky-pink thatched cottage with views over the sea. It was going to be the perfect summer holiday.

Tori rounded the corner in her little sky blue convertible VW Beetle and slammed on the brakes because right in the middle of the road was a large sheep's bum. Several sheep bums actually. The road, as far as she could see, was filled with fluffy white sheep that seemed in no hurry to move or even remotely bothered that they had nearly been mint sauce under the wheels of her car. To top it off there didn't seem to be anyone with them, apart from a mangy old sheepdog who was fast asleep on the side of the road.

As the sheep moved lazily around the side of her car and then crowded around the back, effectively trapping her, she stood up and leaned over the windscreen of her car to see if she could spot anyone who might be in charge of this rabble.

As luck would have it, a middle-aged couple wearing bright yellow Lycra were walking towards her, pushing their bikes along the grassy bank at the side of the road. The woman was striding ahead of her husband who was huffing and puffing in her wake.

'Excuse me, do you know what's going on?' Tori gestured to the sheep, though that was obviously unnecessary.

The woman didn't even break her stride. 'It's Saturday,' she trilled as she strode past.

Tori stared at her in confusion. She said it as if it was the most obvious answer in the world. Tori waited for further explanation, though it was quite clear that none was coming.

'What does that mean?'

The man clearly thought this was a good excuse to stop. 'Everyone knows not to take the west road on a Saturday,' he shrugged, looking after his wife who had the word 'Mindy' emblazoned on the back of her neon vest. Tori wondered idly if her husband was Mork. Seeing that Mindy wasn't looking, 'Mork' slipped a toffee from his pocket and quickly popped it into his mouth.

'Well who's in charge of the sheep?' Tori asked.

'That'll be Trevor, he'll be having his lunch right now. I'm sure if you wait an hour or two, he'll move them along,' Mork said, still huffing and puffing.

'An hour or two?' Tori echoed, incredulously. Her carefully laid plans were starting to crumble. This kind of thing never happened in London, an entire road closed for an hour or two. Everything moved fast there and, if it didn't, drivers felt free to lean on their horns until something was done about the traffic. Though in this instance she suspected leaning on the horn wouldn't achieve a fat lot. 'What should I do for an hour or two?'

'I'd suggest you go and get yourself lunch too. The Cherry on Top does a mean bacon sandwich, best in the village, especially with lashings of brown sauce,' Mork said, dreamily.

'And how would you know that?' Mindy said, suddenly turning round, and he quickly swallowed his toffee before he had finished chewing it. He coughed and cleared his throat.

'Just what I've heard, dear,' he called after his wife. 'Mindy and I are vegan,' he explained to Tori. 'And I'm on a diet, so no lovely, erm, horrible bacon sandwiches for me, but I'm sure you will love them. Just down the hill on the left, blue parasols; it sits right on Sunshine Beach, you can't miss it.'

He trundled off despondently after his wife and Tori smiled at the matching writing emblazoned on his top. Mark. Mark and Mindy. Close enough. Poor Mark, he looked like he'd kill for a bacon sandwich.

She looked back down the hill. The Cherry on Top was Emily's café. Emily had told her to pop in there to collect the keys to Blossom Cottage around three o'clock. Tori had planned to have a drive around the tiny seaside village first and get a feel for the place and meet up with Melody and Isla if they were free, but she guessed that she could change her plans. She looked back at the sheep. It didn't look like she'd have much choice.

She grabbed her bag and locked the car door as she got out, though it was quite obvious that even if some opportunist car thief came along, they wouldn't be able to go anywhere either.

She started her walk down the hill and the sheepdog eyed her with something that looked like a smirk at her predicament.

She fished her phone out of her bag and texted Melody and Isla to say she had arrived in Sandcastle Bay a bit earlier than expected, explained her predicament with the sheep and said she'd be in The Cherry on Top if they were free.

The emerald tree canopy above her provided shade from the sun for a while but as she rounded the corner and the trees cleared she saw the tiny village of Sandcastle Bay for the first time.

Most of the houses that tumbled down the hill were a gorgeous pale yellow with slate roofs that almost glistened blue in the sunshine. Some were round or had round towers, making them look like little sandcastles perched up on the hillside. There was a row of shops all facing out onto Sunshine Beach and a large village green with multi-coloured bunting fluttering gently in the sea breeze. At the foot of the hill there appeared to be a café which was probably The Cherry on Top, based on Mark's description and the navy and turquoise parasols outside the front.

It looked picturesque.

She was leaning back against a garden fence to take a photograph of the idyllic view when she heard the strangest sound behind her. It sounded like a high-pitched squeaky child's toy. She looked over the pale blue picket fence into the garden and saw a flash of black and red. Then the largest turkey that she had ever seen burst out from the garden gate, wings flapping, wattle wobbling under its beak as it launched itself at Tori.

She quickly stepped back and slipped in something slimy, landing on her knees in what was probably sheep poo. There was no time to dwell on that though as the turkey was still propelling itself towards her.

She scrambled to her feet and started running down the hill, her flip-flops flapping against her feet. To her surprise, the turkey chased her all the way down, still gobbling loudly. What would happen if the turkey caught her? Had anyone been savaged to death by a wild and angry turkey before? She guessed she would find out as, impossibly, the bloody bird was gaining on her with every step she took.

CHAPTER 2

Tori made for The Cherry on Top, hoping they might have some kind of security guard or bouncer that would be able to protect her from the turkey, although in the village the size of Sandcastle Bay, it was very unlikely.

The turkey was right on her heels as she swerved through the gate, losing one of her flip-flops in the process. She burst through the door of the café and slammed it behind her, heaving and panting with the exertion of the most exercise she'd done in months.

Everyone turned to look at her, conversation stopping mid-flow. The café was filled with people, mostly over the age of seventy, but in the corner, there was a young dark-haired guy about her age who seemed amused by her arrival. But then she probably did look a state. Her hair had come loose from her ponytail, leaving it in a tangled mess of red curls as it spilled onto her shoulders. Her knees were stained with green sheep poo, though thankfully not her beloved denim shorts, and even her pink sea-shell print top seemed to be marked with something, although that was totally normal for her. Standing there in only one shoe, it wasn't the greatest first impression on the people of the village. She couldn't even catch her breath to explain her impromptu arrival.

'You alright, love?' A blonde-haired girl who obviously worked at the café came towards her, wiping her hands down her apron as she approached. She had cute freckles on her nose, lightly tanned skin – probably from days out on the beach – and looked to be in her mid-thirties. Tori wondered if this was Emily, the girl she had been speaking to about staying at Blossom Cottage.

'Turkey,' Tori managed to get out, gesturing behind her, and the young guy in the corner snorted with amusement.

The girl turned to him in exasperation. 'Jamie, can you not do something to stop Dobby escaping? He's scaring my customers.'

Jamie laughed. 'The way I see it, he's bringing you customers.' He turned to Tori. 'Sorry about him, he's completely harmless. He just loves people and when they run he thinks it's all a game and chases them. He grew up with three dogs, so I'm afraid he thinks he is a dog as well. I've even heard him bark when the other dogs bark – well, at least he attempts it. I better make sure he gets back OK.'

He stood up, slugged down the rest of his coffee and pulled on a baseball cap over his black curly hair. He was tall and broad and cute in that roguish, mischievous kind of way. He passed her a wink as he strolled out the café.

The girl rolled her eyes as conversation resumed around them. 'I'm sorry about my brother, and his bloody turkey. Are you OK, you're not hurt or anything?'

Tori's heart was slowing down as she looked down at herself. 'I lost my shoe.'

Just then Jamie walked back in, proffering her missing flip-flop like a peace offering. Tori gladly took it, sliding her foot back into it before Jamie disappeared out the café again.

'Here, let me get you a wipe for your knees, get rid of those stains,' the blonde girl said as she quickly grabbed a packet of baby wipes from behind the counter. 'These are little miracle workers, I carry them everywhere.'

Tori took one from the packet and wiped away at her knees, surprised to see the green sludge coming off very easily.

'Can I get you a coffee or something to eat? On the house to apologise for your trauma.' The girl was smiling, and Tori smiled too, starting to see the funny side of being chased by an over-affectionate turkey.

'A chai latte would be great.'

The girl's face fell. Tori suppressed a smile. She definitely wasn't in London any more.

'How about chamomile tea?'

The girl's face brightened. 'We have that.'

'And is Emily around?'

'I'm Emily.' She paused for a moment. 'Are you Tori?'

Tori nodded and, to her surprise, Emily threw her arms around her and gave her a big hug. Tori had never really been a tactile person. She hugged her friends and family, but she was never really keen on hugging strangers. But for some reason, this hug felt nice. She had spoken to Emily over the phone and via email a few times and she knew that Emily was chatty and friendly so it kind of felt like she already knew her. Tori found her arms snaking around Emily's back and hugging her too.

'Oh, it's so nice to meet you,' Emily said, stepping back. 'We need someone every year to help with the fruit-picking but we can never get anyone to commit to two weeks. People generally have other commitments. And it's so hard to get the right person for the job, as people come down to Sandcastle Bay and see it as a bit of a holiday and don't really want to commit to the early mornings and late nights of fruit-picking. But Melody said you'd be perfect.'

Tori nodded. 'I'm looking forward to it. I need some time outside, I've been locked away inside with work for the past eighteen months, so I need to be out. I've never been much of a sunbather – I can't keep still for that long, I get too restless – and hiking or cycling isn't my idea of fun, so this seems like a great way to spend a few weeks outside in the fresh air. I don't mind the work, I like to be kept busy and it's a good way to spend some time with Melody too. I've really missed her since she moved here.'

'Melody adores you, that's easy to see, and I'm starting to see why.' Emily stood back to look at her. 'God, my brother is going to fall in love with you.'

'Who, Jamie?' Tori asked, in surprise. He had been cute but not really her type. Hell, no man was really her type. It had been three years since she'd been in a proper relationship and she liked it that way. Luc had broken her heart. And then there'd been Matthew and that had hurt like hell. She wasn't keen to repeat that again.

'No, Parker. He owns Heartberry Farm. He has a bit of a thing for red-heads.'

'I'm not interested in love,' Tori said. That was an understatement. She'd actively run away from it most of her life. Put up her walls, pushed people away. It had worked just fine. No risk, no getting hurt. The two times she had let her barriers down hadn't worked out, so she had now closed herself to the possibility of love completely.

'Neither is he. But doesn't mean you can't have a bit of fun while you're here.'

Tori blinked and laughed. 'Are you suggesting I have some kind of one-night stand with your brother?'

'No, I'm just saying enjoy your time with him; he's a big flirt so enjoy that if nothing else. He's one of my favourite people in the entire world. Don't tell Jamie and Leo I said that, but I adore him. Have some fun with him, god knows he needs it, he works way too hard. And Melody says you do too.'

Tori couldn't deny that. Throwing herself into work was one way that she didn't have to spend time alone at home.

'Look, take a seat and I'll grab your tea,' Emily said as she looked around for a table and pointed to one in the corner.

Tori nodded and made her way over to the table, but before she got there, the door opened, and Melody and Isla Rosewood rushed in.

Melody slammed into her hard, giving a little squeal of excitement as she hugged Tori tight.

Tori smiled as she wrapped her arms around Melody. Then she found herself holding her tighter. She really had missed her best friend.

She felt guilty that, although she had seen Melody a couple of times when they had met halfway between Cornwall and London, she hadn't seen her as much as she would have liked since her friend had moved away. However, with Sandcastle Bay being so far from London and Tori being the lead animator on the film she had been working on, there just hadn't seemed to be the time to make the long trip down here. She thought about the last year since Melody had left London.

Melody had gone through such a tough time with her twin brother Matthew dying in a car accident. The thought of Matthew's death hurt so much. Coming to Sandcastle Bay was always going to be hard as this had been Matthew's home. Tori had been meaning to come to see Matthew even before Melody moved down here but life had got in the way. Or maybe she had let it get in the way but then it had been too late, and Matthew was gone. And now she was here, under completely different circumstances, and she'd be lying to herself if it didn't hurt.

'It's so good to see you,' Melody said, leaning back to look up at her.

'It's really great to see you too.'

Tori looked down at her friend. Her skin was glowing, her eyes shone with happiness. She had been down here less than a year, but it seemed to have done her the world of good.

'You look really well,' Tori said.

'I'm happy here. I really am. I never wanted to leave London or you, but this is home for me now. I can't imagine ever going back.'

'Who knew that our Melody was a country bumpkin at heart,' Isla said as she moved to hug Tori too.

Tori loved Isla. She was a few years older than Melody and Tori, and though that older sister mentality had come with loads of advice about boys and kissing and sex when they'd been teenagers, it also came with a crazy sense of humour and a silliness that Tori adored.

They moved to a table and sat down.

'I can't believe you're here in Sandcastle Bay – it's so far away and a complete pain in the arse to get to,' Melody said.

'It is far away, but that's still no excuse,' Tori said. 'I should have visited you sooner. I'm sorry it's taken this long to get down here.'

Melody waved away her attempt at an apology. 'You have nothing to be sorry for. You were making a movie, that's such a huge deal, especially in the animating field. We couldn't be prouder of your achievements.'

'We know how much work goes into that sort of thing,' Isla said. 'I bet you've been down at the studio night and day.'

'It certainly feels that way, but I should have tried to make more of an effort to get down here.'

'And we could have come up and seen you so we're all as guilty. You're here now, that's all that matters,' Melody said, and Tori loved her for not holding any kind of grudge.

'You had family commitments,' Tori said, glancing at Isla. Matthew's death had such a big impact on all of their lives, but as Isla was now looking after his son, Elliot, her life must have changed the most. She wanted to ask her about it, but it seemed insensitive to word it like that. 'How has it been moving down here, it can't have been easy?'

'It's so different. There's nothing here.' Melody had the biggest smile on her face as she spoke. This was not someone who was suffering in her new home. 'Being a city girl like me, you'll miss everything you love about London. The coffee shops, the amazing restaurants, the entertainment, the shows, the street performers, the fact that every day is different. It's so quiet here and nothing ever happens. It's such a startling contrast. I'm not sure why Matthew loved the place so much.'

The mention of his name was another little kick to the stomach. It hurt more than it should because Tori didn't feel she had any right to grieve over him. Though she supposed they had been best friends long before anything had happened between them. Long before she had pushed him away. Twice. The worst thing was Melody and Isla had no idea that anything had ever gone on between them, or that part of the reason why Tori had put off coming to Sandcastle Bay was that it had been Matthew's home and it hurt to be reminded of him and what she could have had, had she been brave enough to take it.

'I love Elliot so much and I don't regret for one second that Matthew asked me to be his legal guardian if anything was to happen to him,' Isla said. 'Elliot has changed my life, for the better. But it has been hard moving here. I love Sandcastle Bay, there's so much community spirit here, everyone looks out for everyone else and I do love that, but coupled with that is this nosiness where everyone thinks they have the right to comment on your business. And I miss my job in London. Growing up, all I ever wanted was to be a window dresser. After watching *Mannequin*, I wanted to create masterpieces like that in shop windows and I do that… I did that. I trained hard to get where I was, head visual merchandiser in one of the biggest department stores in the world. I travelled the world to advise on different windows or specialised themes and I miss that so much. Not much call for a window dresser in the little corner shop in Sandcastle Bay. But I'm doing OK financially at the moment. Matthew's life insurance finally paid out and that has helped quite a lot, but it won't last forever and while I've been happy to just be there for Elliot over the last year, I will need a job eventually. There are no jobs round here, all the businesses are struggling to stay afloat and my skills are not exactly transferable.'

'Would you ever move back to London, take Elliot with you?' Tori asked.

Isla shook her head immediately. 'He loves it here and I love being able to take him to Sunshine Beach every day and watch him play. I do miss my old life, but I can't go back to that, not with a young child. Early mornings, late nights, all that travel. And what kind of life would he have living in inner London compared to living here? I miss London so much, but I can live vicariously through you.'

'I think you're amazing, I really do,' Tori said. 'You had this wonderful job, this brilliant life in London, this seemingly fabulous boyfriend – although he turned out to be a complete ass – and you gave it all up for Elliot. And I know there was no choice and you don't regret it, but I admire you so much for doing what you did – both of you in fact. I know if I was Elliot's godmother, I would have done the same thing, but leaving London would be so hard. I love my job and I love where I live. I'd miss it so much if I had to leave. I love being able to get something to eat at any hour of the day, and not just burgers but Nepalese, Portuguese, French, Australian, Icelandic if I so wish. I love the theatres and the museums, I'd miss the fast-paced life, where no day is the same. I'd miss the street performers and markets and restaurants and shops. Having said that, this place does have a certain appeal, I can see why you'd be happy here. And, I suppose, even if I did leave London, I would still be doing my job as I can freelance from anywhere. I couldn't imagine giving up a job I loved as well, it would feel like I'd lost some of my identity somehow.'

Isla nodded her agreement. 'It feels exactly like that. Someone referred to me as Elliot's mummy the other day and

I thought, is that all I am now? Isla Rosewood was a name that was recognised in London. Any department store managers or anyone who worked in visual merchandising knew my name. Here I'm Matthew's sister, or Elliot's mummy or "that poor girl".'

Tori took Isla's hand. She had lost so much more than a brother when Matthew died.

'How is Elliot doing?' Tori asked.

'Thriving under Isla's care,' Melody said, proudly.

'I've seen his photos, he looks so happy,' Tori said. 'I can't think of a better person to raise him.' She suddenly panicked that Melody would take offence at that. Tori had never asked her whether she minded that Isla had been asked to take care of Elliot and not Melody. She looked at Melody. 'I didn't mean that you wouldn't do a great job, I just…'

'Oh god, I'm not ready to have children yet. Matthew knew that. Isla is definitely the best person for the job and as the oldest it makes sense that Elliot should go to her. She's wanted kids all her life, whereas I've always been more keen on dogs than kids. I want children some day but not yet. I love Elliot, I love spending time with him and looking after him, but I also love my own space and there's a big difference between being a fun aunt to Elliot and being a parent. Isla is a great mum to Elliot, the best he's ever had.'

Tori knew that was a dig at Sadie, Elliot's real mum, who had left Matthew to raise Elliot on his own when Elliot was only one. As far as Tori was aware, she'd never been heard of since. Apparently, she had emigrated to Australia and pretty much disappeared off the face of the earth.

'And how is he doing with the grief?'

'He was only four at the time, how do you explain to a four-year-old that their dad isn't coming back?' Isla's voice caught in her throat. 'He already knows his mum has left him, though I have no idea how Matthew handled that one. When I first told him that Matthew was dead he simply nodded and asked if we could have lasagne and garlic bread for tea.'

'Then he kept asking when Daddy was coming home,' Melody said. 'It was heartbreaking.'

'He asked if we should put some sandwiches in the coffin in case Daddy got hungry,' Isla said. 'Most of the time he seems fine, his normal, happy, cheeky self,' she added. 'I don't think he totally gets it. He says he misses Daddy and then goes out in the garden and plays with his dinosaurs as if nothing has happened. He's a bit clingy sometimes, especially at bedtime. He had an imaginary friend for a while, though he seems to have gone now. Apparently, that's quite normal, but it freaked me out at the time.'

'I can imagine,' Tori said, shaking her head. Isla and Melody had been through such a tough time over the last year, not only coping with their own grief at losing their brother but helping Elliot to come to terms with his as well.

Emily came over with Tori's drink and a jam doughnut. 'Can I get you two girls anything?'

Isla and Melody shook their heads. 'No thanks, I have to get off shortly,' Isla said.

'Me too,' Melody said.

Emily nodded and left them alone.

Tori took a sip of her tea. 'Where is Elliot now?'

'Mum's got him,' Melody said, an edge to her voice.

Tori pulled a face, knowing the relationship between Melody, Isla and their mum had been strained for several years, mainly since their dad left. While Tori's mum had spent several years after her dad walked out crying, closing herself off from the world and generally feeling sorry for herself, when Melody and Isla's dad left, their mum had dealt with it by being angry at everyone, including her children. Melody, Isla and Matthew, after an initial period of being angry at their dad, had still maintained a relationship with him and their mum hadn't been happy with that either. Since Matthew's death, her grief had manifested itself as anger again, and although she had relocated to Sandcastle Bay to help Isla with Elliot, she made sure that anyone who listened knew what an inconvenience it was.

'And how has it been with your mum?'

'Hard work,' Melody said. 'Nothing Isla does is right.'

'She thinks she should have had custody of Elliot,' Isla explained. 'Although whenever she has Elliot, her idea of playing with him is to sit on the sofa or in a deckchair and watch him play. She wouldn't want another child to look after now, not after all this time. And her ability to find fault in everything would make her a terrible guardian, though she can't see that. I do appreciate her help and Elliot adores her. Whenever she's angry, Elliot giggles and says she has her grumpy pants on which actually makes her laugh, but I do try to reduce the time I leave him with her to a minimum.'

'Well, if you need a sitter while I'm here, I'd be happy to help.'

'That's very sweet, thank you. How are things with you?'

'Yes, please tell me you've managed to get out of the house occasionally over the last year?' Melody asked.

Tori thought about how to answer that question, because if she answered it truthfully, they would worry and feel guilty and she didn't want that. The sad truth was her life had been so intrinsically wrapped up in the Rosewoods' life for so long she didn't really know how to exist without them. She couldn't remember a time when Melody, Isla and Matthew hadn't been in her life. She had grown up with them, playing round their house every day, as she lived across the street from them in London. Melody and Matthew were her best friends, and though Isla was a bit older she still hung around with them a lot. When Tori's dad had left, Tori had spent almost all her time at the Rosewoods' house as her mum's sadness over the divorce meant pushing everyone away, including her.

And then there was her friendship with Matthew. He had been her first kiss when she was thirteen years old. A game of spin the bottle which had ended with a wonderful result. She'd probably fallen a little in love with him then. Although nothing had happened between them after that kiss, they'd stayed really close friends for the next few years, spending a lot of time alone, just the two of them. She adored him. Years later, a few days before he left for his gap year, he had been the first person she had made love to as well. She wasn't entirely sure how it had happened. They hadn't been dating, but a conversation about how much she would miss him had led to a kiss and that kiss had continued until they were both lying naked on the sofa in the most intimate way possible. It had been quite clear there had been these buried feelings between them both for years. After that he'd left and, though they'd stayed in touch, they had never been close again – that is, until shortly before Matthew's death. Probably because she had told him she wasn't interested in having any kind of relationship. She had pushed him away just as she had again years later.

After Matthew had left, her friendship with Melody had remained close. She'd gone to university with Melody. They'd had other friends at school and university but, as with most things, they'd lost touch with them as they'd all slowly moved out of the area or even out of the country. When Melody and Tori had got jobs in London, the natural progression was to get a flat together. They'd spend their evenings with each other at home, watching box sets or meeting up with Matthew and Isla once or twice a week. She had missed Matthew terribly when he had moved to Sandcastle Bay, but she'd still had Melody and Isla. Then, after Matthew had died and Isla and Melody had moved to Sandcastle Bay too, she realised how utterly alone she was. She had good friends at work, but she had never socialised with them before, so they looked at her a little weirdly when she had tried to suggest it. She'd ended up working extra-long hours and even at weekends to try to cover over her lonely existence, although she knew part of that was to try to escape the guilt and sadness surrounding Matthew's death.

She realised they were still waiting for an answer.

'I've been skateboarding,' Tori said, which was the truth, but she didn't need to specify that she'd only been once, maybe twice. 'And I started Pilates.' Although she hadn't made any friends there. She didn't even know any names of the people in her class. They all came to do Pilates not to chat. She sighed. 'I've missed you guys so much.'

'Ah no, I feel terrible for leaving you,' Melody said. 'I've missed you too, leaving you was like cutting off one of my limbs and leaving it behind.'

'Don't feel bad, family comes first,' Tori said.

'You're family,' Melody said. 'I love you. Growing up I wanted to swap you for Matthew and have you come and live with me instead of my stinky brother. I was in bits for the first few months I was down here, and I realised a huge part of that was leaving you.'

Tori knew this to be true. They'd spoken on the phone pretty much every night for the first three or four months after Melody had left. Most of those phone calls had just been Melody crying and Tori crying with her. Matthew's death had hit them both hard. She missed talking to him so much. But losing Melody to Sandcastle Bay had hurt like hell too. And she knew some of her grief about Matthew was tied up in that as well.

'We just need to make this work,' Melody went on. 'I need to come up and see you more and maybe you can come down here more often, but I'm not letting you go.'

'I'm not letting you go either,' Tori said. 'You're way too important to me for that. I definitely need to make more of an effort to come down.'

'You know this problem would be solved if you just moved to Sandcastle Bay,' Isla teased. 'As you said, you can work from anywhere.'

Tori smiled and looked out of the window to the golden sands of the beach. Could she really do that? She loved London but there was nothing there for her any more.

'Look, I have to go, I promised Elliot we'd enter a sandcastle-building competition this afternoon,' Isla said, standing up. 'Shall we meet at The Mermaid pub tonight? We have so much more to catch up on.'

'About seven?' Tori said.

Isla nodded and gave Tori a kiss on the cheek, a proper, warm kiss not an empty air kiss, before she left.

Tori turned back to Melody as she reached across the table and took a bite of Tori's doughnut. Tori didn't even bat an eye; they had always stolen each other's food when they lived with each other.

'Are you really OK about living here? I know you'd never say otherwise in front of Isla.'

'When she called me a few weeks after Matthew's death and asked me to come down here, I didn't know what to do, my life was in London. I know she was scared that she couldn't do a good enough job looking after Elliot, which was definitely unfounded, but I know she felt so alone with this new, huge responsibility. There was no way I could leave her to do it on her own. I figured I'd come down here for a year or two, and once she was more settled I'd come back to London, but that changed almost as soon as I got here. Sandcastle Bay has a way of getting under your skin. I love it here.'

'And is she doing OK with raising Elliot? That has to be tough on anyone. Being a mum is a hard job but suddenly being a mum to a four-year-old is a whole different ball game.'

Melody smiled. 'He's five now. Celebrated his birthday last month. But Isla was born to be a mum; I wasn't lying when I said she was the best person for the job. She has always wanted children and you know she kept asking Daniel about it and he kept putting her off.'

Tori scowled at the thought of Daniel. He had seemed like such a nice guy, she thought he had loved Isla and Isla had certainly thought they were heading for forever. Marriage, children, the whole caboodle. But after the accident, he had wanted no part in raising Elliot. He'd even told Isla that she had to choose between them. Of course, that had taken her about half a second to decide.

'It is hard being a single mum but she loves it,' Melody went on. 'I know she loved her job but here she is genuinely happy, in a way I don't think she was when she was living in London.'

Melody reached across the table to grab a napkin and caught the handle of the teapot with her elbow, sending it flying across the table. Tori grabbed it quickly before it could spill too much of its contents and laughed as she and Melody quickly mopped up the damage.

'Some things don't change,' Tori said.

'Is that tomato ketchup down your top?' Melody said, pointedly.

Tori laughed. 'Probably.'

Melody shook her head, fondly. 'I have to get back to the shop soon too.'

'How are things in the fast-paced world of jewellery making?'

'Good, really good. I'm probably making half what I was when I owned my own shop in London but then the overheads are so much cheaper here and everyone is so much friendlier. It's definitely a slower, more relaxed pace of life here and I really love it. In fact, I needed it.'

Tori nodded. She totally understood that; she felt like she could breathe here.

'You'll have to come down and see the shop.'

'I will, definitely.'

'The whole of Starfish Court is worth a look actually. There's a gorgeous chocolate shop that makes handmade chocolates, there's pottery, glass, and you should check out Stormy Skies, opposite mine. The sculptures in there are incredible. I could honestly spend hours in there looking at them all.'

Was it Tori's imagination that Melody was blushing a little when she was talking about Stormy Skies?

'Klaus makes these wonderful driftwood pieces and Jamie makes these amazing masterpieces out of clay, I've never seen anything like it. What he can do with his hands, it's like magic.'

There was definitely more to this than Melody was letting on.

'Jamie as in Emily's brother?'

'Yes, have you met him?'

'Briefly, he seems nice,' Tori fished.

'He is,' Melody said, her smile filling her face, before she cleared her throat and distracted herself with cleaning the already spotless table. Clearly realising that Tori was seeing way too much in this conversation, Melody stood up. 'I really better get back to the shop, I'll see you tonight.'

'Yes, looking forward to it.'

Melody gave her another big hug before running out the door.

Tori leaned back in her seat with a smile on her face.

'She's going to marry him,' came a voice from the next table. Tori looked over to see an elderly lady with bright green hair sitting at the next table holding a copy of *Fifty Shades of Grey*, though it seemed that the conversation at their table had been much more interesting than the book.

'Jamie?' Tori clarified.

'Yes. They will get married, I have seen it.'

The lady gave Tori the once-over, looking down at her flip-flops, taking in her outfit and then up at her hair. Tori wondered if she passed muster.

'Aidan Jackson,' the lady said, decisively.

'I'm sorry?' Tori asked in confusion.

'That's who you're going to marry.'

CHAPTER 3

Tori stared at her for a moment. 'I think you have me confused with someone else. I'm not marrying anyone.'

'Not yet, but you will,' the lady said.

Emily came over and rolled her eyes at the lady with an affectionate smile. 'This is Agatha, she has a gift for predicting who will marry who,' she said as she cleared away the lady's empty cup and swapped it for another cup of coffee. She leaned over to tidy away the dirty napkins from Melody's spillage from Tori's table and then whispered so only Tori could hear, 'Not a very accurate gift.'

'Some call it a gift, some call it a curse,' Agatha said, taking on a mystical voice.

'Who have you predicted that Tori will marry, Agatha?' Emily said, clearly not taking anything that Agatha was saying remotely seriously.

'Aidan.'

Emily laughed as the phone rang behind the counter. 'Oh well, Aidan and marriage aren't really a good mix.'

'That's because that last woman was a slut,' Agatha said, simply. 'Everyone could see that she was completely wrong for our Aidan. But Tori is his soul mate.'

Emily smirked and winked at Tori as she hurried back behind the counter to answer the phone.

Tori decided to just indulge the crazy old lady's whimsical predictions.

'So, I'm going to marry Aidan Jackson?' she said, taking a sip of her tea.

'Yes, five children.'

Tori choked on her drink.

'Are you here for the Heartberry Love Festival, dear?' Agatha asked, putting her book back in her bag, clearly deciding that tormenting Tori was far more interesting.

'No, I'm not sure what that is.'

Agatha looked surprised. 'You come to Sandcastle Bay at the end of May and you don't know about the Heartberry Love Festival?'

Tori shook her head.

'It's a festival to celebrate the picking of the famous heartberry. You know about the heartberry?'

Tori considered lying and saying she did, but she knew she'd get caught out. Her silence had already let her down anyway.

'The heartberry is a rare heart-shaped red berry that brings luck in love to anyone that eats it. People from all over the world come to celebrate the harvest and taste the berries so they can be as happy in love as the people of Sandcastle Bay.'

Tori smiled at the lovely sentiment of a magical love berry.

'Are the people of Sandcastle Bay happier than anywhere else then?' she asked.

'Happy in love. Lowest divorce rate in the whole country,' Agatha said, proudly.

That was hardly a fair comparison. With one of the smaller populations in the country, of course they would have a lower divorce rate than somewhere like London or Manchester; there were fewer people living here.

'The heartberry is magical, you mark my words,' Agatha said; clearly she could see the doubt on Tori's face.

'So, what happens in this love festival?'

'Well, lots of things but one of the biggest events is the boat race. All the local businesses make their own boat. Well, I wouldn't call them boats as such, some have wings and giant wheels and are more for show than anything else, but they are designed to float on water. Of course, most of them fall apart as soon as they come in contact with something wet but that's half the fun. The boats try to make it to the little island in the middle of the River Star and the villagers from Meadow Bay on the other side of the river also join in. Those that make it can eat the famous heartberry cake or share it with a loved one. There's lots of other things going on, but that's the main event. Then there's always fireworks and dancing afterwards.'

'Sounds like fun.'

'It is and it's also the time in the year that some people receive gifts or tokens of love from their secret admirer.'

'Oh, like a second Valentine's Day?'

'Well yes, but this is much more important in the eyes of the Sandcastle Bay residents.'

'I'll be sure to check it out.'

'Make sure you bring Aidan with you.'

Tori smiled.

Just then the café door was pushed open and the light from outside was temporarily blocked out completely by the huge hulking shape of a man as he stepped inside. He was still silhouetted against the sunlight but, as he closed the door behind him, Tori couldn't help but stare. He was wearing a flat cap and wellies and there was something so ruggedly sexy about that... or maybe it was just him that was ruggedly sexy. He was wearing a pale blue shirt, which bulged out in all the right places, the sleeves were rolled up and he wore it loose over dark blue jeans that hugged his large thighs. Black curls stuck out from underneath the cap, but his face was the thing that she was drawn to. She felt like she knew him, that she had met him somewhere before. He had soft grey eyes and a gorgeous smile which he flashed towards Emily and then waved at Tori. She found herself on her feet. He recognised her too. She saw his eyes flick towards her as she waved back and to her shame she realised he hadn't been waving at her at all but at Agatha.

'Parker,' Emily called him over and he looked away from Tori as his sister talked to him. 'I'm glad you're here, this is Tori, she's going to be helping you up at the farm for the next two weeks. If you're free now, you could take her up to Blossom Cottage so she can get settled in.'

He looked back at Tori and his whole face broke into a huge smile, making her feel slightly less awkward at the embarrassing waving mistake.

He moved quickly towards her, and for a wonderful moment he looked like he was going to hug her. She opened her arms to reciprocate before he opted for a handshake instead. She quickly dropped her arms and tried to make it look like she was simply stretching as she took his hand, but as Agatha snorted with amusement behind her, she guessed that her premature hug had been noticed by her, at least, if not by Parker as well. His skin was rough but warm and she knew she was holding onto his hand longer than was socially acceptable, but she couldn't let him go either.

'Great to meet you.' His eyes shifted down briefly to look at where their hands were still joined but the genuine warmth in his expression didn't falter. 'I'm so pleased to have you here.'

'You are?' Tori asked before cursing to herself. Of course, he meant about helping with the fruit-picking. Not actually her.

'We have a lot of fruit to pick,' he said, skating over her embarrassment.

She nodded. 'I'm looking forward to it.'

What was wrong with her? She was acting like a school girl with a silly crush. She never acted like this around men. For one she simply wasn't interested in a relationship, so men were either colleagues or friends, never anything more. Most of her team were men and, yes, some of them were pretty cute, but she viewed them in that detached way you might view a nice cake: tasty but ultimately bad for you and best to be avoided. So why was she reacting to Parker like this? True, he was probably the most attractive man she'd seen in a long time. Or ever. But nothing was going to happen. So why the bloody hell was she still shaking his hand?

She finally managed to remove her hand from his and, for a brief second, she thought she saw Parker's mouth twitch in a smirk.

'We can go now if you like,' Parker said.

'Don't you want to get something to eat first?' Tori said, wanting a few moments to compose herself before she went anywhere with this man.

'Oh, I've already eaten, I just came in to talk to Emily, but it can wait.' He gestured to the door.

Tori hesitated then wrapped her doughnut up in a napkin and grabbed her bag. Agatha gave her two thumbs up and an over-the-top wink. First, she was trying to set her up with Aidan Jackson, whoever he was, and now Parker. She glanced over at Emily who also gave her a wink. Maybe it was time she invented an imaginary boyfriend to stop everyone in this village trying to set her up with someone. Melody had certainly never mentioned how keen the villagers were to see everyone married off. She wondered if Melody had received this kind of welcome when she had moved there.

She moved over to the counter to pay for her drink and doughnut, but Emily waved away her money.

'Have fun,' Emily said, giving her an enormous grin.

Tori turned for the door which Parker was already holding open for her and then he followed her outside.

A dusty blue jeep sat outside, and he held the passenger door open for her. 'It's cleaner inside than on the outside, I promise.'

'It's totally fine. Melody's car is always filled with McDonald's wrappers and KFC boxes. After being in her car, I can pretty much face anything,' Tori said.

She slid into her seat and, to his credit, it *was* a lot cleaner on the inside.

Parker walked around to the other side and got in too. As soon as he closed the door, his wonderful scent washed over her. It was salty and tangy like the sea air mixed with the clean smell of apples and the spice of ginger. It was heavenly.

She quickly tore her eyes away from him and unwrapped her doughnut, taking a big bite. If she was going to be tempted to have something that was bad for her, she might as well go for the doughnut. The effects wouldn't last as long or be as devastating.

He started his engine and drove off, following the coastal road so Tori had a dazzling view of the sea as the sun glittered over the waves. Children were playing on the beach and dogs chased balls as parents sat back in deckchairs and tried to forget the stresses of the world. It was Saturday, the first weekend of the May half term, so people were clearly making the most of the sunshine before the kids went back to school in a week's time.

'So, is this your first time to Sandcastle Bay?' Parker asked.

'Yes, my friend Melody and her sister Isla live here but I haven't been here since they both moved here about a year ago.'

'I get the impression from what they say about you that you and Melody are really close.'

She smiled. Of course, Melody had talked about her.

'We have been best friends as far back as I can remember. She's always been there. Our mums were friends so we were brought up together. Went to school, college, university together, and then ended up living together in London. I love her. She's like a sister to me. When Matthew died, and she moved down here to help Isla with Elliot, she left this gaping hole behind.'

Truth be told, Tori had been heartbroken by more than just Matthew dying. Losing her best friend to Sandcastle Bay had hurt too.

Parker looked at her sadly for a moment and then back away at the road.

'You're thinking that, if we're such good friends, why haven't I been down here before? I know, I've been thinking the same thing. I live in East London and, despite the optimism of Google Maps saying it's under six hours away, in reality it's more like seven or eight, especially on a Friday evening when everyone is leaving London for the weekend. I had a massive project on at work that has taken over a year to finish and there never seemed to be the time and I know I should have made the time but… it was the first time I'd been asked to take the lead at work and I wanted to prove I could do it.'

She sighed because it was probably just an excuse. There had been many times she'd been aware she was using work as an excuse not to come down here. Sandcastle Bay would always remind her of Matthew and the life she could have had if she'd been prepared to take that risk. Matthew had been one of the reasons she had held back from visiting for so long after he'd died, though no one else knew that.

'I wasn't thinking that,' Parker said. 'I was thinking that Matthew's death had such far-reaching consequences, his family and friends were all affected by it and it's still having an impact now. Not just emotionally but practically too. Melody left her successful jewellery shop in London and opened a tiny little jewellery shop down here and I know she does OK, but nothing like the money she was getting in London. She left you behind and I know she misses you like crazy and it seems you miss her too. Isla is struggling to find work and look after Elliot. And suddenly being a mum to a four-year-old must have been a shock to the system. One foolish moment and it's changed the lives of so many people forever. Including yours.'

Tori swallowed and nodded her agreement and then looked away out of the window for a moment. It was the first time she had really spoken about Matthew's death with anyone. It *had* affected her, and Parker didn't know the half of it.

'Sorry, this is a bit of heavy conversation considering we've only just met. So, first time in Sandcastle Bay, let me give you a brief guided tour. This is Sunshine Beach, the main beach. There are a few little secluded coves in the village but mostly people come here.'

Tori pushed her emotions away just like she'd always done and listened to his little spiel.

'We have a population of just under two thousand people and the village hall is that funny building over there with the red and gold clock tower on the top. It looks small, but it can hold everyone who lives here with room to dance. The village is getting ready for the Heartberry Festival this coming weekend, hence all the fairy lights and bunting they are currently hanging on the village green,' Parker pointed. 'We have one pub, The Mermaid, I think five cafés and two proper restaurants. No McDonald's or KFC here. We don't even have a Starbucks. We do have a very tiny Tesco, but most people get their shopping delivered as all the other shops are more touristy than useful. Even the post office sells more buckets and spades than stamps, I imagine. Up there, at the top of the hill, that large white house is my home and all the land between this fence and the house, and from that little pink cottage over there on the right, which is where you're staying, to the rise of that hill on the left and down to the river on the other side belongs to Heartberry Farm.'

'Wow,' Tori said, taking in the huge expanse. 'You're quite the mogul.'

Parker laughed. 'Well, I guess if I was to sell it I might get one or two million for it, but I certainly don't have that kind of money in my account. Most of it is fruit fields, though some of it is fallow land. This side of the village are the strawberries and raspberries, I also grow apples and blackberries and the heartberries are down by the river and Orchard Cove, which we can't see from here. What else can I tell you? Everyone knows everyone here and if you so much as sneeze the whole village will know about it by lunch time. So if you're not keen on people talking about you – I know I'm not – try to keep a low profile, well at least in public. Half the village will already know that we've driven off to the farm together and will have embellished that story so we're practically engaged or having some kind of sordid affair already.'

Tori laughed. 'Really?'

Parker nodded. 'They're not all bad though. Everyone looks out for each other. If you have a problem, half the village will turn up on your doorstep to help you. I love it here, but I imagine it's very different to London. What are your first impressions?'

'Well, I was forced to abandon my car in a road filled with sheep, I was chased down the hill by an insane turkey that thinks it's a dog and a crazy old lady with green hair has predicted who I'm going to marry.'

Parker laughed. 'That crazy old lady is my aunt.'

Crap.

'I mean she's not crazy, she seems lovely, even if she is a little misguided.'

'It's OK, you don't have to be diplomatic. Agatha is completely bonkers. She has been predicting the marriage of everyone in the village and anyone she meets for as far back as I can remember. She got lucky and accurately predicted the marriage of my mum and dad and hasn't stopped predicting people's marriage ever since. I think she currently has a success rate of eleven couples out of the hundreds she has predicted. Though when you ask her about the ones she got wrong, she says that her predictions were who they were supposed to marry, and she can't be held accountable if the couples get it wrong.'

Tori laughed. 'That's a good get-out clause.'

'So, come on then, who did she predict you were going to marry?'

'Some bloke called Aidan Jackson.'

Parker laughed loudly.

'What, is he hideous? Does he collect stamps? I bet he has a comb-over and wears patchwork waistcoats and enjoys playing tunes on the penny whistle. Does he have bad breath and warts all over his face? I bet he has a pet tarantula that he calls Princess.'

'No, none of those things. So, Emily didn't tell you much about me when you were talking about coming here?'

That was a weird change of subject. Maybe Aidan really was horrible. Or Parker knew him, and she'd offended him by insulting his friend.

'No, not really. We talked about the fruit-picking and the cottage and Sandcastle Bay. To be honest, I didn't even know your name until Emily mentioned it in the café earlier.'

'Parker.'

'Yes, that's right.' Tori frowned in confusion. Had she misheard?

Parker pulled up outside a gorgeously cute cottage that was painted a dusky pink, had a golden thatched roof and flowers crawling up the side of the purple door. It even had a little waterfall at the side of the garden. It was picture-postcard perfect and Tori couldn't wait to go inside and have a look around.

'Welcome to Blossom Cottage,' Parker said.

'It's beautiful.'

'And before we go any further I feel like I should properly introduce myself.'

Tori turned back to look at him in confusion.

'I'm Aidan Jackson, pleased to meet you.'

CHAPTER 4

Tori stared at him in confusion. Finally, she found the words she needed.

'But you're Parker.'

'It's a nickname. When I was a kid, I told everyone I was Spiderman and insisted on being called Peter Parker. I'd introduce myself like James Bond. "I'm Parker, Peter Parker." Parker kind of stuck, well it did for Emily. Everyone else calls me Aidan.'

'But… but… how can you be Aidan Jackson? She's your sister and she's Emily Breakwater and… She's married, isn't she?'

He nodded. 'To Stanley Breakwater, they have a daughter called Marigold.'

How embarrassing. No wonder Agatha seemed so pleased to see the connection between them, well at least from her. Aidan had been nothing but polite so far.

Aidan turned to face her, a smirk on his face. 'So, if we're going to get married you should know a few things about me. I don't like spiders, freaky little buggers, so definitely no pet tarantula called Princess. I don't play the penny whistle, but I can hold a tune or two on the guitar and my triangle skills are second to none. I got a sticker the last time I went to the dentist because my teeth are in such good condition. Well to be fair, I went with Marigold and she got a sticker and she asked why I hadn't got one, so the dentist felt obliged to give me one too. It said, "Winning Smile" so hopefully I don't have bad breath. I don't collect stamps, but I do have a collection of old paint cans in my garage that I've never got around to getting rid of. What else? I can cook a mean curry. My lasagne is pretty good and my beans on toast is the best you've ever tasted. Always fancied being a bit of chef actually, puddings and desserts are the things I enjoy making the most. I'm not particularly tidy, I'm not a morning person and I sing in the shower, probably very badly.'

Tori couldn't help but smile at the brief run-down of his character. 'I'm glad you cleared all that up. If we're going to get married, these are things I definitely need to know.'

'And what about you, Tori Graham, what do I need to know about you?'

Fear suddenly rose up in her at the prospect of any kind of relationship with this man, coupled with a wonderful thrill of excitement which she didn't like at all.

'I don't do relationships,' she blurted out and then immediately regretted it. Aidan was only joking with her and she had suddenly ruined the lovely banter with her silly fears.

He leaned back out of her space, watching her carefully, his eyes soft and gentle.

'Why don't I show you around?' Aidan went to get out of the car.

'No, wait. I'm sorry. I'm not a complete nutter, I promise. I just…'

'Have trouble letting people get close to you. It's OK, I get it. Believe me, I understand. I have absolutely no interest in having a relationship with anyone either. No more jokes about marriage and this…' he gestured to the space between them, 'will be as close as I get to you, you have my word.'

Tori nodded with relief but she was confused by the disappointment she felt too.

'Doesn't mean you can't tell me more about yourself though,' Aidan said. 'Give me the bullet points.'

Tori smiled, glad he wasn't completely freaked out. 'Well, I'm very organised. I plan for everything. Hazards of the job where I storyboard everything before we take any shots.'

'Oh yes, Emily said you were an animator. So you make cartoons?'

'I work mainly with clay and plasticine, but I have done some cartoon work.'

'Sounds like fun.'

'It is, I love it.'

He stared at her for a moment. 'I have a ton of questions about this.'

'You do?' That surprised her.

'Of course, I own a fruit farm. I love it, but it's pretty mundane, it's just looking after and picking fruit. But your job sounds fascinating. I've never met anyone who's an animator before. But we're doing bullet points, so I can grill you about your job later. What else should I know about you?'

'I can't cook. Not at all. I basically live off tins of soup, cheese on toast and bacon sandwiches. Melody used do all the cooking for us. So, if we did get married, you wouldn't be getting a wife that could look after you.'

He laughed. 'I'm thirty-two years old; I'm big enough and ugly enough to look after myself. Besides, I do love a good bacon sandwich.'

'I can make an excellent cheesecake as well, chocolate, raspberry, marshmallow, any flavour really, but it's the one thing I'm really good at.'

'Then I think with my beans on toast and curry and your bacon sandwiches and cheesecake, we'd never go hungry.'

She smiled at this.

'What do you do with your spare time?' he asked.

'I don't have a lot of that, but I have a skateboard and occasionally I dig it out and use it. There's a skateboard park near my house and, though I can't do much, I can at least stay on.'

'Wow, you do surprise me. How on earth did you get into that?'

'I don't know. Matthew was my best friend as a child, he loved it growing up and I always wanted to be as good as he was. My parents bought me one and I taught myself and I suppose I never really grew out of it. The kids at the local park think I'm the cool old lady.'

Aidan laughed. 'You're not old. Not unless you're secretly eighty-five and looking great for it.'

'I'm thirty-one but the kids are all around the age of twelve, so to them I must be ancient.'

'So true. I asked Marigold how old she thought I was the other day and she said a thousand and one. I obviously haven't aged as well as I hoped.'

'You look bloody fine to me,' Tori said, without thinking, and then blushed. Stupid mouth. It would often say things without her permission.

'Thank you.' He smirked at the compliment but obviously decided not to pursue it. 'What else do you do with your time? Bungee jumping perhaps?'

She hesitated to tell him in case he thought she was a complete nerd, but she wasn't there to impress him or have any kind of relationship with him, so what did it matter what he thought of her? Plus, it seemed she had already won brownie points for the skateboarding.

'I like to do origami.'

His face lit up. 'You see, that is something we have in common.'

'You do origami?' That was so unlikely – she couldn't really seem to connect this big, gentle man who owned a farm with the delicate, intricate paper folding of origami.

'I did a twelve-week course when I was at school,' Aidan said. 'It was one of those after-school clubs. I wanted to join the computer games club but that was full, and I was never any good at any of the sports or drama activities, so I reluctantly signed up for origami. I loved it. I have to say I never really pursued it once I finished with the club, but I can still make a great paper flower and a swan. I find myself doing it sometimes when I'm thinking about something. Doing something with my hands helps. Or if I'm stressed out I like to make one, you can't worry too much when you're concentrating on the paper folds.'

'Yes!' Tori was delighted that someone understood. 'I find it so relaxing because some of the more intricate pieces take all of your concentration.'

'See, our marriage will be just fine. Love is completely overrated. A shared love of bacon sandwiches and origami is all we need. Come on, I'll show you around.'

He got out of the car before Tori had time to digest that statement. She knew that love wasn't for her, but it sounded like Aidan didn't believe in it at all. Not that that was any of her concern. She was here for two weeks and then she'd be going back to London. She got out of the car too and walked up the path, which had flowers spilling onto it from either side. Aidan pulled out a large gold key and unlocked the little purple door.

He had to duck to step inside as the door was so small – or he was so big – and after another glance around the picturesque garden with the flowers tumbling out of pots and borders, she followed him into the cottage.

She wasn't sure what she was expecting when she walked inside what was going to be her home for the next two weeks, but it wasn't what she got. Judging by the outside, Tori half expected to see a lot of chintz and perhaps old antique furniture, but it was fairly modern and looked warm and cosy.

There was a large royal blue log burner up one end of the lounge with a thick railway sleeper as a mantelpiece which housed a few candles. The sofa was a beautiful pale duck egg blue with pink cushions and it looked squashy and comfortable. It had wooden flooring which was obviously the original floor and there was a white fur rug in front of the fireplace. A wrought iron twisted metal coffee table stood in the middle of the room with a few magazines stacked haphazardly on one side. Off through an archway she could see the white gloss cupboards of the kitchen.

'Well, I'll give you the "state the obvious" tour. This is the lounge,' Aidan said.

Tori laughed. 'So it is. And let me guess, through there is the kitchen.'

'You're kind of spoiling my tour guide spiel.'

Tori giggled. 'Sorry, go ahead.'

'Through there we have the kitchen. And if you'd like to follow me, I'll show you upstairs.'

In the corner of the lounge was a small spiral staircase which disappeared up through a hole in the ceiling. Aidan seemed to have to squeeze his way up, the staircase creaking and moaning under his weight. Tori waited until he had stepped off at the top before she made her way up, not trusting that the old stairs could hold their combined weight.

She stepped out into a white bedroom with red curtains at a tiny window and a large white bed that took up almost all of the space. There was a large skylight over the bed that gave the room a bright, airy feel.

'Which room is this?' Tori asked, innocently.

He smiled. 'This is the bedroom.'

'Oh, yes, I see that now.'

'Bathroom is through there. When you turn the shower on, give it five minutes for the water to heat up.'

'Right. Are you sure you don't want to show me the shower as part of the guided tour?'

'I think you'll be able to work that one out for yourself. Spare blankets and sheets are in the ottoman. The window jams a little, just give it a shove if you want to open it.'

He gestured for her to go ahead of him back down the stairs, so she carefully did; some of the stairs were very narrow. She walked back into the lounge and smirked at the sight of him trying to negotiate his way back down the tiny stairs and then nearly bump his head on the ceiling.

'I take it, if we got married, we wouldn't be living here?' Tori said. The place was tiny and lovely, but there was no way someone of Aidan's size could comfortably live there.

'No, we'd live at the farm. I can't even fit into that bathroom, which is why it wasn't part of the guided tour.'

He moved into the kitchen and she followed him.

There was a top-of-the-range gas stove that gleamed in the sunlight streaming through the windows and a little wooden table with benches either side. But it was the stunning view of the sea at the bottom of the garden that captured her attention. It seemed to stretch on forever.

'This is the power generator. It doesn't normally stop working but, if it does, give me a call and I will come and turn it back on. But if the power does go out you'll still have gas for the oven and log burners and candles don't require any electricity,' Aidan said.

Tori looked around at the candles that dotted the surfaces. They were unlit at the moment but they clearly had all been used quite a bit.

'There are spare candles under the sink,' Aidan said, as if reading her mind.

'How often does the power generator pack up?'

He pulled a face. 'More often than I would like.'

Tori looked again at the view. So the house wasn't perfect, but that view more than made up for it.

'Dog food is in this cupboard here,' Aidan said, pointing to a tall door.

Tori frowned in confusion. 'I don't have a dog.'

Aidan rubbed the back of his neck awkwardly. 'He sort of comes with the cottage.'

'Who does?'

'Beast. He's some sort of Gordon Setter mix. He's quite big, so will need a bowlful every morning and night. You can leave it outside if you don't want him in the house.'

'What do you mean, he comes with the cottage? Who does he belong to?'

'No one, he just sort of turned up here a few years ago.'

'So, he's a stray?'

'Sort of. He kind of lives here.'

'Why didn't you take him to a shelter, so he could be properly looked after or rehomed?'

'I can't catch him. He hasn't got a collar and he's too strong to be able to restrain for any length of time. Chasing him is all a big game to him. The animal shelter has been out, and they finally caught him after several hours and then he escaped a few days later. He's escaped from them three times. He misses his girlfriend too much.'

'He has a girlfriend?'

Aidan nodded. 'Beauty.'

'Of course,' Tori laughed.

'Although it's more of an ironic name, she's very tatty. She's much more timid than Beast is, she won't let anyone go anywhere near her, and he seems to be quite protective over her. Anyway, we're kind of stuck with him.'

'So, you feed him? Doesn't that encourage him to keep turning up?'

'I suppose it does, but I can't bear the thought of him going hungry.'

'Well, where does he sleep?'

'Um, well, I have a heater in the shed. It's set to come on a timer every night and I've put a mattress and blankets in there too so he's very comfortable. I installed a dog flap as well, so it stays warm at night and he can come and go as he pleases.'

'No wonder he keeps coming back if you treat him that well,' Tori said.

'Some of the people who have stayed here have had him in the house and he sleeps in front of the fire, but don't feel you have to do that if you don't like dogs.'

'I don't have a problem with dogs, I just didn't know that my responsibilities would extend to dog-sitting as well as fruit-picking.'

'There's no dog-sitting needed, I promise. Just put a bowl of food and water out every morning and night. Beast will take care of his own walks and come back at night to go to bed.'

'And what if I forget?'

'Then Beast will probably remind you.'

Tori sighed. 'Any other animals I need to be aware of?'

'Well… no.'

'What does "well no" mean? That doesn't sound like a straight no.'

'Well, Dobby sometimes turns up for a visit. Him and Beast seem to be friends and Jamie can't stop Dobby escaping.'

'The turkey?'

'Yes.'

'The one that chased me down the hill?'

'Yes, but he's very friendly. He probably won't turn up at all, so you don't need to worry.'

Tori glanced again at the view.

'I'm sorry, I know this isn't ideal and the cottage comes with a few tiny issues but…'

'It's fine. Feed the dog, don't worry about the turkey, give the bedroom window a shove if I need to open it, wait five minutes for the shower to heat up and give you a call if the generator packs up. It's fine. I'll be out during the day fruit-picking anyway so…'

His face fell. 'Didn't Emily tell you?'

'Tell me what?'

'The fruit-picking, it takes place at night.'

'What?'

'The berries are best picked at night when it's cold. They seem to retain their juiciness when we pick them at night.'

Tori stared at him. 'But the whole point of me doing the fruit-picking was that I wanted to be outside for a change.'

'You will be but… at night. It's only for a few hours each night, so you'll have plenty of time during the day to enjoy the sun and the sea or go skateboarding or catch up with Melody and Isla. I'm sorry, Emily is normally really good at passing on that information. She must have forgot.'

He was right. The main point of this break was to spend time with Melody and Isla and, if she had to pick the fruit at night, that would give her a lot more time to spend with her friends during the day.

'It's fine.'

'You say that a lot, when really it isn't,' Aidan said.

'No, it is. I agreed to do the fruit-picking and I wanted to spend some time with my friends. So this really does work out better than I planned.'

'OK, good. We don't start until Monday night, so you've got the rest of the weekend to find your way around, catch up with Melody and Isla and meet some more of the locals. If you give me your car keys, I'll get your car later once the lane has cleared. There's milk in the fridge and fresh bread and eggs in the cupboard with some of our famous heartberry jam. Emily has made you some biscuits too, they're in the tin. Is there anything else you need?'

He suddenly seemed in a hurry to leave, probably before she found out any other little problems with the house or extra animals that she was supposed to look after.

Tori shook her head as she rooted in her pocket and handed over her car keys.

'And why don't you come to the farm tomorrow night, I'll cook you dinner to apologise for…' he gestured to the cottage, encompassing all the things she hadn't envisaged when she had agreed to come here.

She tried to find the words that would excuse her from what sounded like a bit of a date but couldn't think of a reason fast enough.

'Seven o'clock OK?' Aidan asked as he inched towards the front door and to her frustration she found herself nodding. 'Good, I'll see you then, if not before, and if you need anything, anything at all, my number is stuck to the fridge.'

He gave a little wave and headed out the front door.

She looked around the cottage and its tiny size and cuteness made her smile, the smile growing even bigger when she looked out at the view again, as she envisioned herself sitting out on the patio every morning, having breakfast.

Her eyes flicked to the fridge where Aidan's number was scrawled on a blue Post-it note, Sellotaped to the door. Her heart skipped, and she didn't like the way it betrayed her like that. No relationships, no men, had been her mantra for far too long, yet it seemed that she had herself a sort of date the following evening.

CHAPTER 5

'You have a date?' Emily all but squeaked at Aidan.

He took his cap off and brushed his hand through his hair as he tried not to look at his sister.

'With Tori?' Emily squeaked again.

'I told you, I told you they would be married,' Agatha called from her corner in the café.

'It's not a date,' Aidan said, not entirely sure what he could call it if it wasn't a date and why exactly he had felt the need to ask her in the first place.

'Sounds like a date,' his brother Leo said, passing him a smirk as he returned his empty coffee cup to the counter. Leo was the same height as him, with the same unruly dark hair, but although he was big and muscular, Aidan was a lot broader and probably stronger. There had been several occasions when they had been growing up that they had ended up in a physical fight and Aidan had won every time. Well, almost every time. He wondered if they were too old for a fight now because he'd like nothing more than to wipe that smug smile off his brother's face.

Leo continued to smile at him as if he knew exactly what he was thinking and didn't care. That was Leo all over, he didn't care about risk. He used to be a fireman until a leg injury forced him to take early retirement. Now he found his thrills working in his own firework display company.

'She's a red-head,' Emily said, knowingly, and Leo nodded as if he understood, as if the colour of Tori's hair had anything to do with it. Aidan had only ever been out with one red-head in his life and that had ended in total disaster, so why Tori's red hair should explain why he had found himself asking her out on a date he didn't know.

'Is she hot?' Leo asked.

'Leo Jackson!' Emily said, her hands on her hips. 'Whether a girl is hot or not has nothing to do with compatibility or chemistry and personality. And thankfully Aidan has a little more class when it comes to choosing women.'

'Is she?' Leo asked again, ignoring his sister.

Aidan didn't answer because Tori was beautiful; those wonderful large green eyes, that cute little nose, her freckles and heart-stopping smile. But Emily was right, there was more to Tori than that. She was quirky. How many girls did he know who enjoyed skateboarding or origami? She was different, and he liked that about her. He had enjoyed their banter and how easy she was to talk to. But that still didn't explain why he had asked her out on a date. *No*, it wasn't a date.

'I just felt bad about the cottage. You know it has more problems every week and with Beast and probably Dobby turning up on a regular basis, and the fact that her idea of spending long sunny days picking fruit went out the window when I told her we had to pick the heartberries at night, I felt like I needed to do something to persuade her to stay, to show her that her trip to Sandcastle Bay isn't going to be a totally horrible experience.'

'Is sleeping with her going to be part of the welcome party as well?' Leo asked, leaning over and stealing a freshly baked cookie from the tray that Emily had just taken from the oven. Emily swiped at his hand, but Leo already had it and took a quick bite before she could snatch it back.

'No,' Aidan said.

'But you didn't feel the need to invite Jim, the fruit-picker we had come stay at Blossom Cottage last year, round to your house for dinner,' Emily said.

'No,' Aidan agreed.

'Or Stefan the year before,' Leo said, through a mouthful of cookie.

'Look, she's good friends with Melody and Isla. They'd both be mad at me if I didn't make their friend welcome. And then by proxy they'd be mad at you. And you wouldn't want Isla to be mad at you, would you,' Aidan said to Leo and had the pleasure of watching him swallow the cookie before he had properly chewed.

Leo coughed. 'No, I definitely wouldn't want that.'

Aidan smiled, pleased that he had managed to turn the tables on his brother. Leo came across as cocky and confident but there was one person he had a soft spot for and that was his friend Isla. Though why he hadn't acted on it, Aidan didn't know.

'It's dinner with an employee, that's all it is. It's not a date, it's not a prelude to something more. Just dinner,' Aidan said, not sure if he was trying to convince himself or his family. He glanced over at Agatha who was smiling ecstatically at this turn of events. 'And what on earth possessed you to tell Tori that me and her would get married?'

'Because you will,' Agatha answered serenely.

Aidan resisted the urge to roll his eyes.

'And because you need someone nice, but someone with a bit of fire, to challenge you and bring you out of this funk you seem to have got yourself into. I think Tori will be perfect for you.'

'She's here for two weeks, she will be spending most of her time picking fruit and any spare time with Melody and Isla. It's hardly going to be the romance of the century,' Aidan said.

Agatha stood up and wandered over to them. She looked sweet and innocent, though anyone who was familiar with her knew this wasn't the case.

'Care to make it interesting?' Agatha said, stealing a cookie from the tray too.

'Oi!' Emily said, though Aidan noticed Agatha didn't get her hand swiped like Leo did.

'What did you have in mind?' Aidan said, knowing his mum would clip him round the ear if she knew he had been encouraging Agatha to gamble.

'Fifty pounds you'll be walking Tori down the aisle within the year.'

Aidan laughed. Tori was sweet and cute, there was a definite spark between them and he knew they'd both get on well at dinner the following night. But she wasn't remotely interested in any kind of relationship and neither was he. At best they might end up having a little fun over the next few weeks, which would finish once she went back to London, but there was never any chance of it turning serious and marriage was something he was never going to do again.

He offered out his hand to shake Agatha's. 'Deal.'

Tori walked along the beach towards The Mermaid. She waved at Mark and Mindy as they jogged past in their high-vis gear and then watched the children playing in the sea. She spotted Melody's mum and Elliot on the beach though they didn't see her. Elliot seemed happy, despite what had happened over the last year. Sandcastle Bay was an idyllic little haven, and the perfect place to raise a child. Her thoughts turned to Isla and Melody and the new life they had built for themselves here. It was a big change for all of them but, from talking to Melody, it seemed they were both happy here and it was the right decision for them all.

The pub was quite noisy and filled with people, probably locals and tourists as they swapped stories about their day. For a moment she looked around the pub trying to see Melody and Isla before she spotted them, Melody waving to attract her attention.

They both stood up to hug her and then they all sat back down.

'How was the sandcastle-building competition?' Tori asked, taking a sip of the cloudy cider waiting for her on the table.

'Great, we won, but then visual displays are kind of my thing,' Isla said.

Tori laughed. 'I'd expect no less.'

She looked at Melody, dying to ask about Jamie, but Melody had been embarrassed earlier when Tori had suspected something, so she wasn't sure whether to push it. They used to tell each other everything, but then she hadn't exactly been forthcoming about what had happened between her and Matthew either.

'How was the rest of your afternoon at the shop?' Tori tried instead, and she was surprised to see Melody blushing again.

'It was good,' Melody said, quickly, a smile filling her face.

Tori glanced over at Isla and saw she was smirking at Melody's reaction. 'Any visitors?'

Ah, Isla knew something was going on too.

'Yes, a few tourists and Mr Davies came in to buy a present for his wife,' Melody said, nonchalantly, as if they were genuinely interested in who had come to her shop.

'Anyone else?' Isla pushed.

Melody smiled.

'And Klaus invited me to Stormy Skies to look at some new sculptures that he and Jamie had done. Well, mainly I think Klaus wanted me to see Jamie's new piece, it was very good. It was called 'Love' and it was this hurricane-style sculpture surrounding a heart, it was so beautiful,' Melody gushed.

Tori looked between the two of them. 'OK, what's going on?'

'Melody's in love,' Isla said, with all the diplomacy and tact of a big sister teasing her younger sibling.

Tori looked back at Melody in surprise. In all their conversations over the phone, Melody had never mentioned that she was seeing anyone. Was something more going on here with Jamie than a little crush?

'Oh shush, I am not in love,' Melody giggled. 'I just love Jamie's sculptures. He is so talented. I can appreciate art without there being something else going on.'

Tori noticed the blush and the fast talking which Melody did whenever she was trying to change the subject.

Isla smirked and Melody saw it.

'You can stop smiling. You have your own crush I could tell everyone about,' Melody said.

'Oh, come on, nothing is going to happen between me and Leo Jackson,' Isla said, and that name jolted a memory. Tori knew that name though she didn't know why. 'He's Elliot's godfather so of course he hangs around. Leo adores him and he's someone nice to talk to and have a bit of banter with. It's never going to be anything more than that. Besides, you know I'm off men at the moment.'

'Hear, hear!' Tori said, raising her glass to chink against Isla's in solidarity.

Isla sighed. 'That's kind of depressing actually, that we've both been so burned in love that we never want to risk our hearts again.'

'I take it you haven't heard from Daniel?'

Isla shook her head. 'I know I should be grateful for a lucky escape. He dumped me as soon as I told him I would be having custody of Elliot, a few days after my brother had died. What kind of asshole does that? And I get that raising a child who isn't his isn't up there on his list of priorities, but we were supposed to be forever, for better for worse and all that. I know we weren't married but we had talked about getting married and having children some day. I feel conned, as if I didn't really know the man I dated for two and a half years. It seems like such a waste of my time. He never wanted a serious commitment from me, he never really loved me – he can't have if he finished things with me so easily. So yes, I feel a bit anti-man at the moment.'

'I still can't believe he did that to you,' Tori said. 'Daniel was supposed to be one of the good guys.'

'I know. I've always thought I was a good judge of character and now I'm doubting that ability,' Isla said.

'Are you still anti-men too?' Melody asked Tori.

'Me and relationships are not a good mix.'

'I don't know why you are both so anti-love. I want nothing more than to settle down with a wonderful man who loves me, raise a family with him, grow old and grey together. I know Luc broke your heart when he cheated on you, we were there, we saw how much that ripped you apart. You were so scared about trusting in a relationship after it destroyed your mum when her marriage fell apart. And he knew about that and he let you down. I get why you would be scared about starting a new relationship, I never want you to go through that again. But just because you've both had relationships that ended badly, that doesn't mean you can never be happy with a man again,' Melody said.

'Men are assholes,' Isla said, decisively.

'What's an asshole?' came a little voice from behind Tori. She turned to see the startling blue eyes and blond hair of Matthew's five-year-old son, Elliot. His eyes were wide as he looked back at Tori. She'd met him a few times when he was much younger. She wondered if he remembered her, though he was really only a baby then. She couldn't believe how much he'd changed in the time that had flown by. Of course, she'd seen photos of him over the last year, but he looked more and more like Matthew every day. Elliot was the spitting image of him and Tori wasn't quite prepared to deal with this younger, cuter, cheeky version of her friend face to face.

She forced the smile to stay on her face and looked up at the tall man holding Elliot's hand.

He had dark curly hair and indigo blue eyes and was so obviously Aidan's brother; the resemblance was striking. He had that raw sexual magnetism that his brother had, the kind that made someone catch their breath. But whereas Aidan was gentle and laid-back, this man had a bit of an edge to him.

She glanced over at Isla, who had gone pink, staring at him like one might stare at a delicious chocolate cake, topped with caramel and marshmallows and everything that tasted good, but you knew was bad for you. Judging by Isla's reaction to him, and as Tori had already met Jamie, this must be Leo Jackson.

Isla recovered herself and held out her arms for Elliot. He immediately climbed up on her lap and she peppered him with kisses.

'How's my favourite boy?'

Elliot grinned and snuggled in closer to her. 'What's an asshole?'

Tori smirked; he clearly wasn't going to let it go.

'It's a not very nice word for some horrible men.'

'Oh. Leo isn't an asshole, is he?' Elliot asked as he played with the crystal raindrop around Isla's neck.

Isla looked up at Leo who was still standing there, not saying anything as he watched the two of them together. She grinned. 'No, he is most definitely not an asshole.'

'Good to know,' Leo said as he sat down at the table between Tori and Isla. He turned and gave Tori a smile. 'I'm Leo Jackson, and you must be Tori Graham. I've heard all about you.'

'You have?' What on earth had he heard, she'd only been in the village five minutes.

'Well, these two talk about you; they tell anyone who will listen how proud they are of you being an animator on all these big films. And Matthew used to talk my ear off about you.'

That was a punch to the gut. Of course, coming to Sandcastle Bay, she was going to meet people who knew Matthew but she didn't think that people would talk about him, especially not with her. In everyone's eyes, she was just his sisters' friend. And then she remembered why she knew Leo Jackson's name. In her many conversations with Matthew, Leo had been mentioned frequently. He was godfather to Elliot. Leo wasn't just someone who had known Matthew. This was Matthew's best friend.

'Matthew used to talk a lot about Tori?' Melody asked in confusion.

'Leo mentioned that this morning, when I said you were coming down here. He said that you and Matthew used to be a thing?' Isla said, dropping another kiss onto Elliot's head. 'I said he was mistaken.'

'How were you a thing with Matthew?' Melody asked. 'He lived down here, we lived in London.'

'We weren't a thing,' Tori said, quickly.

They both knew about her spin the bottle kiss with Matthew when they were thirteen – it had been the talk of the school – but she had never told them about her teenage crush on him, nor the lovely night they had spent together the first time they'd made love. Making a move on your best friend's brother was never the done thing and, as they'd never had any kind of relationship in their teens, there didn't seem to be a lot to tell them then.

'You and my dad were a thing?' Elliot asked, clearly having no understanding of what being a thing was. Tori wasn't entirely sure what qualified as being a thing either, not when it came to her and Matthew.

'No, there was no thing,' Tori tried again.

Leo was watching her carefully. 'Sorry, my mistake. He must have been talking about someone else. To be fair there were lots of girls in Matthew's life.'

Lord, her heart was taking a battering today. That's just what she needed to hear.

'That sounds like Matthew,' Melody said.

Was it? Was that how Matthew really was, and Tori had just never seen that side of him?

'And I hear Dobby took a shine to you,' Leo went on, and Tori was glad of the subject change.

Isla laughed. 'That bloody turkey.'

'Yes, it was quite the welcome party,' Tori said, trying to force away any feelings about Matthew from her mind. What did it matter whether he'd had hundreds of girlfriends? They'd never had any kind of real relationship, not really. One lovely night together when they'd been eighteen; several years later, they'd shared a few months of intimate, close phone calls; and then a few months before he died, one incredible weekend where they didn't leave the bedroom. That wasn't a relationship. She'd refused to give him that and now it was too late.

'And I hear you're going to marry my brother,' Leo said.

Melody choked on her cider. 'Jamie?' she squeaked in alarm and Tori smirked at that telling reaction.

'No, Aidan,' Leo said, smirking at Tori. 'Agatha predicted it and they have a hot date tomorrow.'

'Wow, Tori, you move quickly,' Melody said, laughing.

'Everyone knows that if Agatha predicts a marriage round here, it must be true,' Isla said, dryly.

'I don't have a hot date. It's dinner, nothing more. We'll probably be talking about fruit-picking and other boring non-date topics. Nothing sexy about that at all.'

'Yes, that's exactly what you'll be talking about,' Leo said, sarcastically. 'I hear you two had zero chemistry.'

'Is that what Aidan said?' Tori didn't know why she was hurt by that. It didn't matter if Aidan didn't like her in that way. She was there to spend time with Melody and Isla and pick fruit.

Leo's mouth quirked up into a sexy smile. 'Quite the opposite.'

'Oh.'

Tori smiled and then frowned. She didn't want Aidan to be saying nice things about her. Nothing was going to happen between them and she didn't want the awkwardness of Aidan wanting there to be something.

'Are you and Aidan a thing?' Elliot asked, following the conversation with keen interest, even if he didn't understand half of it.

'No,' Tori said, firmly, making sure they all knew that this wasn't going to happen.

'Not yet,' Leo said.

'Not ever,' Tori said.

Leo smirked as if he thought differently. 'Zero chemistry? That is a problem.'

'There was plenty of chemistry,' Tori snapped. 'Doesn't mean either of us will act on it.'

'You come to Sandcastle Bay, pretty much the capital of love in the UK, in time for the big love festival, to work alongside a man who is single and, by all accounts, "sex on legs" and who you have plenty of chemistry with, and you don't think anything is going to happen?' Leo said.

'I have a lot of willpower.'

'So does Aidan if he wants something,' Leo said. 'Fifty pounds says you go back to London in two weeks having had some kind of fling or *thing* with Aidan.'

'They'll be no flinging, I can assure you of that,' Tori said. She held out her hand for Leo to shake. 'You have yourself a deal.'

Melody laughed and shook her head. 'You picked the wrong person to have a bet with, Leo. Tori is fiercely competitive.'

'We'll see,' Leo said. He turned back to Isla. 'I thought Elliot could stay with me tonight. I know you ladies will have lots to catch up on, and I'm sure there'll be a few glasses of wine and cider involved in that. This way you can stay out as late as you want and not have to worry tomorrow morning.'

'I thought Mum was going to look after him for a few hours,' Isla said.

'Your mum apparently has a headache,' Leo said, dryly, and Isla rolled her eyes. She turned her attention to Elliot, obviously not wanting to say anything bad about his gran in front of him. 'Do you want to stay at Leo's tonight?'

Elliot's face lit up as if it was Christmas Day. 'Can I? Staying at Leo's is so much fun. We watch movies and eat popcorn and he tells me the best stories and makes the most amazing breakfast.'

Isla smiled and kissed Elliot on the head. 'He does make a pretty good breakfast.'

Tori's eyes widened.

Oh.

Leo didn't miss a beat. 'Well, I can make up the spare room and you can stay over tonight after you finish here. That way you don't have to make the long walk up the hill to your house. And then I'll make you both breakfast tomorrow.'

He said it so innocently as if the only thing he was offering was a room to sleep and some breakfast, but Tori got the impression there was much more to it than that.

She glanced over at Melody who smirked and rolled her eyes. They weren't fooling anyone.

'That would be nice,' Isla said, vaguely, busying herself with playing with Elliot's fingers. Elliot giggled as she chased her fingers up his arm like a spider. 'That walk up the hill can be a pain, especially late at night.'

'Good, I'll see you later. Ladies, I'll leave you to it. Come on, squirt, you can help me make some chocolate brownies.'

Elliot lifted his arms in the air and Leo grabbed them, hauled him up in the air and threw him over his shoulder. He walked out of the pub with Elliot hanging upside down and laughing and waving madly as they went.

Tori smiled and waved at Elliot, waiting until Leo had gone before she turned back to Isla. 'So, something *is* going on between you and Leo?'

Isla looked alarmed. 'Of course not. What on earth makes you think that?'

'You're staying over at his house.'

'As friends,' Isla insisted, her cheeks turning a little pink.

'And how many bedrooms does Leo have?'

Isla laughed. 'Four actually. Two spare rooms and Elliot has his own room decorated with space rockets and planets and stars and aliens. And Leo's room. His spare room is very nice, I've stayed there a few times. As friends, nothing more.'

Tori looked back at Melody. 'Are you buying this "just friends" malarkey?'

Melody laughed and shook her head. 'No, but she tells me the same. That nothing has ever happened between them. I don't have any evidence that might point to the contrary, so I guess we'll have to believe her for now.'

'Leo Jackson has had more girlfriends than I've had hot dinners,' Isla said. 'He is not the settle-down-with-one-woman type of guy and if something did happen it wouldn't ever be anything serious between us. For Elliot's sake, if I was to have a relationship with someone, it would need to be with someone reliable, someone who would be there for him no matter what.'

'Leo would do anything for Elliot,' Melody said. 'As you said, he even decorated one of his bedrooms for him, so Elliot could have his own room.'

'I know, he's great with him. He's like the fun uncle, takes him out for the day, does fun stuff, lets him stay up late and eat cake and then gives him back. Doesn't mean that Leo really wants to be a dad to him, marry me, and be a proper family. There's a big difference between the two.'

'Maybe he does, you won't even give him a chance,' Melody said, and Tori smiled at her friend's desperation to see everyone happily married and loved up. 'You say that he has a different girlfriend each week, but I've not seen that from him. I know when we first moved down here he did seem to have a few different girls with him and yes, he does have a reputation for being a bit of a ladies' man, but for months there has been no one on the scene for him. Maybe that's him taking his role as godfather for Elliot very seriously and trying to be a good role model for him. Or maybe it's because he has found the person he wants to be with in you and he doesn't need anyone else.'

Isla waved it away. 'Can you honestly see Leo Jackson marrying anyone, least of all me? Raise a child that isn't his? That's a huge commitment. Don't get me wrong. It's not that I don't want him, I fancy the arse off the man, but I just can't see that he would seriously want anything more than a bit of fun from me.'

'Well, Agatha predicted that the two of you would get married, so it must be true,' Melody said and they all laughed.

'And what about you and Aidan?' Isla said, deftly changing the subject.

'There is no me and Aidan,' Tori said.

They both looked at her as if they didn't believe her. Tori sighed and busied herself with the condensation on the side of the glass. There was no point in pretending that he hadn't had an effect on her. Her friends would see right through her.

'OK, he's the sexiest, most beautiful man I've ever seen, and we did have chemistry. We just sort of clicked and we were only together for a short while and yes, I have been imagining Aidan Jackson doing rude and dirty things to me since he left me at Blossom Cottage earlier today and I haven't had feelings like that in years.' There was a noise from Melody, but Tori kept talking. 'And yes, I'd like nothing more than to run my tongue from his neck down to his—'

'Stop talking, for god's sake, stop talking,' Melody hissed, and Tori looked up to see both Melody and Isla staring in alarm over Tori's shoulder.

Her heart sank, and she screwed up her eyes. He couldn't possibly be standing behind her. Life wasn't that unfair. But, somehow, she knew that he was, she could sense him there. And life had taught her it was spectacularly unfair so why would it change now? She just needed to brazen this out. She would finish what she was going to say so there was no misunderstanding.

She swallowed. 'Down to his… knees. But there is absolutely no chance of anything happening between us. I don't want that and neither does he.'

She opened her eyes and downed the rest of her cider before she could turn around and face him. But clearly he couldn't wait. He appeared at her side, those large muscular thighs filling the gap between her and Melody.

'I bought you ladies a drink,' Aidan said, his deep rich voice resounding above her. She watched his large hands place three glasses of cider in the middle of the table before she plucked up the courage to look up at him. To her surprise he smiled and winked at her. 'You got a thing for my knees, Tori Graham?'

Her mouth was dry, so she took another large swig of cider and then looked back up at him. 'I bet you have very nice knees.'

He smirked. 'If you want, I'll show you my knees tomorrow night.'

'I don't want to see your knees,' Tori said, too quickly. He was playing with her and she needed to give him as good as she got. 'I'd much rather see your elbows.'

His smile grew.

Elbows? Was this her feeble attempt at flirting? She didn't even want to flirt with him but if she was going to she could try to do better than that. She desperately tried to think of something smart and funny to say.

'I like elbows.'

She looked at Melody and Isla who were staring at her in shock, Melody's eyes begging her to somehow recover the situation. But she had nothing.

She looked back at Aidan. Well at least he wouldn't be trying anything with her now. She had well and truly put him off. Problem solved.

To her surprise, he undid the cuffs on his shirt and slowly rolled his sleeves up, so they were above his elbows. His forearms were tanned, smooth and so huge and she had an overwhelming urge to stroke them.

He offered his elbows out, turning them around as if showing them off, and she couldn't help but burst out laughing at the ridiculousness of the situation.

'What do you think? Out of ten?' Aidan asked, a smile tugging on his mouth.

Tori laughed. Then looked back at the elbows, seriously considering them. 'Six.'

'Six?!' Aidan said, incredulously.

Tori shrugged. 'I've seen better. Six and a half then.'

'Wow. I feel hurt. So, you don't want to lick them?'

Tori looked back at them again, hardly believing they were having this conversation. She pulled a face. 'Meh! They look like pork scratchings, all knobbly and weird looking.'

'Well, that's put me in my place. Enjoy your drinks, ladies.'

He turned and walked away, and Tori watched him go and then turned back to face Melody and Isla. They stared at her.

'What the hell just happened?' Tori said.

'I'm not entirely sure,' Isla said. 'I've never seen anything like it.'

'You two definitely have a connection,' Melody said.

'Which I think I just killed. I talked about licking him and how I have a fetish for elbows. Elbows, for crying out loud. There's nothing sexy about elbows. I imagine he's running out of the pub as fast as he can and barricading himself inside his house.'

Suddenly something landed in the middle of their table and they all leapt back in shock. Tori looked down to see a packet of pork scratchings. She whirled round to see Aidan by the door.

'Seven o'clock tomorrow night. I'll have my knees out.'

She grinned, and he walked out. God, this man was going to be trouble.

CHAPTER 6

As Aidan headed up the hill towards where Tori had left her car, he saw Jamie walking his dogs and Dobby. Jamie waved, and Aidan strode over to join him.

'Have you met your new fruit-picker yet?' Jamie asked as Aidan stroked Jamie's black lab, Harry, on the head.

'I have.'

'I felt bad, poor girl. Dobby chasing her down the road when she had only arrived in the village a few minutes before. I didn't know who she was until Emily told me later. I hope Dobby hasn't scared her away,' Jamie said.

'She seems a hardy sort. I think it would take more than a deranged turkey to scare her off.'

'Hey, Dobby isn't deranged,' Jamie said.

'He thinks he's a dog, I wouldn't say he is mentally stable.'

Jamie looked over at Dobby as he followed Ron, Jamie's collie, along the side of the road, cocking his leg up whenever Ron did.

'A little confused maybe, but not deranged.'

'Well luckily for me, Tori doesn't seem to have let it put her off,' Aidan said.

Jamie paused to take a photo of the candyfloss clouds as the sun very slowly started its descent across the sky. He was always taking photos which he would pin up inside his art studio to help inspire him. He loved nature and a lot of his sculptures were influenced by what he saw around him; anything with texture or unusual colours ended up in his pieces somehow.

Jamie turned back to him. 'What's she like?'

How was he supposed to answer that?

'She seems nice,' Aidan said, vaguely. Nice was too bland a word to describe Tori Graham. Extraordinary would be a more apt description. He smiled. They had just talked about elbows. The whole conversation had made him laugh, she was so quirky, and he liked that about her. She was right, they did have a connection and, though they were both wary about getting involved in a relationship, he just couldn't help flirting with her. She liked him too. That much was very clear. Even if nothing was going to happen between them, he was really looking forward to talking with her the following evening and getting to know her better. Hopefully, with some good food and a few glasses of wine inside her, she would relax enough to enjoy herself around him and not worry about what she was saying.

He realised Jamie was staring at him. 'Oh, I recognise that look.'

'There was no look.'

His younger brother was so insightful that there would be no point in denying it. Aidan decided to change the subject instead. Agatha was already picking out the hat she was going to wear to their wedding, he didn't need to add fuel to the fire.

'How's the preparations for the love festival going? Have you made your boat for the race yet?' Aidan asked.

'I'm working on it,' Jamie said.

As Jamie was a very talented artist, working mainly in sculpture, Aidan expected it would be something incredible.

Though whether it would float or not remained to be seen. Jamie wasn't the least bit practical.

'What about you?' Jamie said as Hermione, his greyhound, came bounding over, only just realising that Aidan was there.

Aidan scratched behind Hermione's ears. 'I have the basic shape. I'm adding red and purple balloons to represent the berries and they will hopefully aid with the flotation.'

'Good idea, though sounds like you'll need a lot of balloons if that's the main way you intend to float.'

'The boat is made from wood. What's yours made from, clay?'

'No. Well, there are some parts that are made from Fimo, but those are purely decorations. I had to stop Klaus from making a full-sized figurehead for the front of our craft out of clay. He didn't seem to believe me that it would probably sink it.'

Aidan smiled. Klaus was the other artist who worked out of Jamie's art studio and he was completely over the top in everything he did. A full-sized figurehead seemed very tame for Klaus. Aidan wondered what else he had up his sleeve.

'Leo's shoots fire of course,' Jamie said. 'Apparently the whole thing is rigged with pyrotechnics. But then you'd expect no less from him.'

'Leo's boat gets more extravagant every year. I think most of the village turn out purely to see what he will produce next.'

'He likes to put on a show. He knows it impresses the women.'

'I think there's only one woman he wants to impress these days,' Aidan said.

Jamie laughed. 'I know, but it's not like him to hold back from making a move. Unless he has made a move and she rejected him.'

'I can't see that. Have you seen the way she looks at him?'

'Yes. They have such a weird relationship. They both obviously adore each other but neither of them seem keen to do anything about it,' Jamie said. 'Well, there will be a lot of disappointed women at the festival this year when Leo shares his cake with Isla.'

'I don't know if it will go that far,' Aidan said. The village had a lot to answer for with its loved-up traditions. It was said that if a man managed to sail to the island in the middle of the river and win a slice of the famous heartberry cake, then shared the cake with a woman, that was his way of telling her he loved her. If they ate the cake together they would be happily married. The number of heartberries in their slice was supposed to represent the number of children they would have. It was all very symbolic and, as far as Aidan was concerned, a complete load of rubbish. He went along with it because he owned the heartberries and tradition was very important to the villagers, but he knew it couldn't possibly be true. 'Leo has never shared his cake with anyone before, and neither has he given tokens of love to any woman. I can't see that changing this year.'

'Leo just loves Emily's cake. I don't think it has anything to do with not falling in love with anyone. He holds as much faith in the legacy of the festival as you do. So, are you going to share your cake with Tori this year?'

Aidan laughed. 'You would have a lot more in common with her than I would. She's a sculptor too, of sorts.'

Jamie's eyes lit up. 'Really?'

Aidan frowned at the punch of jealousy to his gut. Why did he want to push Tori onto his brother?

'Sort of, she's an animator, works with clay and plasticine. She's done a few big animated films. And I looked her up and she was responsible for those TV shorts, *Amazing Animals*.'

'Oh, they were really good. Animation is really cool. I'd love to have a go at that. But I would get too protective of my sculptures to start moving them around or destroying them. I'll have to have a chat with her about it.'

Aidan's frown deepened, and Jamie laughed.

'A chat, Aidan, not sticking my tongue down her throat and taking her to bed.'

Aidan smiled and watched him take a picture of a rose, caught between a hedge of brambles and thorns. 'And what about you, anyone you want to share your cake with this year?'

He watched Jamie shove his hands in his pockets and focus his attention on the grassy bank.

'Nope.'

Jamie lacked any kind of confidence at all when it came to women. While Leo seem to have it in spades, Jamie had missed that gene. He'd had his heart broken when he'd fallen in love with Polly Lucas and she hadn't returned his feelings. Other than that, there hadn't been anyone serious for him. His relationships always ended before they'd got off the ground. The girls all thought he was too nice, which made Aidan's heart ache for his little brother. Whereas Aidan was definitely not looking for love ever again, and Leo seemed more than happy to do without it, having fun flitting from one woman to the next, Jamie wanted that: wife, kids, the happy ending. And Aidan felt sad that the girls of the village never took the time to get to know him properly. He thought perhaps that Jamie had a soft spot for Melody but if he did, and if she returned those feelings, neither of them had made it known, preferring the wistful-looks-when-the-other-wasn't-looking approach. *It was clearly working so well for them*, Aidan thought sarcastically.

They got to Jamie's cottage and said their goodbyes before Aidan carried on up the hill to Tori's car, which was thankfully now not surrounded by sheep.

The car was cute, just like its owner. A little blue convertible was the perfect car for Tori Graham. He let himself in and immediately he had to move the seat back, so his legs weren't jammed under his chin. He adjusted the mirrors too, so he wasn't looking at his navel, and then he looked around the car. It was spotlessly tidy, not even a sweet wrapper on the floor. But on the seat next to him was a little notebook and a green pen. Curious, he picked it up and thumbed through it. It was some kind of journal and he nearly put it straight back down again, not wanting to invade her privacy; he should never have picked it up in the first place. But he quickly realised that it wasn't for any kind of personal thoughts, more a record of countless 'things to do' lists, a few sketches of some characters she had probably animated, various dates and meetings, minutes or notes from those meetings. This didn't tell him anything more about her, apart from what she had already said about her being super organised.

He was about to put it back down on the seat when it fell open on the latest page. He smiled when he realised she even had a list of things to do while she was in Sandcastle Bay. 'See Melody and Isla' was at the top, even though she would hardly need reminding of that. His smile grew when he saw, underneath that, it said, 'Pick fruit', and underneath that it had in big letters 'Relax', as if it being on that list would help her to achieve it. Next on the list was 'Visit Matthew's grave'. His eyes cast down to the last thing on the list. He frowned. It was in different handwriting to the rest of the notes and he realised he recognised the writing. In the same green ink, but written in Agatha's spidery handwriting, were the words, 'Marry Aidan Jackson'.

Aidan burst out laughing. Agatha had clearly been up here, spotted the journal and had no scruples about looking through it and even adding her own notes.

He knew Agatha was going to do everything in her power to get the two of them married off within the next year, especially now there was money involved. He was sure this tiny little note was just the start of it.

CHAPTER 7

Tori let herself back into her cottage later that night with a big smile on her face. It had been a lovely evening talking to Melody and Isla, laughing and giggling as if they had never been apart. They'd discussed everything, about Aidan and Leo, how Elliot was getting on and how Isla's mum didn't think Isla was doing a good enough job raising him, which was crazy. Anyone could see how much Isla adored him and how happy he was. They had talked about Matthew, about the fond memories they had of him, and it was so good to talk about him after all this time. They had chatted long into the night until the owners of the pub had come over to kick them out. She had missed her friends so much. She really needed to spend more time down here with them. She could drive down here late Friday nights and leave late on Sundays. She could even fly to Newquay and maybe get a bus or a train the rest of the way. It was definitely more doable than she'd thought.

She closed the cottage door behind her, plunging the little house momentarily into darkness, and she fumbled around for the light switch. There was nothing by the door, which meant the switch had to be somewhere else.

Damn it. She really should have checked where the light switch was in the daylight rather than trying to find it in the dark.

Tori was rummaging around in her bag for her phone, so she could have some light until she found the switch, when suddenly she heard a giant thud upstairs.

She froze.

The noise was followed by heavy footsteps and a scratchy sound that accompanied each step. Suddenly the footsteps were on the stairs and they were coming down them really quickly.

Tori grabbed the door handle, yanked open the door and ran back outside. The footsteps were hot on her heels, so she quickly slammed the door behind her. There was a giant thud as whoever it was hit the door as it slammed in their face and then a groan from the other side and then nothing.

Her breathing was heavy, her heart thudding against her chest as she ran to the other side of the gate, but whoever was in there wasn't following her outside.

Her phone was still clutched in her hand and she quickly thought about phoning the police but then she remembered Melody saying that the local police station, several miles out of the village, was only manned nine to five, two days a week. She guessed the emergency services would take a while to get there too.

She'd call Aidan. His house was bound to be nearby because of the fruit-picking and it was his cottage that was currently being broken into. He could damn well come and do something about it.

She dialled his number, thanking her foresight that meant she had already programmed it into her phone.

It took a few moments for him to answer and when he did he sounded sleepy.

'Hello?'

Evidently, she had just woken him up.

'There's someone in the house,' Tori hissed.

'What?'

'In Blossom Cottage, someone has broken in.'

Immediately his voice sounded clearer and more awake. 'Where are you?'

'Outside the gate. I think he might have knocked himself out. He was running for me and I slammed the door in his face and then after that there was silence.'

'Don't go back in there. There's a dirt track about a hundred yards up the road from your cottage. Head for that and I'll be down in a few seconds.'

The line went dead and Tori looked around, peering suspiciously at all the shadows and up the darkened road Aidan had told her to go up. The place suddenly felt silent and sinister and Tori didn't fancy walking up the road in complete darkness. Sandcastle Bay seemed such a quiet, peaceful little haven and she hadn't even been there twenty-four hours before someone had broken in. And they had been in her bedroom. What on earth were they doing there? Rifling through her underwear, maybe?

She shuddered at the thought of some pervert lying unconscious on the other side of the door and decided the road was probably a much safer option than waiting for the pervert to wake back up and give chase again.

She quickly hurried up the lane, checking over her shoulder to make sure she wasn't being followed. She found the dirt track and fumbled her way up it, over uneven ground and through muddy puddles. She couldn't see a thing. She pressed her phone to get some illumination and a shadow suddenly loomed from the darkness.

'Arghhh!' Tori wailed, swinging her fists and kicking out her legs, her phone going flying.

'Ooof,' came the sound of Aidan's voice as she punched him in the chest. 'It's me, you daft sod.'

'Oh god, sorry, you scared me,' Tori whispered into the darkness.

She saw the shadow reach down and pick up her phone. He passed it back to her and in the light from the screen she could see that Aidan Jackson was wearing only his jeans and boots. No top. All other thoughts went out of her head for a second and she found herself subtly moving the phone around, so she could fully appreciate his chest in all his yumminess.

'Did you get a good look at him?' Aidan said.

'Mmm? No, it was pitch black,' Tori whispered, trying to focus on the situation at hand. 'I only heard him running for me. He sounded big and heavy though.'

'Why are we whispering?' Aidan whispered.

Tori straightened and realised how ridiculous this was. 'I don't know. Will you go and have a look and sort him out?'

Aidan nodded and took her hand and they walked back down the lane towards the cottage. His hand felt nice in hers, warm and safe. As they cleared the trees, the moon lit up Aidan's half-naked body in all its magnificence.

'Right, stay here,' Aidan said as they arrived back at the gate.

He marched off towards the door without any kind of weapon or anything to defend himself. But then it was unlikely that whoever it was on the other side of the door would be bigger or stronger than Aidan, the man was a giant. However, suddenly fearing for his safety, she grabbed a thick branch from the wood store near the gate and followed him down the path, wielding it in the air as if going into battle.

He opened the door, stepping into the darkness, and immediately there was a big scuffle, followed by the sound of Aidan swearing and muttering. As she heard a thud she ran into the cottage yelling and screaming and waving her branch around her.

Suddenly light filled the lounge and as her eyes became accustomed to the sudden brightness she saw Aidan standing by the kitchen door, his hand on the light switch. Next to him a big black fluffy dog who was wagging his tail and looking ridiculously pleased with himself.

She lowered the branch.

'I believe this is your intruder,' Aidan indicated the monster dog next to him. 'Tori, this is Beast. Beast, this is your new landlady for the next two weeks.'

Oh god, it had been the dog the whole time. She had dragged Aidan from his bed because of a dog.

She looked at him to see if he was mad, but she couldn't tell, and she was still very distracted by his chest.

She decided that she would take the defensive route. 'Well how the hell did he get in?'

Aidan suddenly looked awkward, rubbing his neck. 'The kitchen window doesn't close properly.'

'So, an intruder really could have broken in?'

'Well yes, possibly, but that isn't going to happen round here.'

'Didn't stop you running down here in only your jeans to confront my mystery intruder.'

'You should be grateful I stopped to put on some jeans. I was lying in my bed naked a few minutes ago. You sounded scared, I wanted to make sure you were OK. I didn't really think it was an intruder.'

Tori looked at him in disbelief. He had been as worried as she was.

Beast barked and wagged his tail so hard his body shook, and Tori felt herself soften. He really was very cute, in that big woolly dog kind of way. Realising he had secured another fan, Beast came running over and then flopped on the floor, so she could stroke his belly.

Tori knelt down to stroke him. 'You big lump, you gave us all a fright. And what were you doing in my bedroom?'

Beast snuffled against her hand.

She looked up at Aidan. 'I'm sorry for waking you up.'

He smiled, fortunately seeing the funny side. 'You just wanted to have another look at my elbows.' He started showing them off again, turning slightly so they were catching the light, and she couldn't help but laugh. 'Is there anything else you need from me before I go back home? Maybe you'd like me to check under the bed for spiders?'

'Hey, I'm not some little damsel in distress,' Tori protested.

'I could tell that by the way you came storming in here brandishing that branch like an axe.'

'I didn't want you to get hurt.'

Surprise registered in his eyes. 'You came to defend me?'

Tori focussed her attention on Beast again. She didn't say anything. She didn't want to explain that the thought of him getting hurt had actually scared her because that was crazy.

'Maybe I should just check upstairs, make sure everything is OK before I go.'

Tori stood up and nodded. She watched him go upstairs and, giving a little glare at Beast for starting this fiasco, she followed him up.

The bedroom felt so much smaller now with him in it, and although she was only staying there a short time, she had unpacked and made it hers. It felt a bit weird having him in her bedroom. Too intimate.

He was picking a few leaves off the bed, evidently where Beast had been sleeping when she came home. But apart from a few blades of grass and one or two leaves, the duvet wasn't dirty.

'I'm sorry,' Aidan said, brushing the duvet down.

'It's a bit of a cheek that the dog gets to sleep in the bed even before I do.'

Aidan smiled. 'I know, you should at least get to christen your own bed.'

Tori looked down at the bed and back at Aidan in his bare-chested yumminess. He cleared his throat awkwardly at the double meaning of his words.

'Well, I'm sure you want to go to bed now,' Aidan said, patting the sheets encouragingly and his eyes widened as he realised what he'd just said.

Tori decided to tease him. 'Is that how this damsel in distress thing works, you come out and rescue me and I jump into bed with you as a thank you?'

His eyes widened even more. 'No, no, I meant you want to go to sleep… alone, I mean—'

She couldn't help but smirk. 'You come down here, flashing your elbows, and you think I'm going to be putty in your hands.'

He burst out laughing, realising she was playing with him. 'Well, apparently not as they only get a six and a half in your book. If only my elbows were better-looking, we could be having mad passionate sex right now. Instead, I'd better take my elbows back home.'

'I think you should. Maybe next time, wear elbow pads then I won't be thinking about pork scratchings when I'm having sex with you.'

He stepped closer, so she could smell his wonderful sea spray scent. 'Tori Graham, if we were to have sex, the very last thing on your mind would be pork scratchings.'

She laughed. 'Oh, you're so confident and sure of yourself. That's not an attractive feature.'

It was such a lie. His confidence was very sexy.

He chuckled. 'I'm looking forward to dinner tomorrow.'

'It's just dinner, don't be getting any ideas.'

'About you licking from my neck down to my… knees, no why would I even think of that?'

'You're never going to let me live that down, are you?' Tori said.

'Nope, and when we're married, I'll still remind you.'

She laughed. 'Never going to happen. And flaunting your elbows isn't going to change that either.'

'That's just part of the courtship ritual. Like peacocks displaying their feathers, I'm showing off my elbows.'

'Is it working for you?'

He gave her a devastating smile. 'You tell me?'

She smiled and looked away. It was working too bloody well. Him and his chest, his smile, his heavenly scent, his gentle eyes, this whole conversation, even his bloody elbows. The whole package was infuriatingly sexy and endearing. Just a few hours ago he had promised her that nothing would happen between them but now they seemed to have fast-forwarded several steps to full-on flirting. It excited her and scared her in equal measure.

'I should go,' Aidan said, and he turned and walked down the stairs. She followed him down and found Beast had made himself comfortable on the sofa.

She suddenly didn't want him to go, not because she wanted to jump into bed with him, but she was just enjoying his company. He made her smile and she liked that.

She spotted the origami strawberry she'd made earlier.

'I made you something,' she said, and then regretted it in case he thought it was lame. But it was true that she had made it with him in mind.

He turned to her with surprise. 'As a reward for my heroic deeds? Normally the social norm is just to have sex.'

She laughed and picked up the strawberry. She was quite proud of it, the little green leaves and the tiny black dots she'd added after for the seeds. It was a perfect shape too.

'I haven't done this for a while, but you inspired me to do origami again.'

She passed it to him and he held it carefully in his hand, staring at it, turning it over to appreciate all the different folds.

'It's not sex but…' Tori said.

'It's fantastic, thank you.'

'I was going to make you a heartberry but I wasn't entirely sure what they look like and when I Googled it, they really do look like tiny hearts and I thought you'd get the wrong idea if I made you a heart,' Tori gabbled, trying to make this lame gift a bit better.

'That secretly you fancy my elbows? That's not so much of a secret.'

Tori laughed. 'Go home and take your elbows with you.'

Aidan walked to the door and then turned back to face her. Silhouetted against the moonlight he was a wonderful sight.

'Sweet dreams, Tori Graham.'

She smiled at how lovely that was but then he started showing off his elbows as if he wanted her to dream about them and she laughed.

'Go, you need to conserve your energy for tomorrow night.'

'Oh yes?'

'Yes, I want to try this amazing beans on toast. I don't want you burning the toast because you're too tired.'

He laughed. 'I promise, you won't be disappointed.'

Her heart thudded against her chest. He was clearly talking about something else other than beans on toast.

'I'm sure I won't,' she said, enjoying the banter.

He grinned and walked out of the gate, turning and giving her a wave before disappearing into the darkness as he headed up the lane. She closed the door and went and sat on the sofa next to a snoring Beast.

Her heart was still thudding against her chest. There was a huge part of her that wanted to put the brakes on this before it went any further, but maybe it was the relaxed, happy atmosphere of Sandcastle Bay, maybe it was just him, but she felt safe with him. Even if this never went any further than a bit of harmless flirting, she could enjoy that at least.

CHAPTER 8

Tori was sitting outside on the wall of The Cherry on Top, staring out at the sea, waiting for Melody. There was something about this place that just made her smile so much. It felt a world away from London and its fast-paced, non-stop life. It was peaceful and quiet, and everyone seemed so friendly. Already that morning, she'd stopped at the little post office shop to get some milk and been presented with a few chicken drumsticks for Beast from the owner, Mary Nightingale. She'd met Trevor, the owner of all the sheep, who had apologised about blocking the road and given her an apple pie that his wife had made. It was easy to see why Isla and Melody had felt so settled here so quickly. She didn't know if she could ever live somewhere like Sandcastle Bay but there was definitely an appeal to it.

She watched Mark and Mindy jog past on the beach in their high-vis gear again, Mindy jogging way out in front of her poor husband. Mark looked over wistfully at The Cherry on Top as they passed and stopped. He looked at Mindy, who hadn't noticed, and suddenly he started rubbing his leg and moaning about cramp. Tori smothered a laugh. Mindy came running back to help him and he waved her on, saying he would just have a little rest here for a while and then catch her up. After a bit of persuasion, Mindy carried on jogging and, as soon as she was far enough away, Mark hurried into The

Cherry on Top with seemingly no cramp problems at all. Tori smiled to herself. Sandcastle Bay held some right characters.

Nearby a radio was playing the news, reporting a hurricane off the coast of America that was predicted to change course and head across the Atlantic towards the UK. It was hard to imagine this calm, tranquil haven being the victim of a hurricane.

She saw movement along the sea front and looked over. It was Leo Jackson. He had this air of confidence about him that said he didn't care what people thought about him. The way he carried himself, she got the impression that he was angry with the world but that hadn't been the Leo she had met the night before. The Leo who adored Elliot and invited Isla to stay just so she wouldn't have to go up the hill at the end of the night. He saw her and smiled. Tori thought he would just carry on straight past into the café, so it surprised her when he sat down next to her on the wall.

'I'm glad I caught you alone, I wanted to talk to you,' Leo said.

Why would he want to talk to her? He looked out over the sea as if embarrassed to be talking to her about this.

'About Isla?' she asked.

He frowned. 'No, definitely not.'

No, of course not. If something was happening between them and they were keeping it top secret, he certainly wouldn't be asking advice from someone he'd just met.

'About Aidan then?'

'About Matthew.'

'Oh.'

That wiped the smile off her face. She had been sitting there, enjoying the view, feeling the relaxed atmosphere of the place seep into her bones, and now she felt herself tense in response to that one word.

'There weren't lots of girls. I wanted to clarify that. I only said that yesterday to cover over the fact that I had clearly dropped you in it. Matthew talked about you often. In the last three or four months before he died, you were pretty much the only thing he did talk about. He wasn't seeing anyone else. Thought you should know.'

Tori stared at him, emotion clawing at her throat as all those buried feelings for Matthew came flooding back.

'I have no right to care about that but I do,' she said.

'Why do you not have any right?' Leo asked.

'I pushed him away. I told him I didn't want a relationship with him, just before he died.' She paused. 'And that wasn't the first time either.'

She looked at Leo and he sat there patiently, waiting for her to talk if she wanted to, not pushing her for any more than she wanted to give. She had never talked about Matthew with anyone and all these suppressed feelings came bubbling to the surface now.

'We were best friends growing up. Me, Melody and Matthew, and mostly Isla too, would always hang around together, inside school and out. He was my first kiss and later, at eighteen, he was the first person I made love to as well. I don't know why we did, we hadn't been dating or anything. But one night, it just sort of happened. I was scared about getting involved in any kind of relationship, it destroyed my mum when my dad left, and I didn't want to go through that. He was due to go on a gap year anyway, which turned into a gap three years, and so the morning after we made love and he asked what it meant for us now, I told him I wasn't interested in starting anything, that we were better staying friends. I think I hurt him, though he never said anything.

'He left for America and later Australia and I always thought it was for the best. I didn't want to lose him as a friend. We stayed in touch over the years, but we were never as close as we were growing up. I don't know whether it was the distance; he went to university down this way when he eventually came back to the UK, and after a brief stint in London, he got work down here. Or maybe it was that I'd driven a wedge between us after such a wonderful night together.'

Tori looked away over the sea as she remembered the first time she had laid in his arms.

'And Isla and Melody never knew?'

'No. I don't know if they noticed the change between us, but he was away from the UK for three years; of course things would be different between us.'

'Then you got together again years later?'

'Sort of. One night, probably about four months before he died, he phoned to speak to Melody and she wasn't in. We ended up chatting for hours. Then he phoned again the next night and the night after. It was just like old times again. We spoke every day for about two months. It was quite clear that something a lot more than friendship was going on. One night he said he wished he was with me so he could kiss me and I said I wished for that too. The following weekend, he came up. The worst thing was that he told Isla that he had to go away with work and could she come down here and look after Elliot. She leapt at the chance, she loved spending time with Elliot. Melody decided to come down here too. And me and Matthew spent the whole weekend in London making love. After that we'd chat two or three times a day and it was quite clear that Matthew wanted it to be something. He kept talking about me coming down here. I was busy with work so I kept putting him off, but I knew in reality I was scared about getting involved in a relationship again. I'd had one serious relationship that had ended badly and the thought of being in another relationship, especially with my best friend, freaked me out. He knew that too and he confronted me about it. We ended up having a big row and I called things off. I regretted it as soon as I'd done it and I deliberated about whether it was the right thing or not, changing my mind and changing it back again over the next few days. Five days after our row, he was dead.'

She swallowed down the pain of the grief and guilt that lay heavy in her heart, but she felt a bit lighter for finally talking about it.

'And Isla and Melody don't know any of this?'

Tori shook her head.

'In reality, we didn't have any kind of relationship to tell them about. A one-night stand when I was eighteen, one amazing weekend and a few months of flirty phone calls.'

'So, you didn't have a conventional relationship with dates and actually seeing each other on a regular basis, but you guys talked more each day than most happily married couples. I know he wanted you to come down and visit but you were scared. He understood that. So, I know something of your tentative relationship. Whatever it was between you, I know that it was more than just friends; that he absolutely adored you, probably even loved you, so don't dismiss that.'

She swallowed, tears pricking her eyes. Leo was the only person who had validated what she had with Matthew. No one knew about them and when he'd died she didn't feel she had the right to grieve for him to the extent she wanted, at least not publicly. Melody was his sister and she was distraught. Tori had to be there for her, not impede on her grief with her own. Their mum had specified that the funeral be small, family only, so she hadn't gone. Visiting his grave had been one of the things that she planned to do while she was here, though she wasn't looking forward to it. She thought she had let him down somehow.

'He wanted more than I was willing to give, and I will always regret that,' Tori said, quietly. 'We were friends for so long and I was scared of losing that, of trusting in a relationship again. I knew I loved him. I was just too scared to do anything about it. The worst thing was that he died never knowing how I really felt and he probably died hating me too.'

There was silence for a while as they sat on the sea wall, looking out over the waves.

'There was an email,' Leo said, quietly.

Tori looked at him.

'Isla asked me to go through his things, his emails, his computer, take care of anything that needed taking care of. She asked me to email people from work or other contacts and let them know what had happened. There was an email to you in his draft folder. It was written three days before he died. I read it to see if it was anything important and…' he trailed off.

'And?'

'Well, it was, but I couldn't bring myself to send it to you. I didn't know you, though I knew how much he cared for you.

When I casually mentioned you to Isla and asked about your relationship with Matthew, she said that you were just friends. I wasn't sure what to do. People write email messages to people all the time with no intention of ever sending them, just as a way to pour out their feelings, but it's not something they actually want the other person to see. In my mind there was a reason why he hadn't sent that email when he'd written it and not in the following days before he died either. I wondered whether he was still refining it, trying to get the right words, or if he never meant for you to see it at all. I didn't want to betray Matthew. But now I think you should see it.'

'Do you still have it?'

'Yes, I think so. I forwarded it to my own email, just in case. But this was a year ago. I'd need to look for it. Give me a day or so.'

She nodded, wondering what it was Matthew had wanted to say after their row. God, what if it was something horrible, she didn't know if she could cope with that.

'You shouldn't take all the responsibility for the relationship never really taking off. You were both busy with work and long-distance relationships rarely work. Who's to say if he was still alive that it would have worked out between you anyway? I think Matthew's death taught me one thing, that we can't live our life with regrets. Be happy with what you had – a wonderful, very close friendship – and perhaps learn from it in the future.'

'How do I learn from it?'

Leo sighed as he looked out to sea. 'I'm not in any position to give you advice about love, my life is a bit of a mess when it comes to that side of things. But sometimes you have to take a risk because the reward can be amazing. If you think the reward is good enough, then you shouldn't let fear get in the way. If it doesn't work out at least you tried, rather than regret that you didn't.'

Tori nodded. 'Very true, but in many cases, it's a lot harder than it looks.'

'I know. In life it's very easy to take the safe path, where you think you'll never get hurt, but life is short, and we never know what is around the next corner. Life can change in the blink of an eye and no matter how careful you are, how safe you think your life is, you will always end up getting hurt one way or another.' Leo grinned. 'The other path is much more fun so maybe take some risks now and again.'

Tori smiled. He was so right. She had been so careful with her heart and in one awful moment she had lost Matthew, and then Melody shortly after when she had moved to Sandcastle Bay. She had ended up hurt anyway so maybe it was time to have some fun.

He looked down the beach and stood up. 'Melody's coming. I'll let you get on.'

'Thank you for talking to me.'

He nodded and moved away, and Tori watched him go. 'Leo.'

He turned back to face her.

'He loved you too. Whenever we'd talk, your name would come up often. I could tell he adored you.'

He stared at her for a few moments and then nodded and walked away.

A few seconds later Melody bounced up and gave Tori a great big hug. 'Hey, you. Did I see you talking to Leo?'

'Oh, yes, not anything important, just, well, mundane stuff really: weather, Sandcastle Bay, nothing special,' Tori said, vaguely, hating that she was lying to her best friend. She didn't know why she didn't feel she could tell Melody the truth. When she and Matthew had started their… relationship, it had been just two friends catching up. She'd told Melody he'd called, and they'd chatted for a bit, and Melody clearly hadn't thought anything of it. And at that time there really wasn't anything to it. When he had called the next night to talk to her this time, not Melody, Tori still hadn't mentioned it to her friend and it became this private thing, a wonderful, delicious secret just between them.

As time had gone on, it became even harder to tell Melody, because how did she tell her friend that she had been flirting and chatting with her brother every day for four months, or that they had secretly spent the weekend making love, while Melody and Isla had been babysitting Elliot? She felt bad about that, but Matthew had deliberately lied to his sisters so he could spend the weekend with her and she didn't want to betray him by telling the truth. After his death, it became almost impossible to tell Melody and Isla. She didn't want them to think Tori was laying some claim over him and the lie over that weekend sat heavy on her conscience. What was the point of hurting them over a relationship that had never really taken off? Melody seemed to take her word for it, which made Tori feel even worse. Melody linked arms with her and they walked into the café.

The place was quite busy, again filled with elderly couples. Mark was sitting in one corner, eating what looked suspiciously like a bacon sandwich. She gave him a wave and he blushed guiltily, moving the menu stand subtly in front of his plate so she wouldn't see what he was eating, but it was a little too late for that. Melody made for the corner where there was one table empty and Tori followed.

'I think I might get the waffles,' Melody said, excitedly. 'Emily makes the most amazing waffles and then you can get either savoury or sweet toppings. The cheese and mushroom toppings are delicious, but then so is the banoffee. Maybe I'll get both.'

Tori smiled at her friend, at how something as simple as a great lunch could make her so happy. 'That sounds good, shall I go and order? My treat.'

'Oh no, let me pay. You've come all the way down here to see us, I can at least buy you lunch.'

'Well, if you buy me lunch, I'll buy the pudding,' Tori insisted.

Melody smiled. 'Deal.'

Emily came over to take their order and, after she had written it down, she nudged Tori. 'So, hot date with my brother tonight?'

'It's not a date, just dinner,' Tori tried, knowing it was no good. 'And why didn't you tell me yesterday that the Aidan Jackson that your aunt was predicting I would marry was the brother I was going to work for?'

'I've mentioned Aidan before, in our emails, I'm sure I have. I thought you knew.'

'No, actually you never mentioned his name, just referred to him as your brother. I didn't really think much of it at the time. And yesterday you called him Parker.'

'Oh yes,' Emily laughed. 'Sorry. But I hear you two have hit it off already, so maybe Agatha will be right after all.'

Tori shook her head, laughing. 'Never going to happen.'

'We'll see,' Emily said, disappearing back behind the counter.

Tori turned back to Melody. 'What is it with this village and their desire to see everyone married off?'

'I think it's the silly legend surrounding the heartberries and that all those that eat them will be happy in love. They have this heartberry festival which is basically a big festival of love every year, I guess they have something to prove to the outside world. The more loved-up couples the better. Don't take it personally, they try to get everyone together.'

'Who are they trying to fix you up with?' Tori asked and watched Melody blush.

'The other Jackson brother.'

'Jamie?' Tori had guessed as much. 'He seems nice.'

'He is, he's so lovely. Of course, Agatha announcing to the world that me and him would get married has made him keep his distance a bit. Bit awkward really when we work in the same courtyard and get to see each other every day. His studio is right opposite my shop, I literally look out my window and see him working away. He's caught me staring a few times, but I've caught him staring too. He never really says a lot to me, smiles at me, occasionally waves. I've tried talking to him a few times, but I never know what to say to him.'

Tori had wandered round Starfish Court that morning, a little alleyway just off the beach that had a collection of crafty shops, including Melody's jewellery shop, a pottery store, a shop that sold handmade chocolates, Jamie's art studio and a few others. It was a cute little place. Melody had been dealing with a customer at the time, so Tori hadn't gone in, but she had seen Jamie and he had been staring across the alley into Melody's shop at the time. Maybe the two of them needed a little help. Tori shook her head at that thought. She didn't like the villagers interfering in her love life, why should she interfere in Melody's?

Just then the door opened, and Agatha walked in. Tori almost didn't recognise her at first, her hair was a candyfloss pink today.

Agatha went over to the counter to chat to Emily, no doubt putting in her order, and then came straight over to their table and plonked herself down.

'Love the hair, Agatha,' Melody said.

'Thank you, thought I'd go pink, it is the colour of love. I might even add some red for the festival.'

'And do *you* have a date for the festival?' Melody asked, and Tori liked that she had turned the tables on Agatha for once.

'Well, I'm hoping that sexy Stefano from the Italian might ask me. He's been giving me the eye every time I walk past. Of course, at our age, it could be cataracts or glaucoma that makes his eyes go funny, not me, but we'll see,' Agatha said.

The café door opened again and this time Jamie walked in with a young pretty blonde in a pink flowery dress. They were laughing and chatting easily, and Tori wondered what Melody's reaction would be to seeing him with another girl.

She glanced at Melody. Although she was looking wistfully over at Jamie she didn't seem too perturbed about the other girl.

Tori noticed that some of the old folk had gone quiet since they had walked in and some were even glaring at them, well mainly at the girl, not Jamie.

'That's Rosie,' Agatha whispered. 'She and her wife Eva have just moved to Sandcastle Bay. They have a young daughter, Merry. But nobody is particularly happy about them being here.'

Tori stared at her in shock. 'Because they're gay?'

It seemed strange that in the twenty-first century there were still people who had homophobic views, but for a whole village to think like that really surprised her.

Agatha looked aghast. 'Of course not, what kind of back-ward regressive place do you think this is? We have several gay people that live here in Sandcastle Bay, no one cares. No, it's because they've opened up a tattoo studio in Starfish Court. Rosie is a wonderful tattoo artist and her wife does body piercings. Many folk think that Sandcastle Bay and especially Starfish Court is not the right place for a tattoo studio. Starfish Court has been associated with art, sculpture, paintings, jewellery making for many years, it's supposed to be a place of culture and art. Tattoos are not everyone's idea of culture. The young people of the village think it's great. The old fogies are too stuffy in their way of thinking.'

'But tattooing is a form of art,' Tori protested.

'I know, I think it's wonderful. The village needs some fresh life. These people need to wake up and move with the times. I'm going to do something about it,' Agatha said.

'You going to get a tattoo then?' Tori teased.

Agatha nodded. 'That's exactly what I'm going to do. Rosie! Rosie dear, come over here.'

Tori's eyes widened in surprise. Agatha was well into her eighties. Was she really going to get a tattoo?

Rosie smiled at Agatha and wandered over, leaving Jamie by the counter.

'Rosie, I would like a tattoo,' Agatha said, loudly, so everyone in the café could hear. 'I've always wanted one but never got around to doing it.'

'Oh, that's great,' Rosie said. 'What would you like?'

Agatha faltered, clearly not having thought that far ahead. She looked over at Tori for some suggestions.

'I've always fancied getting a dragon,' Tori said. 'Maybe you could get your favourite animal.'

'Yes, there you go, me and Tori will come and get a tattoo on Monday. She'll get a dragon and I'll get a giraffe.'

Tori's eyes widened in shock and Melody giggled.

'Wait, I'm not sure if I want something permanent. I can't change my mind if I don't like it. And I'm not sure if I want something that would be visible all the time.'

'Of course, you do,' Agatha said. 'What's the point of getting one if no one sees it?'

'Lots of people have them hidden,' Rosie said. 'It's a private thing just for them or for their partners to see. If you're not sure you want to commit to something permanent, I could do you a henna tattoo, they wash off in a couple of weeks, then you can get used to having it before you go for something permanent.'

'Well, that might be a good idea,' Tori said.

'And maybe somewhere a bit discreet,' Melody suggested. 'So if you really didn't like it, no one else would see it. Maybe on your back.'

'I can do that,' Rosie said.

'Let me choose one for you,' Agatha said, excitedly, clearly getting into the swing of things. 'If it washes off anyway, why not let me choose one for you, something that I think would suit you perfectly.'

Melody subtly shook her head at that suggestion, but Tori was distracted by Emily's assistant who came over with a tray and placed their order on the table before hurrying back behind the counter.

Tori picked up her mug of chamomile tea, playing for time before she answered. Did she really trust Agatha to choose something tasteful for her? Although, if it was going to wash off in a few weeks and it was hidden on her back, it didn't really matter what tattoo she had done. And if it made Agatha happy then why not? If Tori was going to follow the fun path for a while, she could start with something small like a temporary tattoo.

'Sure, you can choose for me,' Tori said.

Melody's eyes widened in shock, but Tori just shrugged. What was the worst that could happen?

Agatha clapped her hands together happily. 'I have the perfect design for you. I'll draw it out and bring it along on Monday.'

'Great. I might even get my belly pierced,' Tori said.

'I might get a piercing too, maybe a nose stud,' Agatha said. 'I've always thought they look so exotic.'

'Oh, my wife can do that for you.' Rosie looked really pleased to have this new custom, even if it was through an unlikely source. 'I better get back, she'll be wondering where her lunch is. I'll see you Monday. Pop in any time.'

Rosie moved back over to the counter and took a brown paper bag from Emily, before waving goodbye to them and Jamie.

Jamie took a brown paper bag from Emily too and was just about to leave when Agatha called him over.

'Jamie! Come and join us for lunch,' Agatha yelled across the café.

'I probably should get back,' Jamie said, eyeing Melody who had suddenly gone several shades of pink.

'Nonsense, that young Klaus can take care of things for a bit, surely you can spare a bit of time for your dear old aunt. I might be dead in a week and then you'd regret not having lunch with me.'

Jamie smirked and then came across the café toward them. Agatha immediately shuffled around and grabbed a seat from a nearby table and pulled it over, so it was next to Melody. Jamie awkwardly sat down in the empty seat.

He cleared his throat. 'Hi Melody.'

'Hi,' Melody said, smiling at him and then, clearly embarrassed, she focussed her attention on her food. She scooped up a bit of cheesy waffle on her fork but before it reached her mouth it splatted on the table, which actually was a step up from splattering down her top, which was what normally happened with Melody.

Jamie handed her a napkin as she blushed furiously. He then opened his bag and spent a long time unpacking his lunch onto the table.

Silence descended in their little corner of the café and Tori looked at Agatha in exasperation. Agatha rolled her eyes.

Jamie turned his attention to Tori. 'So, how are you settling in? I hear you had an intruder last night.'

Agatha gasped. 'Someone broke into Blossom Cottage?'

'No, Beast turned up to give her a welcome party,' Jamie laughed. 'Apparently he was hoping to spend the night in Tori's bed.'

Tori marvelled at how easily he could talk to her and with Rosie when he had come into the café, but found it so impossible to talk to Melody.

'He didn't spend the night in my bed. I drew the line there, but he did sleep on the sofa. He was gone again this morning when I got up, no doubt off to terrorise some other poor unsuspecting soul, but I guess he'll be back again tonight for his dinner.'

'Oh, that bloody dog,' Agatha said. 'I don't know how Aidan expects to run a professional holiday let from the cottage when it comes with a stray dog. It's hardly a selling point.'

'What can he do though?' Tori said. 'He's called the animal shelter to come and get him and he's escaped from them three times. Blossom Cottage is Beast's home.'

'Aidan encourages him. You know there's a mattress and a heater in the shed, so the dog has somewhere to go if it can't get in the house.'

'I think that's really sweet that he's done that,' Tori said before she could stop herself and Agatha's eyes lit up.

'You think he's sweet? Oh, this is wonderful, you like him. Oh, you two would be perfect together.'

'No, I just think it's sweet, it's not—'

'I knew it!' Agatha said, practically bouncing out of her seat.

'There's nothing to get excited about, we barely know each other,' Tori tried.

'But you do have your hot date tonight,' Jamie said, grinning as he added fuel to the fire.

'Oh yes, you do,' Agatha said. Rooting around in her handbag, she pulled out a handful of condoms. Jamie choked on his sandwich and Melody stifled a giggle as Tori stared at them in horror. There were five strawberry and three chocolate-flavoured ones and they looked like they had probably expired a long time ago. 'Take these just in case.'

'Agatha, why do you have condoms in your bag?' Jamie asked.

'Well you never know, do you dear? One day, I might go into Stefano's Italian to get my meatball Bolognese and he might just decide to have his wicked way with me right there on the restaurant floor or on one of his pristine white tables. I mean, just because it hasn't happened yet doesn't mean it will never happen. I like to be prepared.'

'Well, I don't want to ruin your chances by taking all your condoms,' Tori said, trying to push the condoms back across the table towards Agatha.

'Oh, no need to worry, I have loads in here.' Agatha peered in her oversized handbag. 'There's probably fifty of them in there. I have mint-flavoured too but I find that a bit tingly. You take them and go and enjoy yourself.'

Melody snorted, and Tori was aware of the muted conversations in the café as everyone tuned in to what was being talked about at their table. She looked around and saw a few people looking over in their direction. She firmly pushed the condoms back across the table.

'It's not a date Agatha, no matter how much you'd like it to be, it's not. It's dinner and he will probably want to talk me through the berry-picking and how to do it,' Tori said. Though she was aware that, after their interactions the day before, they had already progressed much further than talking about work.

'Berry-picking, my arse, what do you need to know? You pick berries off the plant, it's not rocket science. And my sources tell me that you said you want to lick him all over, so I definitely think you will be needing these.' Agatha pushed the condoms back towards her.

'What sources?' Tori said. Surely Aidan hadn't told his aunt what she had said.

'Mary Nightingale from the post office was in the pub last night at the next table to you. She said it was quite an informative evening.'

Tori stared at her in shock and replayed everything that she'd said. Even after Aidan had gone there had been much talk about him. What else had they said that had now worked its way back to Agatha?

'I'm not denying that I find your nephew attractive,' Tori said, awkwardly. 'But nothing is going to happen.'

Agatha pushed the condoms even closer to Tori. 'Take them, just in case. You never know when the mood will strike, one of those wild, impetuous, go-with-the-flow moments.'

Tori sighed and decided that just taking the condoms and discreetly changing the subject was a lot easier than arguing against it.

She picked them up and shoved them in her bag.

Jamie laughed. 'Eight condoms. Looks like Aidan is in for a wild night.'

'I've been reading this *Fifty Shades of Grey*,' Agatha said, rummaging in her handbag again. 'That bondage stuff does sound like a lot of fun. Why not give it a go?'

Agatha produced a pair of red furry handcuffs, a blindfold and something long, black and sparkly that looked like it might be a vibrator but there were other bits coming off it, so she wasn't really sure. Thankfully, it was still in its wrapper and Tori was too afraid to ask what it was.

Jamie's laughing went up an octave and even Melody was no longer trying to suppress her laughter, her shoulders shaking, tears running down her cheeks as she laughed so hard.

'What the hell is this?' Jamie said, picking up the black thing.

'It's a vibrator, dear,' Agatha said, simply, and Jamie let it clatter to the table and then burst out laughing again. Melody put her head on her arms, her whole body shaking with laughter.

'I'm not taking those,' Tori said, looking around the café and realising everyone in the café was suddenly taking a strong interest in what was happening on their table. All other conversations had fallen silent and some people were openly laughing at their exchange.

'Look, just put them in your bag, you and I both know I'm going to win this argument, so you might as well take them now. I'm not saying whip them out on your first date tonight, but maybe on the second date you might like to try a bit of spice in your sex life.'

Tori grabbed the stuff and shoved it in her bag in the desperate attempt to stop this conversation once and for all.

'You're going to be sorry I took these once Stefano decides to have his wicked way with you,' Tori said.

'It's fine, Mary Nightingale runs a sex toys catalogue in her spare time, I get a discount. You should have a look yourself.' With impeccable timing, Agatha produced the catalogue. 'You never know what Aidan might be into.'

Tori rubbed her forehead. 'You're going to be so disappointed when I see you next and you hear that the only thing that happened tonight was dinner and conversation.'

'Ah yes, but it depends on what the conversation is about,' Agatha said, waggling her eyebrows.

'Berries and berry-picking I expect,' Tori said and looked around the table at three disbelieving faces.

Tori sighed because she didn't believe that either.

CHAPTER 9

Aidan opened the oven and checked on the chicken kievs for the tenth time. He'd wanted to do something different than his usual curry or lasagne for Tori, though he was beginning to wish he'd stuck to what he knew to be on the safe side. He wanted to impress her, and he didn't know why. Neither of them were keen on starting anything, both trying to protect their hearts, but they seemed to be accelerating towards something without either of them being willing to put on the brakes. He lifted the foil on the dauphinoise potatoes and, once satisfied they hadn't dried out completely, he closed the oven door again.

He eyed the candles on the dining table and wondered if they were too much for a supposedly non-romantic night. But there was no time to think about that as, outside, Tori was approaching his house. She was wearing a pretty yellow dress that sparkled with gold sequins and the setting sun glinted against the gorgeous red curls of her hair. There was something so… magical about her. He didn't like the way his heart thudded in happiness at seeing her again. Dating, relationships and women went against all his self-imposed rules, but he was enjoying himself too much to walk away.

He opened the back door and leaned against the frame. Her whole face lit up at seeing him and that warmed parts of him that hadn't felt warmth for a very long time.

She drew closer and her eyes cast down to his arms. 'You've got your elbows out again.'

He laughed as he looked down at his rolled-up sleeves.

'Well I thought it might stop you jumping me as soon as you walked through the door. It is supposed to be just dinner, remember?' he said, playfully, though he wasn't sure if he was saying that to remind himself.

'You don't need to worry, I have super-strength willpower, I will be perfectly behaved. I didn't know whether to bring anything—'

Tori suddenly tripped up the doorstep and went flying. He managed to reach out and catch her before she hit the floor, but her handbag and its contents went cascading all over the kitchen.

'God, are you OK?' Aidan asked, helping her back to her feet.

'Yes, I'm fine,' Tori said, a little breathlessly. 'Thanks for the lightning reflexes.'

'Ha, no problem. Though I thought you said you were going to be perfectly behaved and that nothing was going to happen. You haven't even been here five minutes and you're already throwing yourself at me.'

Tori laughed. 'It's obviously your animal magnetism. It's my kryptonite. I clearly can't keep my hands off you.'

'Understandable,' Aidan said, and Tori laughed again. 'Here, let me help you with your stuff.' He watched Tori's face fall, her eyes widening in horror.

'Oh god no, please don't,' Tori said.

He cast his eyes to the pile of debris scattered over the floor and spotted a condom, several condoms in fact. Flavoured ones judging by the bright colourful packaging. His eyes caught something else. Shit. There was a pair of red handcuffs, a blindfold and what looked suspiciously like a vibrator. What the hell kind of dinner had she planned for their first non-date?

He cleared his throat. 'Well… when you said you didn't know what to bring tonight, normally social etiquette suggests a bottle of wine or a box of chocolates, not… a vibrator.'

'They're not mine,' Tori said, falling to her knees and hastily stuffing all her things back into her bag. 'Bloody Agatha and her meddling. She insisted I brought these things tonight. They're hers. I tried to tell her it was just dinner and even if it was a date I certainly wouldn't be needing a bloody vibrator but, in the end, it was easier to just take them than argue with her. You know what she's like. Everyone in the café overheard, so probably half the village thinks I'm here for a night of sex and debauchery now. I was going to empty my bag before I came, but I forgot.'

Aidan laughed, with relief. 'She doesn't give up, does she? We need to get her back for this.'

Tori looked up. 'What did you have in mind?'

'I don't know, we can discuss it tonight. Though no matter what we do, it won't make any difference to her interfering.'

His eyes fell on her notebook, which had fallen open on the most current page. On it was an incredible detailed pencil drawing of him. He knelt to pick it up, but Tori snatched it away before he could even reach for it and it disappeared back inside her bag along with her bondage paraphernalia.

He didn't know whether to say anything, but she seemed even more flustered and embarrassed about that than about the bondage gear, so he decided to let it lie for now. Instead he picked up her keys and purse and handed them back to her without a word.

'There's some prawn crackers you can nibble on while I get dinner ready. And some heartberry chutney you can dip them into. Can I get you a drink? I have wine or beer.'

'A beer would be great,' Tori said, zipping up her bag firmly and hanging it up over the back of the chair.

He pulled a bottle out of the fridge, cracked open the top and passed it to her. She took a long swig and he smiled because yet again she had surprised him. In her pretty dress and with her red curls cascading down her back. He'd presumed she was the kind of girl who would appreciate a glass of wine. He clearly shouldn't make assumptions.

'So, for our "just dinner non-date" tonight, I figured we should stick to neutral topics of conversation. So, tell me more about Heartberry Farm?' Tori said.

He stared at her for a second. If she thought he was going to spend the whole night talking about berries and fruit-picking she could think again. He wanted to get to know her, every single thing. But he'd let her have it for now, let her become comfortable with the evening before he started on any of the personal subjects he wanted to talk to her about.

'It's been in my family for several generations. It is one of only three places in the world that grows heartberries and the only place in Europe. We also grow apples, strawberries, blackberries and raspberries but the heartberry is the most important, according to the villagers anyway.'

'And the heartberries are magical?' she teased, as she picked up a prawn cracker and popped it in her mouth.

He smiled and went to the oven to retrieve the dinner. 'Don't let the villagers hear you mock the heartberries. They take their traditions very seriously.'

'They actually believe the berries are magic?'

'A lot of them do, especially the older generation.'

'Do you?'

He served the chicken onto the plates and scooped out the dauphinoise potatoes as he thought about his answer. He didn't believe eating certain berries could possibly have an impact on anyone's life, he'd never believed in the power of the berries, but he guessed he had even more reason to doubt them now.

He placed the plates on the table. Tori sat down, and he sat opposite her. He poured out two glasses of water from the jug he'd put on the table earlier.

'Me and Imogen ate the heartberry cake at the festival of love two years ago shortly before we were supposed to get married. She jilted me at the altar, literally left me standing there in my best suit surrounded by all our friends and family and I never saw her again. So, I don't hold a lot of faith in everlasting love and certainly not in the power of the heartberries.'

Her face fell. 'I'm so sorry. What a shitty thing to do. She never contacted you to explain?'

'I got a text from her to say she was sorry.' There had been more to the text than that, though he wasn't going to go into detail. 'I wasn't looking for explanations at that point. If she was the sort of person that could do that, I think I had a lucky escape.'

'And you had no indication that it was going to happen?'

He took a bite of the chicken, the cheese oozing onto his tongue. Mixed with the garlic and herbs, it was the perfect combination. Maybe it was good to push yourself out of your comfort zone occasionally.

He swallowed. 'Looking back, I knew. I knew something wasn't right. Imogen was getting more and more stressed as the big day grew nearer. And it wasn't just the normal wedding nerves about everything going smoothly, it was obviously nerves about getting married, about being married to me for the rest of her life. Going by the rumours that I heard after she had left the village, she was sleeping with someone else as well.'

'Oh no, that's even worse. I'm so sorry you went through that.' She took a long swig of her beer and then put the bottle down carefully on the table. 'My ex cheated on me, I know what that kind of heartbreak feels like.'

He studied her, wondering whether to push it or not. 'Is that the reason you're not interested in a relationship?'

She turned her attention to her chicken for a moment and he thought she wasn't going to answer.

'There are many reasons for me not wanting a relationship. I suppose Luc was one of them.'

He waited quietly to see if there was any more, whether she'd even want to talk about it. Seeing him patiently waiting she sighed and picked up a prawn cracker, nursing it in her hand before she put it in her mouth.

'My dad walked out on us when I was ten. Just decided he didn't want our family any more and that the woman he had been seeing was much more preferable. I'd like to say that there were arguments, that my parents' separation had been brewing for a long time, but I can't. They were happy together, they laughed and kissed and cuddled. We were a happy little family. Turned out he had a girlfriend and a son a few months younger than me. When Mum was pregnant with me, he was sleeping with someone else. I don't think Mum could ever forgive that. He used to work away from home a lot – it turns out all those nights he was away with work, he was staying with her, living with his other family. And in the end, he chose them over us.

'I haven't seen him since he walked out. I don't know whether he tried to contact me and my mum wouldn't let him or whether he just drew a line under the years he spent with us and started a new life. It doesn't really matter either way. I guess I realised then that men can't be trusted. Mum was devastated. She was utterly heartbroken, and I've never seen pain like it. For years, she would sit around and just sob. It hurt so much that there was nothing I could do. But as I grew up, watching her never getting over it, I vowed very early on that I was never going to let a man get close, so he could hurt me that much. I wouldn't put myself in that position.'

This made so much more sense. Tori wasn't just wary of relationships because of some git of an ex-boyfriend, this was something much deeper.

'But you did have a relationship, with Luc?'

She nodded. 'I never wanted a relationship, with anyone. Luc was… charming and attentive and wouldn't take no for an answer. He slowly wore me down and I agreed to go out on a date with him. We had fun, we talked easily. One date led to another and another and soon we were dating. I was so wary about falling in love with him, I never wanted to be vulnerable or hurt in the same way as my mum. He knew about my trust issues and he assured me that I could trust him and one day I realised that, despite my best efforts, I had fallen in love with him. My first relationship and I knew without a doubt that this would be very different to my mum's relationship. I knew Luc would never hurt me. Turns out he was exactly like my dad. He had been sleeping with someone else for six months before we broke up. That really hurt. The fact that I had been so hesitant to give him my heart and when I did he just squeezed it to a pulp.'

He went to the fridge and got two more beers. 'And there's been no one for you since?'

She paused. 'No.'

The hesitation led him to believe that there *had* been someone.

She picked up the bottle of beer and cracked open the top. 'I kind of had a bit of a thing with Matthew.'

That surprised him. Matthew had moved down here when the girl he'd been seeing fell pregnant with Elliot. They hadn't lasted long after Elliot had been born and Sadie had left him to raise Elliot on his own. There hadn't been any girlfriends for him since, he hadn't left Sandcastle Bay very often and Aidan would have remembered if Tori had come down.

She must have seen the surprise in his eyes.

'We grew up together. When my dad left, and Mum fell apart, I spent a lot of time round Melody and Matthew's house. Both of them were my best friends. He was the first boy I kissed and the first man I made love to, although we didn't have any kind of relationship back then. We stayed in touch over the years and later we became really close. We'd chat every day on the phone and it became something much more than friendship. He came up one weekend and we ended up sleeping together. He wanted me to come down here and see him, but I was scared. I didn't want to get hurt again and I didn't want to lose Matthew as a friend. God, I did love him though. I know that sounds crazy because we weren't dating in the conventional sense. Anyway, we ended up having a big row about my unwillingness to commit and…'

She stared at her beer bottle sadly.

'He got himself killed in that car accident?'

She nodded.

He let out a deep breath. 'I'm so sorry. I didn't realise you had any kind of connection to Matthew, other than him being your friends' brother.'

'Melody and Isla don't know. I never told them, partly because there didn't seem to be anything to tell them about. Matthew and I had this weird relationship that mainly took place over the phone, and he lied to them about where he was that weekend he came up to see me and I didn't want to cause a rift between them by telling them the truth. And it became this wonderful secret that was just mine and Matthew's. And after he died it definitely never seemed the right time. But yes, we had something. I'm not sure what you'd call it, but we had something. I let myself fall in love with him. I refused to let anything happen for fear of getting hurt and I lost him anyway and that hurt in ways I couldn't possibly imagine. And now I think love is just way too painful and something that should be avoided at all costs. Men can't be trusted.'

Aidan was taken aback by this.

'I understand your wariness. But that's a huge generalisation that all men can't be trusted.' He wasn't sure why he wanted to change her mind; it was better for them both if nothing happened between them.

'I don't have any great role models. My dad left, Melody's dad left. Luc cheated on me, Matthew bloody left me too, although not by choice. Are your parents still together?'

'My dad died, so no.'

She swallowed. 'I'm so sorry.'

'It was a very long time ago. Mum remarried, she's blissfully happy, living up in Scotland now. But from where I'm standing there have been several women who have walked away from relationships too, Matthew's ex and mine. Women aren't perfect either.'

'No, we're not. I think relationships in general should be avoided, someone always gets hurt.'

'Agreed.'

They fell silent and Aidan couldn't help the huge stab of disappointment over this decision. Tori looked disappointed too. They had flirted with each other, they both knew that it was likely to lead somewhere and now it seemed they'd talked their way out of it.

He watched her as she continued to eat her chicken, slowly chewing each mouthful.

'So, tell me more about these traditions that the villagers hold so much stock in,' Tori said, seemingly forcing a smile onto her face as she tried to change the subject.

He pushed away his disappointment and tried to formulate a response, but his mind couldn't focus. She was trying to keep things professional, friendly, but not let it go any further when it was quite clear that neither of them wanted that. There was a connection there that he'd never felt with anyone before and he wanted to explore that even if it didn't go anywhere.

It was crazy, they came from different worlds. She lived in London, probably had a hectic and exciting social life going to glamorous parties and mixing with movie types. He owned a fruit farm and had nothing to offer her. It was a recipe for disaster. When he had been engaged to Imogen he had worried that what he had to offer was not enough to keep her interested and he had turned out to be right. She was always bemoaning the lack of great shops and nightclubs. She wanted more than life in Sandcastle Bay, she wanted more than spending the rest of her life with a boring fruit farmer and he'd last heard that she had emigrated to Los Angeles and was auditioning to be in movies. Surely this thing with Tori would never lead anywhere. But for some reason he couldn't leave it alone. He was drawn to her, like a mouse drawn to cheese in a trap. He knew it was going to end badly but he couldn't stay away.

'Hang on, back up a moment. Did we just agree that nothing was going to happen between us?'

She swallowed. 'I thought we agreed that yesterday when we first met. We were in the car. You said that you wouldn't push anything with me.'

'Things have kind of moved on since then. You've been ogling my elbows for one.'

She laughed.

'Look, this doesn't have to be… something. But we could…' he trailed off. What was he suggesting? He didn't really do casual relationships. He couldn't not get emotionally involved when he was with someone and he definitely didn't want to get emotionally involved with Tori and then watch her leave in a few weeks. He had avoided relationships of any kind since Imogen had jilted him. He had kept his heart locked away and that had worked just fine. But for some reason, Tori made him want to step out of his self-made cocoon where it was safe and he could never get hurt. More than anything he wanted to explore what would happen when they both let their guard down. It wasn't just a sexual attraction either, it went way deeper than that.

'I leave in two weeks,' Tori said, quietly.

'I know.'

'So, are you suggesting we have some kind of fling?'

He studied her and, despite her earlier protests about getting involved in any kind of relationship, she suddenly didn't seem so opposed to this idea.

He leaned across the table and took her hand, running his thumb across her wrist. She didn't take her hand away and he distinctly felt her pulse start to race at his gentle touch.

'I'm saying... let's keep an open mind.'

She clearly thought about this for a moment and then broke into a huge smile. She held up her beer bottle.

'To... possibilities.'

He grinned and chinked his beer bottle against hers. 'To all those wonderful, delicious, glorious possibilities.'

She smiled and, keeping her hand in his, she finished off her dinner.

CHAPTER 10

She stared at her fingers entwined with his and wondered why she wasn't more bothered by this wonderful turn of events. While she was scared by it, she was also enjoying this connection and she kind of wanted to see what would happen between them more than she wanted to hide from it. She was choosing the fun path. For once she was going to take a risk.

They'd finished their dinner a long time before and chatted well into the night, neither keen to break this connection between them. She tried to remember if she had ever held hands over dinner with Luc and she didn't think she had. She wasn't particularly tactile, and he hadn't been either, but she loved the way Aidan was gently stroking the back of her hand with his thumb. It was sweet and wonderfully intimate too. He made her laugh and they seemed to have endless things to say to each other, as if they were old friends catching up on all the years they had missed out on seeing each other.

He stood up and her hand fell from his. It felt cold without him. He took their plates to the side and served up what looked like Eton mess with a mixture of berries.

'Do I get to try the coveted heartberry then?' Tori indicated the mixed fruit he was spooning into the bowls.

'Nope, not until tomorrow night. We aren't allowed to start picking the fruit until the night of the May full moon.'

'What, really?'

'That's the optimum time, apparently.'

He placed the two bowls on the table in front of him, and she looked at the strawberries and raspberries that were soaking into the meringue.

'Is that one of the village traditions?' Tori asked as he sat down opposite and took her hand again. Her breath caught in her throat at this simple gesture.

'Yes, and it's a right ball-ache, let me tell you. It will take us about two to three weeks to clear the field, but we have to be done before the next full moon, because around then the heartberry fields always flood.'

'Is that to do with the weather? I've heard there's a hurricane in America they think will head out over the Atlantic towards us.'

'No, that shouldn't really affect us. We don't normally get floods from the weather at this time of year. The heartberry field sometimes floods in the winter, with all the bad weather we get, but all the fruit is gone then. No, the June flood is a tidal flood, you can predict it down to the day. It only lasts a day or two, but any fruit left in the heartberry fields is ruined if it isn't harvested before the flood.'

'Why not start picking the fruit earlier then? Surely the villagers wouldn't want to see the crop wasted.'

'Traditionally it was always picked after the May full moon. They believe that it's the moonlight that gives the berry its special love powers and picking the fruit before would mean it's less effective in its love- and happiness-spreading capabilities.'

Tori laughed. 'That's ridiculous.'

'I know. But one year I did sneak out to pick a few baskets of berries a few weeks ahead of the full moon. We'd had a good crop that year and I'd wanted to get ahead because we had more fruit than usual. Every single berry I picked was a lot tarter than usual and I ended up throwing most of the early berries away. They simply weren't ready for picking. And, despite me doing it under the cover of darkness, the villagers knew, and I didn't hear the end of it for weeks afterwards.'

'OK, so if you can't do it before the full moon, why not move the heartberries, grow them in a different place so they don't get flooded?'

'The salt water moistens the ground for the next year's crop. The heartberries thrive in these conditions, which is why they don't grow in many places around the world. It's not really a major problem – with some help from whoever stays in Blossom Cottage, we can normally get all the fruit picked. It's just a bit frustrating that the villagers' traditions are so restrictive, especially as we are only allowed to pick the fruit at night.'

'Another of their traditions?'

'Yes, but I have to agree with this one. For some reason the berries picked at night do taste better.'

'And you don't have any restrictions on how you pick the strawberries and raspberries?'

'No, I can do whatever I want with them. It's only the heartberries they care about. The strawberries and raspberries are also open to the public to pick their own. The public are not allowed to touch the heartberries. They have to be picked in a special way.'

Tori smiled and shook her head. What kind of place was she staying at with all these weird traditions?

'If the berries require handling by a virgin, you might be a bit out of luck.'

Aidan laughed loudly. 'Thankfully not.'

'Any sacrificing of goats? Because I'm not sure I can get on board with that either.'

'No animal sacrifices, we're not barbarians.'

'OK.'

'We just sacrifice whoever stays in Blossom Cottage at the end of their stay. But it's for the good of the berries, so you'll be OK with that, won't you?'

'Of course. Just make it quick.'

'Well we burn them at the stake, so it's over fairly quickly.'

Tori laughed. 'So, tell me what I'll be expected to do tomorrow night. Are we talking naked dances?'

Aidan hesitated and then his smile grew. 'Yes, definitely naked dances. It's tradition.'

Tori smiled, she loved his wonderful mischievous streak. 'And will you be dancing naked too?'

'Oh no, it's just the women that dance naked. Nobody wants to see me dangling free, it'd be enough to turn the fruit sour if I was to dance for them.'

Tori doubted that.

'So, I'll be dancing naked and you'll be picking the fruit.'

'Yes,' Aidan said, slowly. 'That's exactly what I'll be doing, picking the fruit and not paying any attention to you what-soever.'

Tori laughed.

'No, there are no weird traditions with picking the fruit, you just have to do it gently. Coax the fruit off the stalk. It's very easy to squash the fruit because it's so small and you don't want to lose half the crop being heavy handed.'

'OK, so you can show me that tomorrow. Do all these traditions bother you?'

Aidan shook his head. 'The heartberry farm is as much the villagers' as it is mine. It's been in my family for hundreds of years; who am I to start breaking the traditions now?'

'And is this what you wanted to do, be a fruit farmer?'

Aidan straightened in his chair. 'I know it might not seem like much of a job to you—'

'Wait, that wasn't what I meant. There is absolutely nothing wrong with being a fruit farmer. I imagine it's wonderfully peaceful and if it makes you happy then that's great. It's just you mentioned before that you always fancied being a chef and I wondered if that was your dream but, because you inherited the farm, looking after it was something that you were expected to do rather than what you wanted to do.'

His face softened. 'You remembered that from my ramblings yesterday?'

'You said you wanted to make desserts and puddings.'

He smiled. 'I did. I do. I loved cooking growing up. I always fancied being a chef. But I always knew that the farm would be passed down to me or my siblings and, as the oldest, I knew it was likely to come to me. My dad died when I was quite young and my mum, me and my siblings managed it for a while and then I took it over as soon as I was old enough. Leo and Emily never wanted to do it, and though I think Jamie would have been happy to, he was always so talented in art and sculpture that it was important he was free to do that. I didn't mind so I was happy to take it on. I've taught myself to do various desserts over the years, but I've never done anything more than that. I could hardly set up my own pudding or cake shop when I've got the farm to run too. It's fine – as you said, the job is very peaceful and rarely stressful. I do enjoy it, even if I don't love it, and I couldn't sell the farm on. The future of the heartberries could never be assured if I was to sell it. The heartberries bring a lot of tourism and money to the village and I don't want to do anything to risk that.'

Tori thought about this for a moment, the way he emphasised the money being brought to the village. She thought about Blossom Cottage and how there were certain things that needed to be repaired or replaced. Aidan didn't look as if he was the lazy sort. What if he simply didn't have the money to do these things?

'Does it bring a lot of money to you?'

Aidan paused, and she realised that was way too personal.

'Sorry, I shouldn't have asked that, it's just that—'

'No, it's fine. No, it doesn't, not really. I probably make more money annually from renting out Blossom Cottage as a holiday home than I do from the heartberries, and I don't make a lot from that. In fact, I would make much more money if I was to dig up the field and plant strawberries or grapes or any other kind of fruit instead. Most of the heartberries are sold locally, not just within our village but the surrounding towns and villages. Every café, pub and restaurant in Sandcastle Bay will buy them from me to make cakes, cookies and various desserts. About twenty percent of my crop will be frozen and sold across the UK and probably another ten percent sold abroad. But it's expensive to ship it abroad so I don't make a lot of money from that either. Beyond the local villages, it's mainly bought by hotels and posh restaurants across the UK as some kind of extravagant garnish or for weddings where people have heard of the legend of the berries and want to bring extra luck and romance to a marriage. But it's such an unknown fruit. Many people don't know it exists so there isn't much demand for it.'

'Do you advertise? Tori asked and was surprised when he shook his head. 'Really, not at all?'

'The locals take almost everything I have.'

'Could you grow more?'

He nodded. 'Yes, if there was a need. There is no need.'

'There could be if you advertise. Even if you can't sell the fruit, you could sell the end product. So, you don't make any of the jam or cakes here?'

'No, Emily makes all that and a few other local people do.'

'But that would tick that box for you. You could make cakes, pies and desserts from the fruit you grow here and sell it under the Heartberry Farm label. You could make very simple things, but also more elaborate fruit desserts too. I mean, I know it's not as simple as that. You'd have to get a proper kitchen if you were to make the stuff here and I presume someone from a professional body would need to check it over, I'm not sure how it works, and I imagine you'd have to get a certificate in food hygiene or something, but that's relatively easy to do. You say you've taught yourself to make various desserts over the years, you could start by offering them. Selling cakes, cookies and pies across the UK would be much more attractive than just selling the berries. I'm sure Emily would help you.'

He smiled, and she could see he was thinking about that idea. 'I'm sure she would.'

'We just need to launch you as a new brand. Advertising would help with that.'

'I couldn't afford proper advertising, certainly nothing on the TV.'

'It doesn't have to be, you can make a thirty-second video commercial and put it on social media, Facebook, Twitter, Instagram. You could even put it on YouTube. If you make it something unique or funny, people would be more willing to share it.'

'I wouldn't know the first thing about doing something like that.'

'This is what I do,' Tori said, excitedly. 'When I'm not making animated films, I do freelance stuff like this. Clients come to us, sometimes with no ideas for what they want their adverts to be, they just want an advert. We come up with an idea and once it's approved then we go away and make it. I could make you something.'

He stared at her in surprise and then frowned. 'I couldn't afford to pay you much. I'm not sure how much these things cost, but I imagine it might be quite a bit beyond my budget.'

'I'd do it for free. I love this kind of thing. I've spent the last eighteen months working on an animated film and, as much as I love it, it's so constraining. I've been wanting to do more freelance stuff ever since I finished shooting on the film, I find it so creative and liberating. I have my plasticine with me. We can have a chat about what you want and then I can come up with a few ideas. The design and modelling of the character might take a while, because getting the right character can be tricky, but I imagine I'd be ready to shoot in the next week or so. I have my green screen too, so I can add in a background later in post-production. Or we don't have to have a background at all, it can just be white – sometimes something simple works best.'

Tori pulled her notebook from her bag and started scribbling down some ideas, the thrill of creating something from start to finish buzzing through her. It had been too long since she'd done something like this.

'I could make a talking heartberry, then you could use him as your logo or mascot. Ooh, merchandising would be another good angle to make money. If the advert proves successful, you could make mugs, t-shirts or even cuddly heartberry characters and sell them. Kids love that sort of thing. The possibilities are endless when it comes to merchandising – phone cases, sofa cushions, mouse mats, notebooks, bags – and it all helps to get your image and your company out there. I'll come up with some rough ideas over the next few days and then we can discuss it together, but I definitely think we need some kind of logo like a smiling heartberry going forward, something that will help all your potential customers associate the fruit with you. It needs to be something memorable and cute. I'll come up with a few designs and you can choose which one you like the most.'

She looked down at her notebook and started roughly sketching out a heartberry figure with oversized shoes and big cute eyes. It looked like a walking heart – she needed to actually see the berries and then she could make the character look more berry-like. She had already Googled a heartberry but she needed to see the real thing. Colouring would be key; the end model would need to look shiny and juicy. She sat back and studied it for a while, suddenly desperate to get her colouring pencils. Thankfully she'd brought them with her, but they were back in Blossom Cottage at the moment. She started drawing a different berry character before she remembered where she was.

She looked up and saw Aidan was smiling at her.

'I'm so sorry, I got carried away there. When you stare at plasticine models all day, you sometimes forget how to be social. Coming to dinner with someone and then spending the night drawing in my notebook is hardly good etiquette.'

She reluctantly shoved her notebook back into her bag.

'I've never seen anyone so passionate about their work before. It's a wonderful thing to see,' Aidan said.

'Do you not enjoy your job?'

'I enjoy it. Growing fruit is a peaceful and often easy way of life. I can't say I love it to the same degree that you clearly love your job. Tell me more about it.'

'I do love my job. I was fascinated watching Morph when I was a kid and how he could just change shape at will. Later, when I realised that was all done with plasticine and stop-motion animation, I knew what I wanted to do with my life. I loved making little short films about animals when I was at college and university, something that would only have a running time of a few minutes but would take several weeks or months to make. No one was allowed in my room in the university dorms because there was always a plasticine character in action – well as much action as it could be when we only move them a few millimetres for each shot. But later, those little shorts were seen by someone who worked for one of the main TV stations and the idea got turned into the show *Amazing Animals* that was on TV a few years ago. It was so fantastic to get a break like that and to see my work on screen. After that, I got commissioned for lots of different adverts for big and small companies. I travelled to California, actually worked in Hollywood for a few weeks at a film studio there almost straight out of university. I've had jobs in Paris, Germany, and I've got one in New York in a few months' time. I've just finished an eighteen-month stint on a stop-motion animated film which will be out in cinemas probably later this year and I loved that. But I love seeing a project through from beginning to end, coming up with an idea, turning that idea into sketches and then plasticine models and then shooting and editing the final piece. So working on your advert is a dream come true for me.'

He smiled as she spoke, not taking his eyes from her face as he really listened to what she said. He was so easy to talk to.

He leaned back in his chair when she had finished. 'Well, this advert and merchandising sounds like a great plan, but I will pay you. I couldn't possibly let you do all that work for free.'

'I promise, this is like a fun hobby for me, it doesn't feel like a job. You can pay me in heartberry cake or free strawberries.'

'We can discuss terms later, but this sounds like something fun and I'd love to work with you on it. Honestly, I could do with a bit of help at the moment. I make some good money from the sale of the fruit but it's not really enough. I'm not struggling, not really, but… there are always unexpected outgoings. A new roof on Blossom Cottage set me back over twenty thousand last year and I just don't have the money for those kinds of things.'

'I'll help you. Adverts on social media can't really do any harm. We'll work something out.'

He smiled at her. 'Thank you.'

She focussed her attention on the Eton mess for a few minutes, tasting the sweet fruit and the crunchy meringue as her mind bubbled over with ideas.

She realised that Aidan was watching her with a smile.

'You're still thinking about the advert, aren't you?'

'I'm sorry. Was it that obvious?'

'That you weren't in the room with me, yes a little. Your eyes were filled with so much excitement and happiness. I doubt that I was the one giving you that reaction.'

'Oh, I don't know. You already know I have a thing for your knees and elbows.'

He laughed. 'I knew it, I knew you fancied my elbows. All that stuff about them being only six and a half out of ten was rubbish.'

'You got me. They're the sexiest elbows I've ever seen.'

His laugh got louder. 'You're different, Tori Graham.'

She swallowed the lump of meringue. Was that a bad thing? All this talk of elbows, was it too weird for him?

'Hey, different is definitely a good thing,' Aidan said, softly. 'I've talked to you tonight, really talked, and you're a great listener. I feel I have nothing of interest to say to a lot of the women round here. Quite honestly, some of them have nothing of interest to say to me either. There's a group of women, they meet every week and discuss all the celebrity magazines, who is dating who, the clothes they wear. I know nothing really happens in Sandcastle Bay, but why the lives of celebrities hold so much interest, I'll never know. You're different from all of them. And I really, really like that about you.'

She smiled, feeling inordinately pleased by his words.

The clock above the fireplace started to chime and Tori looked up, realising it was one o'clock in the morning.

'Oh, god, I didn't realise it was so late. I'm so sorry. I bet you have a ton of work to do tomorrow and now you'll be tired. You should have thrown me out, not let me keep talking all night.'

'I think tonight has been one of the best nights I've had in a long time,' Aidan said. 'I had no intention of throwing you out.'

'I've enjoyed tonight too. It's a shame it's over.'

There was a pause as they both stared at each other, the atmosphere in the air suddenly changing between them. She had never slept with anyone on a first date before, that kind of level of trust took a long time to build, but there was suddenly a large part of her that wanted Aidan to ask her to spend the night with him.

They continued to stare at each other and she felt like he was thinking the same thing. But he didn't say anything, and she realised he wasn't going to.

'I should probably go.'

He stood up. 'I'll walk you home.'

Disappointment hit her in a great wave, but then she'd said all along that it was only going to be dinner. She hadn't said anything to give him any clue that she might want to take it further. He was being the perfect gentleman. If something was going to happen that night, then she had to be the one to instigate it and there was no way she could do that. What if he turned her down? He liked her, seemed to be attracted to her, but it didn't mean he wanted to jump into bed with her. God, why was she even thinking like this? She was never like this with men. Even with Luc, sex had been something that he always instigated. It had been nice but never passionate, not the kind she and Melody used to watch in the movies where the couples were tearing each other's clothes off in a desperation for each other. Luc had never been desperate for her. She had never wanted his hands on her with the same urgency that she wanted Aidan to touch her now.

She stood up too and Aidan picked up her bag and handed it to her, standing so close she could smell his wonderful scent. He towered over her and for some reason his height and strength were such a turn-on.

He stared down at her, his eyes casting to her lips for a fleeting second before he stepped back.

'Oh, I got you something,' Aidan said.

He moved to the side and came back with a bunch of flowers. But as he got closer she realised they were all made from paper. They were all different styles, shapes and sizes and looked more beautiful than any real bunch of flowers.

'Oh, origami flowers, how lovely.'

It was such a sweet gesture and knowing how long it must have taken him to make and fold made all the difference.

'I know it wasn't a date but, I just wanted…'

'These are wonderful, thank you.'

'What are your plans for tomorrow?' He moved to the door and held it open for her. The night really was coming to an end.

'I'm going with your aunt to the tattoo studio. I believe she has decided to get a giraffe.'

She stepped outside, clutching her flowers.

'You're kidding? Though why I'm even doubting that, I don't know. Nothing will surprise me with Agatha. Are you getting one too?'

'I'm not sure I'm ready for something permanent, Agatha has persuaded me to get a henna tattoo. It'll wash off in a few weeks.'

'You're a bad influence on my aunt,' Aidan said, closing the door behind them.

'I think she's a bad influence on me. Let's not forget she was the one who handed me a vibrator and sent me off on a date with her nephew.'

Aidan laughed. 'She really is one of a kind. We still need to think of a way to get her back for that and all her general interfering.'

'Oh, I'm sure we can think of something.'

Aidan slipped his hand into hers and she looked up at him. 'I don't want you to fall, there's a few potholes as we walk down the drive and it is dark.'

'Good point and who would help you with all the fruit-picking then?'

'Yes, and the naked dancing.'

She smiled. 'That too.'

'You probably want to take a nap tomorrow afternoon,' Aidan said.

She looked up at him and laughed. 'I don't think I've taken a nap since I was a toddler.'

'Trust me, we'll probably be working from midnight until four, you'll definitely need a nap.'

'Do you nap?'

'I love a good nap. I rarely get the chance to do it, but this time of year, it's kind of a must. I can't really work all day and all night. Naps are great, you should try it.' He paused. 'It's even better when you nap with someone.'

Her cheeks burned red and she was thankful that the blanket of darkness masked that. Was he suggesting that she join him for a nap? Good lord, this flirting malarkey was a minefield. With Luc, she hadn't had to worry about any of that, he had pursued her. She hadn't been keen to start anything, and he had seen that as something of a challenge. With Aidan, there was a huge part of her that wanted this, and she wasn't used to these feelings or the things she should say and do as part of the courtship ritual. Should she offer to join him for a nap tomorrow? Unless he wasn't suggesting she join him at all and it was just a general comment. Then another horrid thought vied for attention in her head. What if he did this kind of thing with all the fruit-pickers that stayed in Blossom Cottage? Flirted with them, napped with them, slept with them.

'Do you nap with all your fruit-pickers?' Tori blurted out before she could stop herself.

Aidan laughed. 'Last year, I had a sixty-year-old, bearded man called Jim help me with the heartberries. Jim was definitely not my type.'

'Beard too scratchy for you?'

'Something like that. And the year before I had a Swiss man called Stefan. I was most definitely not his type. His boyfriend turned up after the first week and… well, their sexual antics were the talk of the whole village. Either they liked a lot of outdoor sex or they liked getting caught. The year before that there was a nice lady called Annie.'

'Did you nap with her?'

'She loved a good nap. The few times I came round to Blossom Cottage, she was sleeping in the armchair. We didn't nap together though. She was sixty-nine. She made a point of telling me because she celebrated her birthday while she was here, and she didn't want anyone to think she was seventy. She was a tiny bit too old for me. And I wasn't suggesting that we took a nap together, just that naps in general are better with someone else.'

'Oh, right.'

They walked in silence for a while, surrounded by the darkness.

'Unless you want to of course,' Aidan said.

She swallowed.

'Want to what?' She needed clarification of what she was agreeing to before she made a fool of herself again.

Aidan didn't answer straight away, but finally he did.

'Take a nap with me.'

Oh god. She had suddenly never wanted anything as much in her entire life. But did 'nap' actually mean they would simply sleep in the same bed as each other or was it code for sex? Should she turn up in her pyjamas or dressed in leather and bring a collection of sex toys? She snorted at that image. Sex had never been anything kinky for her and nor would she want it to be. She'd quite like the sex to be something a bit more than nice. But nothing too weird. But what if Aidan was into all that stuff? He'd recognised what the vibrator was without any problem. She was so woefully underprepared to start any kind of relationship again. The whole thing just scared her, flirting, napping, kissing and having sex again scared her. Letting her heart get carried away with it all scared her, despite her best intentions not to let it happen. She kind of got the feeling that if anything were to happen between her and Aidan, it would turn into… something. And she really didn't want that.

She realised that she was taking way too long to answer, her stupid brain overthinking everything. She opened her mouth to speak, although she still didn't know what her answer was going to be, but Aidan got there first.

'Ignore that offer. That's hugely inappropriate. Taking a nap is something you do with someone special. Not someone you don't even have something with.'

'There are rules for when you can take a nap with someone?'

'Oh yes, there are different stages of a relationship. It's like a fruit, there are four main stages of growing a berry. You have the bud stage where the possibilities of fruit are wonderful and exciting – that's the hand-holding, flirty-conversation, sweet-looks, admiring-elbows stage of a relationship. Then the bud turns into a flower and it's pretty and smells amazing. That's the kissing and mad passionate sex stage and some couples will never get past that part. The berry is the same – the flower will sometimes never produce a fruit, it just withers and dies.'

'So where does napping come in? Stage two?'

'No, not yet. Stage three is the difficult stage, where the flower turns to a berry. The berry is small and hard for a while and some might never grow bigger than that. This is the stage where the couples try to make it work, to take it further than just sex and kissing, to see if they have anything worth fighting for. Some of them just don't have what it takes. Sometimes the berry is fully formed but tastes really bitter. That's those couples that nearly make it, the ones that get as far as the altar but then one of them fails to turn up. And then stage four is the berry that's ready for picking, the big fat juicy berry that's perfect in every way. Those are the relationships that are going to last, the happy-ever-after type relationships. Although to be honest, I'm not sure such a thing can really exist.'

'No, I'm not either. So where does napping fit into all of that?'

'Stage four, I think. The perfectly, blissfully happy stage.'

Tori thought about this and decided that he was right. Cuddling in bed with someone was far more intimate than sex. It was no wonder the prospect of it had freaked her out. She knew it meant something more.

They arrived back at her cottage and Aidan walked her right up to her door.

'Go on inside, I'll wait here until you get the light on,' he said.

She let herself in and, leaving the door open, so moonlight filled the lounge, she found the light switch and flicked it on, noticing Beast was fast asleep on the sofa again.

She came back to Aidan and wasn't entirely sure what the right thing to say was. Should she invite him in for coffee?

'Thank you for tonight, I had a wonderful evening,' Tori said.

'I did too.'

He hovered on her doorstep for a moment and then bent his head and pressed his warm lips to her cheek. 'Goodnight Tori.'

He turned and walked away, disappearing into the darkness, and she reached up and touched her cheek where the feel of his kiss tingled on her skin.

She came inside and shut the door behind her, leaning against it. She found a huge smile spreading on her lips because it seemed that Aidan Jackson had just moved very quickly on to stage two.

CHAPTER 11

Tori sipped her chamomile tea from a bone-china cup and smiled as she looked around the little haven that was Rosie's tattoo studio. It wasn't at all what she imagined it would be. She'd expected red walls, big posters of skulls, drawings of snakes and examples of different tattoos on the walls with heavy metal or rock pounding out of the speakers but that wasn't the case at all. The shop was largely white with cherry blossoms painted all over the walls as if you'd just stepped into a forest. Little silvery and gold fireflies dotted the walls too as they flew around the blossoms. Soft classical music was playing and all the ideas for tattoos were kept away in books. It was tasteful, and she couldn't think for one minute why the locals would have anything against it.

She was tired today and this place was calm and relaxing and exactly what she needed. She felt like she'd just stepped into a spa and would soon be going to have a massage, not getting some scary tattoo on her back.

She looked over at Eva, Rosie's wife, who was curled up in a chair reading a book. 'You have a beautiful shop here.'

Eva looked up and smiled. 'Thank you. It's a reflection of Rosie, she's so girly and sweet. I have to say I love it too, but don't tell her that.'

Tori smiled at the obvious love Eva had for her wife.

She looked around the studio and yawned. She *was* tired. After returning to the cottage the night before, her mind had been buzzing with Aidan and their sort of first kiss. Knowing she wouldn't be able to sleep, she had spent hours drawing out different heartberry characters for Aidan to choose from and even drafted out a script and a rough storyboard of the advert too. For some reason this project excited her. It happened sometimes, a company would come to her with an idea for an advert and it inspired her so much she would work round the clock, so she could get started on it. She had finally crawled into bed around four this morning, so she was definitely looking forward to her nap later.

She flicked through a book of tattoo ideas that Rosie had designed, trying to decide what she would get if she were ever to go for something permanent. Rosie was clearly very talented, her designs were so intricate but, as well as the usual tattoos that Tori would expect to see, there were loads of really unique and creative ones. Amongst others, the book was filled with beautiful Disney tattoos and elaborate Harry Potter ones.

She looked out of the window at the little pieces of sea glass hung about the courtyard, sparkling and twisting in the gentle sea breeze.

She needed this today. The following day was Matthew's birthday and she had been thinking about him a lot since she'd come down here. A year ago, he had been alive, laughing, smiling, full of life, with no idea that three weeks later his life would come to an abrupt and sudden end. They had Skyped on his birthday – they didn't do it all the time as Matthew's

Wi-Fi connection was particularly bad, but they did from time to time. She had sent him a cake with the Millennium Falcon on it because he loved Star Wars and she had wanted to see his reaction when he opened it. He had laughed loudly when he'd seen it and declared it the best cake ever.

God, she missed talking to him.

She had thought about visiting his grave while she was here but what would she say to a headstone? That headstone was not a representation of him, always laughing, so full of energy and happiness. And the headstone wouldn't talk back.

She felt like she should do something to mark his birthday, though she had no idea what. And every time she thought about him, it hurt, so she was grateful for the distraction of getting a tattoo with Agatha.

Agatha had settled on a silhouette of a giraffe against the setting sun and had been behind the curtain having it inked onto her shoulder for the last two hours. Little whoops of excitement, sometimes pain and mostly laughter kept drifting out from the curtains and Tori smiled that she was obviously enjoying herself. Despite her interfering, Tori really liked Agatha.

The buzzing noise stopped, and she heard Rosie say she was getting a mirror so Agatha could see the finished tattoo properly. A few moments later, Tori could hear gasps of delight.

'Oh Rosie, dear, this is wonderful. I've never seen anything so beautiful before. Let's go and show Tori.'

The curtain was pulled back and Agatha hopped out of the chair and offered out her arm for Tori to see.

'Oh wow. This is amazing,' Tori said. The giraffe was only three inches tall but held so much detail, she could even see the bumps of the muscles in the body and the fur on the giraffe's head. 'Rosie, you have a wonderful talent.'

'Your turn now,' Agatha said, nudging her towards the chair.

'For a henna tattoo, not a real one,' Tori confirmed, and Rosie nodded.

'Agatha tells me that she has a design for you?'

Tori sighed. She didn't know what Agatha had planned but she had agreed that Agatha could choose. She was wearing a backless vest, so she could let the henna dry without smudging it, but after today she could hide the tattoo under her normal clothes and no one would ever see it until it faded away, so it didn't really matter.

'I'd like something with those beautiful flowers,' Tori tried.

Agatha shook her head. 'My design doesn't have flowers.'

'I'm sure we can incorporate some though,' Rosie said, clearly trying to find a middle ground. 'Let's see the design.'

Agatha fished it out of her bag and discreetly tried to pass it to Rosie so that Tori wouldn't see.

Rosie's eyes widened and then she looked at Tori. 'Are you sure about this?'

'Why, what is it?' Tori asked.

'You agreed,' Agatha said. 'You said I could choose.'

Tori looked at Rosie. 'It's fine. Whatever it is. It'll wash off in two to three weeks anyway, right?'

'Sometimes a lot less, it depends how oily your skin is. Where are you having it done?'

'The top of my back.'

'Perfect,' Rosie said. 'No one will see it there.'

That filled Tori with a whole heap of confidence.

'Why don't you go and sit in the chair? If you could sort of straddle it so you're facing backwards, and I'll just wrap Agatha's tattoo.'

Tori went to straddle the chair and she heard Rosie explain that Agatha would need to take off the wrapping in a few hours' time and how to clean it.

Rosie came back to her and pulled on a pair of gloves. 'If you really don't like it, come back to me tomorrow or in a few days and I can draw some flowers over the top of the bits you, umm… don't like and I won't charge you anything.'

'Am I really not going to like this tattoo?' Tori asked, quietly, not wanting to offend Agatha by not liking her design she had worked hard on.

'It's just… an acquired taste I think,' Rosie said, diplomatically.

Tori remembered what Leo had said about sometimes taking a risk. This wasn't even a big one, but she had to start somewhere.

'It's fine, whatever it is, it isn't the end of the world,' Tori said, decisively.

'OK then,' Rosie said.

A few seconds later she felt the cool dye being applied to her skin at the very top of her spine and Tori cringed, wanting to change her mind. She kept her mouth shut because how bad could it really be?

'What do you mean I can't see it?' Tori said, trying to crane her neck to see over her shoulder.

'You have to let it dry,' Agatha said, having just appeared round the curtain with a pink stud in her nose. 'It'll be crusty for a few hours and you're not going to see it at its best.'

Tori looked at Rosie hopefully, to see if she had a different answer.

Rosie nodded. 'Agatha is right. Let it dry, then brush or rub off the crust with a towel, then you can take a shower to wash away any remains. It will be dark orange at first and go dark brown to black over the next twenty-four to forty-eight hours. But yes, it's best to view it when you've rubbed away all the left-over henna.'

Eva moved round to look at Tori's tattoo.

'Oh Rosie, this is stunning,' Eva said, proudly. 'You're so talented at stuff like this. It's so beautiful.'

'Really? It's beautiful?' Tori asked.

'Yes,' Eva said, and Tori sighed with relief. She had been wrong to doubt Agatha. 'I mean, totally hilarious but beautiful.'

Tori looked at Eva. 'What do you mean, hilarious?'

'Well…' Eva gestured at the tattoo. 'Not hilarious. just…' Clearly having no more words to describe it, she decided to change the subject. 'What do you think of Agatha's nose stud?'

'It looks great,' Tori said, because actually it really suited her.

She turned her attention back to the matter in hand. The tattoo was beautiful and hilarious, how did that work exactly? She racked her brains for what it could be.

'Can you not just give me a little clue about what the tattoo is?' Tori asked.

'No,' Agatha said quickly before Rosie or Eva told her. 'Don't spoil the surprise.'

Tori sighed but really, how bad could it be?

'How much do I owe you?' Tori asked Rosie.

Rosie shook her head. 'Come back and pay me if you're happy with it and if you're not then come back and I'll change it for you.'

'OK, thanks,' Tori said. She looked at her watch and realised she was supposed to meet Melody and Isla for lunch in a few minutes. 'Oh, I better go.'

'Thanks for coming with me,' Agatha said.

Tori smiled. 'I won't say it was my pleasure as I found the whole experience a bit traumatic, especially not knowing what exactly was being inked onto my back. But I'm working on doing things that take me out of my comfort zone, so I suppose this was good for me. I'll save the thanks for when I've actually seen the tattoo.'

Agatha grinned. 'You're going to love it. I think Aidan will like it too.'

'Well sadly he won't be seeing it. As I've already told you, nothing is going to happen between us.'

'You can still show him. You don't exactly have to whip off your underwear and jump into bed with him to show him, it's at the top of your back,' Agatha said.

Tori rolled her eyes and shook her head with a smile. 'See you later.'

She arranged her scarf loosely round her shoulders, so no one would see the tattoo just in case it was something crazy. She might ask Melody and Isla what the tattoo was as soon as she was out of sight of Agatha and her strict rules, though if it was something embarrassing, it might be better if no one saw it. She thanked Rosie and walked out the shop and straight into Melody's shop, which seemed to dazzle and sparkle from every surface with all the beautiful jewellery pieces that Melody made.

Isla and Elliot were already there. Elliot was trying on a beautiful diamond and sapphire tiara and giggling about how he was a king, and everyone should curtsey and bow to him.

Tori immediately went over and swept down into a big bow. 'Your Majesty. How can I be at your service?'

Elliot burst out laughing.

She watched him as he tried on several oversized rings and she noticed that one had a price tag of several hundred pounds, Melody didn't seem to mind at all. Isla was watching him with absolute adoration in her eyes. Elliot was cute, cheeky, adorable and seemed to find amusement in everything. Just like his dad. It was strange to think that if she had taken a risk with Matthew and the relationship had turned into something serious, or even marriage, she would have been Elliot's step-mum. That prospect hadn't deterred her when she was having her sort of relationship with Matthew but with hindsight what kind of mum would she have been to this little boy? She doubted she would have done as good a job as Isla was doing.

'It's Daddy's birthday tomorrow,' Elliot said, cheerfully and unexpectedly, giving Tori a kick to the gut at the mention of Matthew. 'We're having a party with a big cake and afterwards we are going to go to Daddy's grave and Isla says I can take him the cake though I can have some of it, but we'd leave Daddy a slice, even if he can't eat it, he might see it and be happy we left it for him. We're going to make the cake this afternoon and it will have a picture of the Millennium Falcon on it because Daddy loved Star Wars, and he had a cake with the Millennium Falcon on it last year and he loved it, so I wanted to do it again. Though Isla says that she isn't good at drawing, so it might not look like the Millennium Falcon, but we can give it a go. Are you going to come to the grave with us?'

'I, er…' Tori stumbled over an answer because she wasn't sure. She'd never felt she had ever properly had the chance to say goodbye to Matthew, but she couldn't really go with Isla and Melody, could she? What if she cried when they were there, they'd want to know why. But maybe she should go. Maybe it would be easier to visit him if she went with friends.

'You're Daddy's friend, you should come,' Elliot said.

Oh god.

'Yes, Matthew was my friend,' Tori said, carefully.

'You should come to the party actually,' Isla said. 'You guys were close.'

Tori swallowed. Did Isla know? A party might be easier than going to the grave.

'I'd like that. And you know what, my drawing skills aren't bad, I could help you with the Millennium Falcon on the cake,' she said to Elliot. 'You guys could make the cake and I could do the Millennium Falcon on a cake topper and bring it to the party.'

'Yay!' Elliot said. 'Daddy would like that. He liked you a lot. He will love that you are there tomorrow.'

Oh crap. She was about to get outed by the cute adorable five-year-old and there was nothing she could do about it. She needed to change the subject fast.

'They used to talk on the phone every day,' Elliot went on. 'He liked talking to her. He was always smiling after.'

'Oh no honey, I think you might have confused Tori with someone else,' Melody said as Isla watched Tori carefully.

'No, I'm not confused,' Elliot said, angrily. 'He loved her, he told me.'

Tori had no words, emotion clawed at her throat, her battered heart thundering against her chest. She and Matthew had never said those words to each other. He'd died before she had plucked up the courage to tell him how she felt, pushing him away instead because she was scared of the emotions she'd been feeling. All those months they'd spoken on the phone and she'd been too scared to do anything to change their relationship from the wonderful friendship she had with him into something more. One wonderful weekend was all they had to show for their relationship, making it look a lot more casual than it was.

'I think you might have misunderstood,' Melody tried again.

'No, I didn't,' Elliot said, clearly getting upset.

'No, he didn't,' Tori said, quietly. 'I don't know about the love part because we never said that to each other, though I know that I loved Matthew. But Elliot is right about the other part. We talked every day on the phone for about four months before he died.'

Isla nodded. 'Elliot said as much this morning when we were talking about you. After what Leo said in the pub the other night, I guessed something went on between the two of you. Though I wasn't sure to what extent.'

Melody stared at her. 'You've always been good friends. Was it more than that?'

Tori nodded, hating that she would have to tell them about that weekend that she and Matthew had both lied to them.

She swallowed, nervously. She'd never wanted it to come out like this. 'He was actually the first person I…' she looked at Elliot, 'had a sleepover with.'

Her friends' eyes widened in shock.

'When we were eighteen. Nothing happened after that for many years, he was away, but a few months before he died there was… another sleepover.'

Tori looked at Melody, wondering if she would be angry or upset. The very last thing in the world she wanted was to upset Melody. Though it seemed that Melody didn't know how to react either as she stared at Tori as if she didn't know her.

'You never told me,' Melody said, quietly.

'I'm sorry.'

Tori wanted the chance to explain, to tell her everything, but the words were stuck in her throat.

Finally, she spoke. 'Shall we go to lunch and I promise to tell you both everything.'

Isla nodded and eventually Melody did too.

'I want to hear everything as well,' Elliot said, not wanting to be left out.

'I promise.'

CHAPTER 12

As it happened, Marigold, Emily's daughter and Elliot's best friend, was 'working' behind the counter and as soon as they walked into The Cherry on Top, Elliot wanted to help as well. He was currently standing behind the counter, with an apron on, giggling as they ate a few cookies. Occasionally Emily would get them to take a food order over to the tables, but that was as far as the helping went.

'I can't believe you never told me,' Melody said, sadly, after Tori had explained everything about her relationship with Matthew.

'I'm so sorry, I never meant to hurt you or deceive you. I just wasn't sure how you would react to it and I didn't want to upset you. The first time we made love, it was this wonderful little secret that was just mine and Matthew's. He was going off to America on his gap year so nothing more was going to happen and then later when we started talking on the phone, I didn't know what it was going to be, only that I really bloody liked him. That weekend he came to see me, I had no idea he had lied to you about going away with work until he told me what he had done. I didn't want to tell you guys the truth and drop him in it and hurt you both at the same time. It just felt like a harmless little lie. I couldn't tell you we had slept together then when he was supposed to be in Paris with work. I really am sorry.'

Melody was quiet, and Tori had no idea what to say to make it better.

'We all have secrets,' Isla said and then turned to Melody. 'You've not exactly been particularly forthcoming about your feelings for Jamie. And my… *friendship* with Leo is beyond complicated, I certainly don't want to talk about that either. Sometimes the "keeping it a secret" part can be one of the best bits and interference from other people, even if it is well-meaning, can taint or ruin it before it's even started. Tori, I don't blame you for not telling anyone. I saw or spoke to Matthew quite regularly over the last months of his life and he was so happy. If you had any part to play in that then I think I owe you my thanks more than anything else. It was good to see him smile again.'

'Isla's right,' Melody said. 'I think it's lovely that your friendship with Matthew turned into something more. You made each other happy and that's all we ever want from a relationship. But also, I feel unbearably sad for you too. You never got to see the relationship develop into something more, you never told each other how you felt.'

'I feel so guilty that I ended it just before he died. I hurt him, and I never got the chance to fix things, to tell him how I really felt.'

'Matthew adored you, anyone could see that. Growing up, you guys were so close, it's only natural that closeness would turn to something more,' Isla said. 'You felt safe with him and he knew everything about your dad leaving and how much that ruined you. He knew about Luc and how scared you were of getting involved with another relationship; he should have been a bit more patient with you. If you loved him, then I bet he knew that, or at least suspected your feelings, which I imagine led to his frustration when you started to back off. But knowing Matthew, if he loved you like Elliot says he did, then he wouldn't have given you up without a fight. He spoke to me the night before he died, said he was planning to come up to London to see us the following weekend. My guess is that was something to do with you. I don't think he died still being angry at you. He loved you, and you don't just switch that off.'

'I hope you're right. Maybe it would never have worked out between us if I had taken that step – once we were together our bad habits might have wound each other up. He might have hated my tidiness or how much attention I give my plasticine models and I might not have been able to bear him leaving his shoes lying around. But yes, I will always wonder what could have been. I will always regret what we didn't do.'

'If that isn't an advert for seizing the day, I don't know what is,' Melody said.

'I know. Leo said as much as well. He said there will never be a safe path. And he is so right. We can eat all the right things, never drink, never take drugs or smoke, never get on a plane just in case it crashes, and we can still die under the wheels of a bus one day or from some horrible disease. We might live our lives avoiding risk, push love away just in case we get hurt, but we'll still get hurt one way or another. I was afraid of getting hurt, but losing Matthew hurt more than any broken relationship ever could. So maybe it's time to embrace life a bit more, take a few risks, step out of my comfort zone.'

'That Leo is a wise man,' Isla said, with a smile.

Tori nodded. 'He really is.'

'We're actually having a memorial celebration tomorrow,' Melody said. 'Just us and a few of Matthew's friends. It was Leo's idea. Instead of marking the day of Matthew's death, we decided we would celebrate his birthday instead. You should come.'

'I'd really like that.'

They fell silent for a while and Tori played with the last few crumbs of her sandwich, then she turned to Isla.

'I want to hear about your complicated relationship with Leo.'

Melody giggled, and Tori was relieved the tension of the conversation seemed to have lifted.

Isla sighed, looked over at Elliot to make sure he was occupied and then around the café to check no one was listening. Sensing that this was a big secret, Melody and Tori leaned in close.

'OK, if we're sharing secrets, I'll tell you one of mine. Leo proposed to me.'

'What?' Tori said. That hadn't been what she was expecting at all.

'What?!' Melody squealed, almost bouncing in her chair as she clapped her hands with excitement.

Isla rolled her eyes. 'I know, it's ridiculous. I said no, of course.'

'Why?' Melody asked, her face falling at the happy ending fading away.

'Because he asked me to marry him out of some weird duty to Matthew, because he thinks Elliot needs a dad and because he doesn't want me to worry about money. He knows things have been… a little difficult financially since Matthew died. Leo didn't ask me out of love. He just wants to take care of us.'

'Oh, that's so sweet,' Melody said, the possibility of a happy ending reappearing again.

'I know, it is, but I'm not going to marry someone just so I'm financially supported.'

'He actually said those were the reasons he wanted to get married?' Tori asked. Leo didn't seem the romantic sort who would get down on one knee and declare his love for Isla, but he must have said something nice, something that showed he had some feelings for her.

'This was several months ago, though he has asked me quite a few times since then. But yes, there was no big fancy proposal, not that I'd need one of those. I'd gone round to pick up Elliot after he'd spent the night at Leo's. We were having coffee and he said that he'd been thinking that we should get married. I didn't know what to say at first but eventually I asked why, and he told me that he wants to take care of me and Elliot, that he didn't want me having to worry about getting a job or money.'

Tori sighed. The man clearly needed a few lessons in romance. She'd seen the way he looked at Isla, it was obvious there was something there that was much more than friendship and that this flat proposal came from somewhere beyond just wanting to take care of them.

'No man is going to give up their single life and get married to someone they don't love, just to take care of them. If money was an issue, then why not just give you the money. There's more to this than what he is offering,' Tori said.

'I agree,' Melody said. 'That gesture is so sweet, it's obvious he cares about you.'

'I know he cares about me, but I don't need taking care of. Me and Elliot are fine.'

'But just think of all the incredible sex you'd have,' Tori teased.

Isla laughed. 'I have, believe me, I have thought about that a lot. But if we're not marrying out of love would we even have that arrangement? Or would we have separate bedrooms and live only as friends? Would he continue to date other people, bring them back to his house? I don't think I could bear seeing that, my fragile heart couldn't take it. But then if we did have sex, there would be something quite seedy about me sleeping with him in return for money and a roof over our heads, no matter how amazing the sex was. I want to get married for love and I won't settle for anything less.'

'And do you love him?' Melody asked.

Isla sighed. 'Yes, no… maybe. I don't know. We're good friends, maybe that's as much as it will ever be.'

Elliot came running back, halting the conversation from going any further. At least for now. 'Can I have a slice of banoffee cake?'

'Of course, tell Emily that I said it was OK.'

Elliot ran off again.

'OK, can we change the subject before he comes back?' Isla said.

Tori cast around for a suitable topic. She spotted Mark at the next table eating a large cream cake that probably wasn't very vegan either or, if it was, she didn't think Mindy would approve. Isla was right, everyone did have their secrets.

'I suppose I should share my secret as well, though it's not too much of a secret,' Melody said. 'I'm in love with Jamie Jackson and I'm not talking a silly little crush. I mean head over heels, can't sleep, can't eat, crazy in love with him. And he's the first person I've felt this way for too.'

Isla leaned forward. 'Ah no Melody, I knew you fancied him, I didn't realise you loved him.'

'Your first love?' Tori said, gently.

'I know. Does love always hurt this much?' Melody asked.

Tori and Isla nodded.

'Then maybe it is best to be avoided,' Melody sighed.

Tori didn't want Melody to think that way. She might have given up on love for herself, but it didn't mean she didn't want to see her friends with their happy ever afters.

'Have you done anything about it, have you told him how you feel?' Tori said.

'I think he knows.' She covered her face with her hands. 'I kissed him.'

Tori's eyes widened, and she quickly glanced at Isla, who clearly had no idea this had happened either.

'When was this? Did he kiss you back? What was it like?' Tori asked, a million more questions bubbling in her head.

'After Matthew's funeral. I was a mess. Went to a pub and got myself blind drunk. Jamie looked after me. I knew him, of course. Every time I'd come down and visit Matthew, the Jackson brothers were always with him. I had a little crush on Jamie for years. He stayed with me that night in the pub, made sure I drank plenty of water, practically carried me back to the hotel I was staying at. And that's when I kissed him. I don't remember much, only how he held me in his arms like I was something precious, I remember his grip on me tightening, his tongue in my mouth and how I'd never felt that incredible when kissing anyone before. It seemed to go on forever, but in reality, it was probably only a few seconds before he pulled away. He didn't say anything, just helped me into the hotel and into my room and, for a wonderful moment, I thought he was going to stay with me, but he simply took my shoes off and then covered me with the duvet and left. We have never spoken about it since. Of course, now, I've moved down here, and I live practically next door to him and bought the shop just opposite him, I bet he thinks he's got himself a right stalker.'

'Oh, love,' Isla said. 'It sounds like he kissed you back though.'

'I don't know, maybe he did, maybe he was just trying to get away from me politely,' Melody said, sadly.

Elliot came running back then with a large slice of banoffee cake and a big pile of squirty cream with sprinkles on the top.

Tori looked around the table at her two friends. All their love lives were a complete mess. Maybe the festival of love would sort them all out once and for all.

Later that afternoon, after she had spent a while making a Millennium Falcon cake topper, and some time working on Aidan's advert, Tori pulled on her strawberry-print pyjamas and got into bed, feeling a bit ridiculous for taking a nap. She was tired, but she couldn't remember the last time she had slept in the middle of the day. She lay staring at the ceiling for a moment before she rolled onto her side and closed her eyes, hoping that the warmth of the bed would send her to sleep. It didn't. Maybe Aidan was right, maybe taking a nap with someone was infinitely better.

Feeling silly and giddy, she grabbed her phone from the side and took a photo of herself lying in bed and then texted it to Aidan with the message, *Getting ready for my nap, any tips for getting off to sleep?*

To her surprise, he texted straight back. *Nice pyjamas.*

The next text he sent contained a photo and, as she opened it properly, she could see it was Aidan, lying in bed, with only a sheet clinging to his hips, only just covering his modesty. Was he naked under that sheet? God, he looked amazing, his hair all messed up, his eyes sparkling with amusement.

He sent another text.

You need something to cuddle up to.

She smiled and deliberately didn't take the hint. *If only Beast was here.*

Ha, I bet he is a good cuddler. I'll see you at the farmhouse at 11.

Want to make it a bit earlier, I can show you what I've been working on for your advert.

Sounds good. Come by at 10.30 then. I hope you have sweet dreams, Tori Graham, I know mine will be.

What will you dream about?

Beautiful girls in strawberry print pyjamas.

She smiled, squeezing her phone to her chest as excitement bubbled through her. She wasn't sure what was happening here, but she knew she wanted more of it. She closed her eyes and imagined him lying in his bed, thinking of her, and her smile grew even bigger. If she could get to sleep now that her heart was galloping in her chest, she knew she'd have some very sweet dreams indeed.

To her surprise, she did sleep, and she slept a lot. Maybe it had been the eighteen months that she had spent on the animated film finally catching up with her, or maybe it was the sea air or that she had spent most of the night before awake, working on the advert instead of sleeping, or maybe because she'd had such wonderful dreams that she didn't want to leave them. Whatever it was, she had been in bed for nearly three hours.

She got up and made herself a pot of tea before going outside to sit on the decking. She watched the sun as it began its slow descent into the sea, leaving plum and candyfloss pink trails through the sky, although it wouldn't set properly for another hour or two yet.

She grabbed her notebook and started sketching out some more ideas for Aidan's advert and the mascot, using her fineline pens to add colour to her drawings so they slowly came to life. She was excited about this and how it would finally look and as the ideas bubbled through her she even started making a rough model out of plasticine too. The one she would use for the advert would be bigger, but at least showing Aidan what the model would look like would help him to visualise it better than her sketches and storyboards would.

Tori suddenly realised that she'd lost several hours to her sketches and modelling. The sun had set a long time before and solar lights were lighting up the decking without her even realising, though the pale sky and bright full moon still illuminated the garden almost like it was day time.

She got up and hurriedly made herself a bacon sandwich for her tea, slathering it in a thick layer of ketchup before tucking in. She'd seen Beast sniffing around outside near the shed, but she wasn't sure if he'd gone in there to sleep or snuck off to terrorise the rest of the village again. But she poured out some food and left out some fresh water just in case. Judging by what she'd heard from various members of the village, he got his food from plenty of other sources, not just her, so she wasn't too worried if he had missed dinner from her that evening. He was probably tucking into steak and chips somewhere else.

Tori decided it was time to look at the tattoo. With all the talk about Matthew with Melody and Isla that afternoon, she'd not had the chance to ask them what the tattoo was, and she hadn't been entirely happy about showing people when she still had no idea what it was herself.

She stepped into the shower and a brown crust fell onto the cubicle floor as she brushed a towel across her shoulders. She turned the shower on and washed away any remnants before washing her hair and finishing off her shower.

Tori stepped out into the tiny bathroom and looked in the mirror over her shoulder at the tattoo, but the mirror was quite steamy. She wiped it down with a towel and pulled her hair up out the way and had a look again, but she still couldn't see it properly as it was in the middle of her shoulder blades.

She needed another mirror but there wasn't anything in the bathroom. She quickly moved into the bedroom and rooted around in her handbag to find a tiny hand mirror, noting that she was running out of time and would need to be up at the farm soon. She quickly rushed back into the bathroom and, turning her back to the big mirror, she held up the tiny mirror in front of her and moved it around until she could see the tattoo. But she still couldn't make out what it was. The lighting in the bathroom was particularly dim and, although she could see it was a heart with flowers around the outside, she couldn't make out the patterns on the inside. She moved the mirror around and tried to step back, closer to the big mirror, but the sink was in the way. Maybe the patterns were just Celtic swirls, though she wasn't sure what would be so hilarious about that. But it definitely wasn't writing, no declarations of love for Aidan. It had crossed her mind that that was what Agatha had done, especially as she had been so adamant about Aidan seeing it. She sighed. She would have to get Isla or Melody to look at it the next time she saw them, for now she needed to get up to the farm. Luckily, Aidan wouldn't see it, whatever it was, because it'd be hidden away under her hoodie.

She quickly got dressed, pulled on her wellies, gathered together her sketches and her heartberry model and left Blossom Cottage.

CHAPTER 13

Aidan was waiting at the bottom of the drive for Tori, not wanting her to walk up the bumpy path in the dark on her own. The full moon was shining brightly, stars pin-pricking against a black velvet sky. It was warm, the heat of the day still lingering. The perfect night for picking the heartberries.

He hadn't slept well that afternoon, his head too full of Tori Graham in her pretty strawberry pyjamas. It was funny, the pyjamas were not what he would class as typically sexy if he'd seen them in a shop, but there was something very sexy about Tori in them, lying in her bed, her hair in scarlet waves over the pillow. That photo had been so innocently taken but it had stirred in him so many emotions.

He saw the flickering torch light coming from Blossom Cottage and, as Tori rounded the corner, he couldn't help but smile.

She was dressed in little denim shorts, her long legs disappearing into bright purple wellies. She was wearing a baggy red hoodie, her hair swept up into a high ponytail under a tweed flat cap, just like the one he had worn the first day they had met.

She grinned when she saw him waiting for her and then doffed her cap as she did a little bow.

'My Lord.'

He laughed. 'My Lady.'

She did a little twirl. 'Will I pass muster? I saw the cap in the village and thought if I'm going to be a fruit farmer for a few weeks, then I needed the right uniform.'

God, she was so lovely.

'You more than pass muster,' Aidan said, softly.

He offered out his hand and she smiled and then took it.

'How was your nap?' he asked as they walked back up the drive towards the farm.

'I had wonderful dreams,' she said, looking up at him.

Aidan hoped those dreams were about him.

'So, we've got time to look through your ideas for the advert. The lantern ceremony won't be starting for a while yet.'

'The what?'

'Many of the villagers will bring lanterns and candles down to the field to help light it up for the heartberry-picking.'

'You don't have floodlights or something a bit more... modern to light the fields?'

'Yes, of course but this is all part of the celebrations. It's how it was done hundreds of years ago. So, we still do it today. Well, only for tonight, we have proper lighting for the rest of the time.'

'Oh, that's really sweet,' Tori said. 'And when does the naked dancing start?'

He laughed. 'Any time you want.'

They walked in silence for a while as Tori looked up at the moon and the stars.

'Are you going to Matthew's memorial thing tomorrow?' Tori asked.

'Yes, I wasn't sure if you were going, what with Melody and Isla not knowing about the two of you.'

'They know now. Elliot kind of outed me this afternoon. Apparently Matthew talked about me a lot with him. I'm relieved more than anything. I've been wanting to tell them for a while and the longer I left it the harder it was.'

Aidan thought about Matthew and wondered what his friend would make of this tentative relationship between himself and Tori. He looked down at Tori who was frowning slightly as she was clearly deep in thought. Was she thinking the same thing? Was it too soon for her to be moving on? It had been nearly a year, but she had loved Matthew and that was difficult to get over, if she ever could. Her relationship with Matthew had been a strange one – one weekend, a few months of phone calls – but he was sure that her feelings for Matthew didn't run any less deep just because they hadn't been together in the conventional sense.

'Is this weird?' Tori said.

'What?'

'Talking about Matthew when we're…' she trailed off, clearly not really knowing how to describe what she had with Aidan. She gestured to their joined hands to sum it up.

'When we're… something?' he supplied, rather unhelpfully.

'Yes. If you were talking about your ex all the time, it would be weird.'

'It's different with Matthew. You didn't split up, he died,' Aidan said. 'I know you pushed him away, but in my mind that was a bump in the road more than anything. And you're not talking about him all the time. Matthew was my friend, it's only natural that you would want to talk about him with someone who knew him. I suppose my only concern is you and whether you're ready for… something with someone else.'

She didn't answer at first and he patiently waited, running his thumb over the back of her hand as they walked along. She had made it clear from the first time they met that she wasn't interested in a relationship, but now they were embarking on some kind of fling. Had that been mainly to do with him? Had he pushed her into this?

'I loved him, and I do miss talking to him every day. I regret that I never really gave our relationship a chance but who knows what would have happened if we had, whether it would have worked. And you're right, it's different when your ex dies to just splitting up. My love for Luc ended the second I found out he had cheated on me. I hated him for doing that to me. I loved Matthew long after he had died. So, I don't know when the right time is to move on with someone else after a loved one dies but I do know that this… thing between us feels right. Whatever it is, whether it lasts a few days or a few weeks or it lasts a hell of a lot longer, it feels right. I never want to look back on these few weeks and regret the things we didn't do, and I certainly don't think I'd ever regret the things we did do.'

Aidan nodded as they approached the back door of the farmhouse. He wasn't going to regret it either.

'And what is it you think we're going to do?' he teased.

'Well you've already shown me your elbows, multiple times. It's just a slippery slope from here on in.'

He laughed. She was quick, and he liked that about her. He glanced down at her beautiful smile filling her face. There was a lot that he liked about Tori Graham.

He let her into the kitchen and the bright lights made him blink for a few seconds as he closed the door behind them.

He turned back to find that Tori was already unpacking her sketchbook, notebook and a small box from her bag. Her hair shone in the glow of the light in the kitchen and he wanted to run his hand through it. She smiled at him, filling him with feelings he hadn't experienced in a long time. It had been years since he'd had anybody mooching about in his kitchen, but she looked comfortable here and he wondered vaguely what it would be like if she was here all the time. He quickly pushed that thought away. She was leaving in a few weeks. Whatever happened between them, it would probably never go beyond the few weeks that she was here. He stepped closer to her, inhaling her wonderful scent. But he was damned well going to enjoy himself while she was here.

'So, I have drawn out a selection of five heartberry characters for you to choose from,' she said, laying out five sheets of paper. 'He needs to be cute if we are going to go down the merchandising route, something that might appeal to children too, so I kept that in mind while I was designing them.'

He forced his eyes away from the beautiful woman in front of him to look at the drawings. They were so detailed, shaded and coloured to look 3D, almost popping from the page.

'These are amazing,' Aidan said. 'You have such a talent for this.'

'Which one do you like the best?'

All the berry characters were cute and appealing, but he loved the one with the twinkle in his eye, wearing a flat cap.

'I like this one,' he said, touching the page.

Tori grinned. 'I'm so pleased you chose him, he's my favourite too. This is Max. We can come up with different names for the berries if you don't like Max, but naming them

helped the characters to become more real in my head. And…
I've already made a rough model of him.'

She opened the box and pulled him out carefully, placing
him on the table.

'Oh, he's brilliant, can I touch him?'

Tori nodded, and he picked up the berry character and held
him in his hands. It was quite a bit heavier than he thought
it would be as he turned it round in his hands.

'You've captured the shape of the heartberry perfectly and
made him come to life,' Aidan said. 'He looks cheeky and
friendly and endearing.'

'Oh, I'm so happy you like him. So, I've been thinking
about the story for the advert. I thought it could be a bit of
a love story as the heartberry is famous for bringing people
together. So maybe our Max could be looking for love.'

'I like that.'

She picked up a stack of paper with drawings in little boxes,
kind of like a comic book.

'These are storyboards which will help to give you a visual
for the story. It's a bit of a work in progress at the moment,
but I thought it could be a bit like the Ugly Duckling, in that
Max doesn't know he's a heartberry and he knows he doesn't
belong with the other fruit.' She pointed out the relevant
drawings for that part of the story and then moved on to the
other drawings. 'He tries to find friends with the strawberries,
the raspberries and apples but they know he isn't one of them.
The heartberry is so unique he can't find any fruit that is even
similar to him. He travels far and wide and eventually comes
to Heartberry Farm where he finds lots of berries just like him
and even a female berry called Jenny, who he falls in love with.'

He smiled at the last few pictures of Max, holding Jenny in one of those classic romantic dip poses and then winking at the camera and throwing his cap over the lens. It was fun and catchy and her enthusiasm for the project shone through it.

'I love it,' Aidan said.

'Really?' Her face lit up.

'Yes, I really do, it's perfect. I think people will really like it.'

'Well, we can do some fantastic merchandising with it too. Make cuddly Max and Jenny toys. I can put you in contact with some great merchandising companies who will make all this stuff for you. It's tricky because you don't want to spend thousands on merchandise if no one buys it, but equally you want to have some stuff available to buy straight away if the advert proves a success. We can get the companies to provide some samples of a few popular products, like soft toys or t-shirts and mugs, and have them on your website to start off. If we start getting orders in for them, we can look at ordering more merchandise.'

'Sounds like a great plan,' Aidan said.

Tori clapped her hands together excitedly. 'I'm so happy you like it. Is there anything you want to change? I can make changes to Max or the story or—'

'It's perfect.'

She smiled, and Aidan loved the way it filled her whole face. 'Are you sure?'

He glanced down at her purple wellies.

'Maybe Max or Jenny could wear purple wellies.'

Tori grinned. 'I love it. I can do that, no problem. I can't wait to get started on this. You'll have to come round to Blossom Cottage when I start and see me shooting it. It gets a bit dull as we only make very tiny movements on the models. There are twenty-four frames in a second and we normally make around twenty-four to thirty frames a day, so it won't look like the berries are moving at all, but you can at least pop by for a little while and see how it's all done.'

'I'd really like that.' He glanced across at the clock and realised they needed to go down to the field. He sighed reluctantly. He could have sat and talked to her all night. 'We better go, the villagers will be waiting.'

'OK, no problem.' She packed away her drawings and carefully put Max back in his box. 'Let's go, boss.'

Tori watched as Aidan put a Thermos flask and a blanket into a large rucksack which was already half-filled with Tupperware boxes and foil parcels.

'Are we having a moonlight picnic?' she asked, excitedly. The thought of it was so romantic, lying on a blanket under the stars surrounded by candles. Maybe they might even share their first kiss.

He paused for a moment. 'I'd like to say I'd planned a nice romantic midnight picnic for us, but actually I was just bringing some snacks for later when we have a break.'

Her little romantic bubble popped. She had to stop herself getting carried away.

He must have seen her disappointment. 'I mean, it is sort of a picnic, there's a blanket and food…' he trailed off. 'I'm rubbish at romance stuff.'

'A sort of picnic sounds lovely.'

He swung the rucksack onto his back, grabbed his torch and took her hand again as he led her back out of the farmhouse. She smiled at how right it felt to be holding hands with him. He was doing just fine on the romance side of things.

'The heartberry field is right down by the coast so we'll take the jeep. That way we can load all our berries into the back when we're done. It will be quite a big harvest as the fruit we get tonight will be used for the heartberry festival at the weekend, for the famous heartberry cake, jams, biscuits and other desserts. So tomorrow I'll drive the berries round to all the local businesses and I expect I'll sell out in a few hours. Many places have already put in a big order.'

He opened the car door for her and she swung herself up into the seat, then he walked round to the other side and got in. He started the engine with a roar and they bumped down the track towards the moonlit sea.

As they rounded the corner, a large field opened out in front of them filled with hundreds of lanterns glowing gold in the darkness.

'Oh,' Tori said, taking in the beauty of the night. 'It's a bit like *Tangled*.'

He suddenly started singing, launching into, 'I See the Light', the big romantic number from the Disney film.

She stared at him listening to his beautiful voice as he sang every word perfectly.

'You know the songs from *Tangled*?' Tori asked, in surprise, when he stopped.

'The hazards of having a five-year-old niece. Marigold has made me watch it a hundred times.'

There was something so lovely about the thought of this big man watching Disney films with his niece.

Aidan pulled up to the field and Tori was surprised by the number of people standing around the edge.

'OK, the way this ceremony works is that we will have to wait until midnight to pick the first berry. I'll taste it and tell everybody how great it is and then they will all leave. We can both start picking berries then but, whatever you do, don't eat any.'

'I can't try one?' After hearing so much about the heartberries she was keen to sample them herself.

'Of course, you can but not while anybody is there. The magic of the heartberries is supposed to be most potent at midnight on the first full moon, which is why the fruit we pick tonight will be used in the famous cake for the big festival at the weekend. If we tried them together I have no doubt that the whole village would be planning our wedding before sunrise. Just wait until they've all gone and then we can regroup and taste them together.'

'Oh OK, we don't want to give Agatha any more fuel,' Tori said.

'No, definitely not. She doesn't need any more encouragement. So, we both have trolleys and I've already left stacks of empty punnets on them. Simply fill each punnet, put the lid on and put it on the trolley. When the trolley is full, load it into the car, and take a new stack of punnets.'

'Sounds easy enough. What about this special picking method that you were going to show me?'

'Yes, I can show you that, it's very easy.'

He got out and Tori climbed down into the field too. She followed him to the first row and smiled as he exchanged pleasantries with everyone that he passed. Several people gave her winks or nudged each other and smiled as they walked past, clearly having decided that they were already together or that the heartberries would work their magic over them. A few were a lot more blatant, asking Aidan if she was his girlfriend, which he politely smiled at but didn't answer.

Aidan stood by the first bush and in the light of the lanterns she could see little gleaming red berries. The bushes were waist height which Tori was thankful for as it meant that she wouldn't have to bend down a lot like she would if she was picking strawberries.

She looked up at Aidan. 'So, we just wait?'

'Just another minute,' Aidan said quietly, as he checked his watch.

'Shall I start doing the naked dancing to entertain the troops?'

Aidan laughed. 'I'm sure they would appreciate that.'

Down in the village, Tori heard the clock strike midnight and it seemed the villagers held their breath in anticipation of the first berry being picked.

As the last chime of the bell rang out into the darkness, Aidan picked a berry off the bush and popped it in his mouth.

'Tastes amazing,' Aidan called out to the waiting villagers. 'Even better than last year.'

There were claps and cheers of approval from the crowd and then they placed their lanterns on the ground and slowly dispersed, disappearing off back in the direction of the village.

As the villagers walked away, Aidan turned to Tori. 'I say that every year. So, you don't pull the berry off from the middle of the fruit, you put your fingers near the stem and gently tug it away from the stalk like this.'

She watched him tease the berry off the bush.

'Why don't you have a go,' Aidan said.

He took her hand and with his fingers over hers he showed her the amount of pressure to apply to the berry. Her breath caught in her throat. She had never thought of berry-picking as something that was sexy before, but with his hand on hers, standing alone with him in the velvet darkness, it suddenly really was.

She popped the berry off the stalk and held it in her hand.

'Taste it,' Aidan said softly.

She checked the field and saw that they were now completely alone. She put the berry in her mouth, biting it and letting the juice slide over her tongue. Aidan was watching her the whole time, and for some reason it was sexy as hell.

'Well, what do you think?'

She had been so distracted by him watching her intently that she hadn't really processed what it tasted like but now she could appreciate it. It was sweet and tangy and fresh and not like anything she had ever tasted before. She swallowed.

'It's wonderful,' she said, unable to take her eyes from his. 'So, if this berry is so magical, what happens now? We kiss and fall head over heels in love?'

He didn't say anything for a moment then he smiled. 'Let's see, shall we.'

He bent his head and kissed her.

CHAPTER 14

It was so unexpected that for a second or two Tori just stood in shock as his soft mouth brushed against hers. But as he moved away, clearly realising she wasn't returning it, she grabbed hold of his jumper and pulled him back to her, kissing him too. He brought his hands to her face, cupping her gently. She slid her hands round his neck, stroking the back of his head and fingering his black curls. He moaned softly against her lips and it was such a turn-on to know she had this effect on him.

He moved his hands down her back, holding her closer against him, and eased her mouth open, tasting her.

His wonderful scent surrounded her, the feel of his stubble against her skin was incredible and he tasted amazing.

He slid his arms around her, so he was hugging her tightly, his whole body wrapped around hers and the kiss continued.

This kiss was everything. It was so gentle, so lovely. She had never been kissed like this before with so much adoration.

She moved her hands down his back and then slipped them under his jumper and t-shirt, caressing his bare skin at the base of his spine. At her touch, the kiss changed to something more needful and urgent – the kiss suddenly wasn't enough, she needed more.

Aidan pulled back slightly, still holding her against him but leaning his head against hers, his breath unsteady.

'I think if I was to kiss you for much longer, I'd be stripping you naked and taking you right here amongst the berries,' he said.

Tori laughed. 'I think I'd be OK with that.'

'Let's go back to the farm,' Aidan said. 'Forget the berries.'

She smiled, not entirely sure if he was joking. 'And what would we tell the villagers when there are no berries in the morning?'

'They'll understand, the passion and the magic of the berries took over us.'

She pulled back slightly to look at him. 'Is that what this is?'

'I have no idea what this is, but I'm loving it. What about you, have you fallen head over heels in love with me yet?' he teased.

Something pulled in her heart. 'I think I could definitely fall in love with you, Aidan Jackson, if you keep kissing me like that.'

He smiled. 'I'll keep that in mind. But we should get on with the berry-picking.' He kissed her on the forehead and pulled away, out of her arms. 'I'll take this row and you take that one. I'd like to clear six rows tonight. There's a head torch on your trolley, it'll help you see the berries more easily.'

Tori wasn't sure what to make of this sudden about-turn. She knew the berries needed to be picked and maybe he needed to focus on that rather than what they could be doing if they were back at the farmhouse.

'Yes boss,' Tori said.

He laughed and caught her hand, pulling her back towards him. 'We'll take a break at one and I plan to use it doing more of this.' He kissed her briefly on the lips, lingering that moment too long as if savouring her.

He released her, and she smiled as she moved into the next row, spotting the trolley that was waiting for her. She slipped on her head torch and picked a berry. Holding it in her hand, she had her first proper look at it. It was about the size of a blueberry but had a definite heart shape to it. Now, having had a chance to study it, her ideas for Max started solidifying in her head. She could see exactly where the eyes would be and even where the hands and feet would go.

'Oi, Graham, I'm going to need a faster picking rate than one an hour,' Aidan called over and Tori laughed.

She popped the berry into the punnet and started picking some more, quickly filling the punnet, pressing the lid on and then moving on to the next punnet. She looked at the berries, all red, juicy and shiny in the punnet, and then glanced over at Aidan who smiled at her. Was there really something in these berries that could make people fall in love with each other? Because something was definitely happening between them, something wonderful, and she didn't know whether to be delighted or terrified by it.

She moved down the row, methodically clearing each bush before moving on to the next. It was quite therapeutic in that way that doing something repetitive and easy helped to clear the mind. But every time that she glanced over at Aidan, he seemed to be watching her with a big smile on his face. It made her feel all warm inside.

She had bent over to pick another handful of berries when something large skimmed over her head, and straight into the back of her hood. She quickly tried to flap her hood around to remove whatever it was, but the thing was struggling so much she couldn't free it. A second later the thing fell down the neck of her hoodie and down her back and as she wiggled around she heard the distinctive squeal of a bat.

Aidan had reached the end of his row when he heard a shriek of terror from Tori. He looked over and in the light from the lanterns he saw her running around in a weird kind of dance, her arms flailing, seemingly being attacked by invisible forces. He dropped his punnet and ran over to help her.

She was desperately trying to get her top off, screaming and wailing like she was possessed. He grabbed at her hoodie and yanked it off, inadvertently taking her t-shirt with it so she was standing in only her bra and shorts. But as he did something small and black zoomed out from the inside of her clothes and he realised she had been accidentally attacked by a bat.

'Oh God, are you OK?' Aidan asked, watching her drop her hands to her knees and bend over as she tried to catch her breath. She didn't seem fazed at all that she was half naked.

'Yes, I think so,' she panted. 'I've never had an issue with bats before, but I think I've just developed a new phobia. God, the bloody thing was all over me.'

'They have quite sharp teeth and claws; did he scratch you?'

'He might have done, it does feel a bit sore,' Tori said.

'Let me have a look.' Aidan moved round to her back and she straightened and turned slightly so she stood more in the light and he could see more clearly. He ran his hands gently over her back. There were a few small scratches but nothing serious.

'I think you're OK.' His eyes suddenly fell on the tattoo and his heart stopped as he stared at it. What the hell was this? Yes, they'd joked about marriage and they'd just been talking about falling in love, and if he was honest his feelings for her had grown very quickly, beyond something that could be considered casual. But this was a little creepy.

'So, you got your tattoo?' he said, touching it with his fingertips.

'Oh god.' Tori turned around, so he could no longer see it. 'Is it OK, do you like it?'

'It's…' he trailed off, because really, he had no words to describe what he'd just seen. 'Nice.'

It wasn't really nice, although it had obviously been done by somebody with a lot of talent. But he could hardly tell her that he found it a bit freaky. It was flattering, he supposed, in a kind of stalkery bunny-boiler type of way.

'Oh God, you don't like it, do you?'

'It's just a bit… much. I mean, I saw your drawing in your notebook when it fell out on my kitchen floor last night and I thought that was quite sweet but this…' He really didn't want to upset her, but she must know that this was a bit weird. They'd known each other for three days.

Tory stared at him in confusion. 'What drawing?'

'The one of me.'

'Oh that. That was just a doodle.'

'That you've now had tattooed onto your back.'

Her eyes widened in horror. 'What do you mean? It's just flowers and a heart.'

'With a picture of my face inside.'

Her mouth dropped open in shock. 'Your face inside a heart?'

'Yes.' Why did she seem so surprised by this? Was he mistaken? He quickly moved behind her to look at the tattoo again. His face stared back at him; there was no denying that it was him. He cocked his head. Was it possible that she had asked for the face of someone famous and it had turned out looking like him by mistake?

Tori turned back to face him. 'Your face is tattooed on my back?'

'It sure looks that way,' Aidan said in confusion.

She suddenly curled up in a ball, screaming with frustration into her hands. 'I'm going to kill her, I'm actually going to kill her.'

'Who?'

Tori looked up at him, her cheeks burning red with embarrassment. 'Your lovely aunt Agatha.'

Pennies started to drop into place. 'She had something to do with the tattoo?'

'I stupidly agreed that she could choose my tattoo, I don't know why. I just thought it would make her happy. I figured it was on my back, no one would see it and it would wash off in a few weeks so where was the harm. She wouldn't let me see it when it was finished, and I couldn't see it properly when I got out the shower tonight, I just thought it was a heart with patterns inside. Oh my god, I cannot believe I have your face tattooed on my back. I'm going to kill her.'

Aidan stared at her and then burst out laughing. He offered out his hand and pulled Tori to her feet. 'She really is going all out to get us together, isn't she?'

'Yes, it would break her heart if we actually hated each other.'

'I've been thinking about that. Her whole plan hinges on that she has predicted we will get married to each other. What if we were to show interest in someone else instead? You could perhaps go on a fake date with Leo or Jamie,' Aidan said, bending down and picking up her hoodie and passing it back to her.

'Oh god, she would die, her best laid plans unravelling right before her eyes. Though I can't see Leo agreeing to that and I'm not sure Melody would be too happy if I went on a date with Jamie. I do like that idea though.'

'Leo has quite the mischievous streak; well he used to. He's been way too serious over the last year. I suppose losing your best friend does that to you. But he's always loved winding Agatha up – even as a child he used to love playing practical jokes on her. Maybe this would be a good thing for him too.'

'OK, we'll ask him. Although none of this will be necessary once I kill her for this ridiculous tattoo. What was she thinking? Did she really think that you would be impressed by it?'

'I was a little freaked out if I'm honest. I'm very relieved that this wasn't your choice.'

'Believe me, this is a million miles from what I would choose. I was thinking I might go for a dragon, not the face of a man I've just met. That's creepy. I'm going to go back and get it covered tomorrow. I can't walk around with your face on my back for the next few weeks. Someone is bound to see it.'

'The villagers would love this.'

'No one needs to know,' Tori said, panic starting to show in her eyes.

'If Agatha has her way, I'm sure half the village already knows,' Aidan said.

Tori groaned, and he felt sorry for her. She hadn't been here long enough to put up with this crap from his aunt. He pulled her into a hug and held her against him.

'Hey, when we get married, this will be one of those funny stories we tell our kids or tell people when they ask how we met.'

She laughed and pulled out of his arms. 'I don't think I can ever marry you, I couldn't bear the smug satisfaction from Agatha that she was right. I'm going to carry on picking fruit now before my cheeks match the colour of the heartberries. We'll just pretend that none of this ever happened.'

'OK, agreed.'

He watched her turn back to the bushes and start picking berries again. He wanted to make this OK for her and he had an idea of how he could do that.

❧

'So beautiful,' Tori said, as she lay back on the picnic blanket and stared at the millions of stars twinkling from the inky sky.

After the incident with the bat, they had carried on working until two o'clock, clearing four out of the six rows between them. They had taken a break and had spent it kissing, eating and kissing some more.

'I agree,' Aidan said.

She glanced over at him and realised he was staring at her and not the stars.

'Smooth,' she laughed, rolling over on top of him.

He wrapped his arms around her, holding her against him. She stared down at him. This felt so comfortable and so right. Lying here with him, it felt like they had been doing this for years.

She frowned slightly. Things seem to be moving so fast between them, well, they were for her. She meant what she'd said earlier after they'd kissed. She could definitely see herself falling in love with Aidan Jackson and that worried her. Because, in reality, what kind of future could they have together, two people who didn't want any kind of relationship for fear of getting hurt again? Could she really put her past behind her and let herself fall in love again? What if he didn't return her feelings? What if he let her down? Love hurts, and she had spent most of her life trying to avoid it. Could her relationship with Aidan be that different? And what if they both managed to get past their fears and make a go of it? Could it really work? She lived in London, he lived in the most westerly corner of the UK. It was crazy to get involved with him. The sensible part of her head was screaming at her to untangle herself from this mess before her feelings grew any deeper, but her heart was loving the way he was looking at her right now, the way he was stroking his hand through her hair and his kiss which was not like anything she'd ever experienced before.

She sighed because right now her heart was in charge and she just couldn't walk away from him.

He stroked his hand down her cheek, running his thumb across her lips as he stared at her with complete adoration. 'What's going on in that beautiful brain of yours?'

'Nothing.'

'I doubt that. Your mind is constantly buzzing and for the last few minutes you've had a frown and this sadness in your eyes.'

'Just… thinking about us.'

'Ah, I see. Want to slow things down?'

'No,' Tori said immediately, her heart speaking for her. She bent her head and kissed him, and he slid his hand round her neck to cup her head. He kissed her back, slowly, leisurely, as if he had all the time in the world and not just a few weeks before things would come to an end between them. 'I'm just worried about… tomorrow.'

'I'm pretty sure that tomorrow I will still feel the same way as I do now, that I'll still want to kiss you and I'll still be imagining doing dirty wicked things to you.'

Tori laughed. 'I meant the future.'

'Oh, I see.' He smiled because he'd known exactly what she meant. 'In my experience, it's better to enjoy today and worry about tomorrow when it arrives.'

'And that approach works for you, does it?'

'It's working out for me just fine right now. There's no point in worrying about what might happen. Worrying isn't going to change that.'

'I like to be prepared.'

He smiled. 'And where's the fun in that?'

She grinned because he was so right and, for this holiday at least, she had promised herself she would take the fun path.

'Look, we have something special here, you know that,' Aidan said. 'And the only way we can tell if what we have is worth fighting for is to enjoy this for the next few weeks. If it turns out to be nothing, then we would have had an amazing few weeks and you leave here with some happy memories. If it's something more… well, we'll cross that bridge when we come to it.'

She looked down at him and something inside her said he was worth the risk. It was probably her foolish heart but, right here in his arms, she was enjoying where her heart had taken her too much to listen to her head. She bent her head to kiss him again.

'OK,' she whispered against his lips.

He rolled her, so he was pinning her to the ground. 'Good, now let me show you all my dirty plans for you.'

She laughed. 'Sadly, we have berries to pick.'

He groaned. 'I can't believe you're choosing berries over hot sex.'

Her heart leapt at the thought of sleeping with him, but she wasn't sure if she was ready for that yet.

'I think we'll save the hot sex for that elusive tomorrow. As you said, we should enjoy today, which means right now we have berry-picking to do and we'll deal with tomorrow when it comes.'

She pushed him off her and he let her up.

'Well, we have about two hours until sunrise so we're technically already in tomorrow.'

'Still no sex.'

'Damn it.' Aidan got up and she helped him to pack away the picnic.

'Whenever we do, it'll be all the more amazing because we waited for the right time,' Tori said, not entirely sure she believed that or why she was waiting or when exactly the right time would be.

He snagged her around the waist and held her against him, kissing her briefly on the lips. 'I have no doubt it's going to be amazing. Whenever you're ready.'

She smiled. 'Maybe tomorrow.'

His eyebrows shot up. 'The elusive tomorrow, or the real tomorrow?'

She pulled out of his arms and walked back towards the rows of heartberries. 'You'll have to wait and see.'

CHAPTER 15

Aidan had never really considered himself to be a romantic man. He knew what to do to tick those boxes for the women he dated but romance wasn't something he'd ever really considered he needed in his own life. He had seen plenty of sunrises and could appreciate their beauty but, for some reason, standing on the shore of the small beach next to the heartberry field, holding Tori's hand as the sun rose over the sea, he could suddenly appreciate it in a whole new light. Was it crazy to think he wanted to watch every sunrise with her?

She leaned into him and he wrapped his arm around her shoulders and kissed her head.

'What a beautiful sunrise,' Tori sighed happily.

They had worked throughout the night as Tori had shown no sign of stopping and managed to clear ten rows between them. It was only half past five but already the warmth of the day was surrounding them.

The waves were lapping gently onto the sand, but he knew later, at high tide, it would be a different story, the waves crashing onto the rocks at the back of the beach in great swells.

'So, you own your own beach?' Tori said.

'No, I don't think this is mine. I mean, there is no way of accessing it unless you walk over my land or climb down the cliff over the rocks or come by boat, so I guess technically it's mine. But I've heard somewhere that all beaches are public property and

I've seen quite a few people on here in the summer months and it's never occurred to me that they're not supposed to be there.'

'It's so peaceful here. I feel like we're standing on the edge of the earth.'

'Well, there is nothing out there between us and Canada. The Scillies are over there towards the left but if we could travel west in a straight line from here, we wouldn't reach land again until we hit Newfoundland. We get the full force of any storms that come across the Atlantic, the rest of Sandcastle Bay and Sunshine Beach is a little more protected by the headland over there, but the storms gather force across the Atlantic and hit here on Orchard Cove. Sometimes the heartberry field floods in the autumn and winter months because of the storms but not normally this time of the year, apart from the tidal flood at the end of June.'

'But there's that big storm coming now, I heard more about it on the news,' Tori said. 'There was that hurricane that was supposed to hit Florida, Hurricane Imogen, but it veered off at the last moment and they think it will travel across the Atlantic. They think it will hit here with eighty mile an hour winds somewhere near the weekend.'

'I know. It figures that almost two years after Imogen, my ex-fiancée, wreaks havoc over my life, Hurricane Imogen is back to finish the job.'

'Are you worried? I know you said that the weather never normally causes floods at this time of year but hurricanes are unpredictable. We have so many heartberries to pick, we'd never clear the field before the weekend.'

'It could be a problem. With the supermoon we had last night, we'll have really high tides, so with the storm, it wouldn't take a lot to send the sea over into the field. But the storm could change course again, head south towards Europe, or north towards Ireland and Scotland, or blow itself out completely before it gets here. There's no point worrying yet. We won't know what damage it will do until it hits, if it even gets that far.'

She looked up at him and smiled. 'You're not really a worrier, are you? You seem so calm and laid-back about most things.'

He shrugged. 'Worrying isn't going to change what will happen. I can only do what I can do and stressing over possible outcomes in any situation won't help anything.'

'That's a great quality to have. I worry about everything; what I've said, what I should say and do. What other people's reactions will be to something I've said and done, whether I should do something, whether I shouldn't.'

'How does that work out for you?'

She laughed. 'It doesn't.'

He smiled. 'Maybe you should try my way for a while. Whatever will be, will be.'

'Maybe I should.'

He laughed because he knew it wasn't that easy. 'Look, I'll take care of the worries for the farm, you don't need to worry about that for me.'

'OK.'

'And you never need to worry about what you've said and done around me, just be yourself.'

She nodded.

'And the rest…' he gestured to the two of them. 'We'll work it out together.'

'Que sera, sera.'

'Exactly.'

She nodded and leaned back into him.

He looked back out over the sea and wished he was really that laid-back about them. He wanted her to enjoy what they had and not worry about where it was going, but in truth he wasn't relaxed about the two of them at all. He felt like something important was happening here and he didn't want to lose that.

As Tori walked back down the drive with Aidan, she felt energised, full of life, more so than she had in a long time. Aidan had suggested they stopped berry-picking at four, but she had felt so awake, adrenaline coursing through her as if she'd just ridden on a rollercoaster, that she insisted they carried on for a bit longer, knowing that it would help Aidan if he had more of the full moon harvest to sell.

She looked up at him as he held her hand. Being with him made her feel alive.

They reached the front doorstep of Blossom Cottage and she suddenly wondered if he was expecting her to invite him in and whether in fact she should. She wanted to continue kissing him, she knew that much. But it was too soon to take it any further than that. Wasn't it?

He leaned down and kissed just between her eyes.

'Stop worrying,' he said.

'I'm not,' Tori lied.

'You get a little crease here when you're worried.' He ran his thumb across where he'd just kissed her. 'What are you worried about?'

She smiled at how well he knew her already. But there was no point worrying, she had to remember that.

'Nothing, it's OK.'

He hovered, and she wondered if he wanted to kiss her. She didn't say anything, just waited to see if he would make a move. But he didn't do or say anything either.

She decided to tease him.

'Would you like to come in and tuck me up?'

He grinned. 'Is that a euphemism?'

She laughed.

He paused. 'I'm not expecting you to sleep with me. It'll happen when you're ready and I'm happy to wait. And if it doesn't happen, then that's fine too.'

She smiled. God, she really bloody liked this man. Luc had pushed and pushed her into going out with him and then it had moved to sex probably a little too quickly for her liking. Aidan was incredibly laid-back and she liked that about him.

'I'm glad to hear that but I was just teasing; you seemed to be hovering.'

'Oh.' He pushed his hand through his hair. 'It's silly but I don't want this night to end. It's been wonderful.'

'It really has.' She smiled and stepped up onto the doorstep, so she could kiss him. He moved his hands to her waist and kissed her back. Every time they kissed it was so sexy, so lazy and slow, his tongue sliding against hers in gentle sure movements. He was so confident, and she loved that about him.

He pulled back slightly and kissed her on the forehead. 'I think this might be my best summer ever, Tori Graham.'

She stroked his face. 'I think it might be mine too.'

'I'm talking about the berries, we've got a good crop.'

She felt her heart fall in disappointment before she saw the twinkle of amusement in his eyes.

'I was talking about being here in Sandcastle Bay, it's such a pretty village. I definitely wasn't talking about us.'

He grinned. 'Why don't I pick you up for the memorial later, say eleven? We could go for a drive along the coast first, there's some lovely viewpoints.'

She nodded. 'That would be great.'

He kissed her briefly. 'Sweet dreams, Tori Graham.'

'Oh, I'm sure they will be.'

He smiled and walked away.

She headed into the cottage and closed the door, noting that there was no sign of Beast this time and she wondered idly where he was. She put some food down for him outside the back door, noticing that the bowl she'd put out for him the night before had actually been taken. Maybe Beast had dragged it into the shed. She'd look for it later.

She walked back inside and upstairs to her bed. She was tired now and starting to ache a little. She pulled off her top and her shorts and flopped face down on the bed. The sun was pouring through the skylight and she couldn't be bothered to move to close the blinds.

She closed her eyes and felt herself falling asleep with a huge smile on her face.

Aidan knocked on the door of Blossom Cottage later and then turned and looked out over the valleys and hills that made up Heartberry Farm. The sun was shining again, making the fields look like meadows of emerald and gold. The sky was a wonderful gas-flame blue today. It was a great day to remember a friend.

He turned back to the door, which was still closed. He peered through the window next to it but there was no sign of life inside. He knocked again and waited a few minutes but there was still no response.

He turned the handle and it opened. So, she hadn't locked it earlier that morning, which made him frown, although he couldn't remember the last time he had locked the door on his own house. He stepped inside.

'Tori?' he called.

There was no answer. Maybe she had gone out.

He wondered what to do for a moment, whether to wait for her or go on to the memorial celebration without her, although they still had plenty of time before it started. He'd planned to take her on a coastal drive first, so she could see more of the village and the local area.

He decided to just check upstairs in case she was in the shower, although of course he wouldn't go in there, but he could at least hear if the shower was running from the bedroom.

Aidan climbed the stairs and smiled when he saw her face down on the bed, fast asleep. She'd pulled a sheet over herself at some point, so it was half covering her back and legs, but she was wearing very little else. The morning light caught her hair like fire, her skin was a wonderful pale cream, her long lashes dusting her slightly freckly cheeks. She looked glorious.

He wanted to crawl under the sheet with her and hold her as he slept beside her.

Aidan grinned when his eyes fell on the ridiculous tattoo. He wouldn't tell her but several people in the village already knew about her tattoo, they'd spoken to him about it that morning. That had to be Agatha's doing; she wasn't going to leave this alone.

He sat down next to her on the bed and stroked his hand through her hair.

She stirred slightly, a smile spreading on her face, although her eyes didn't open. He stroked her again, his hand lingering on her back, relishing the feel of her skin.

She stretched and her eyes fluttered open and then closed again. 'What a wonderful way to be woken up,' she said, sleepily.

He kicked his shoes off and lay down on the bed next to her. She didn't hesitate, immediately cuddling up to him and laying her head on his chest with her arm around his stomach.

How had they arrived here so quickly? A few days ago, they had sat outside Blossom Cottage on Tori's first day where they both had said they weren't looking for a relationship, and that nothing was going to happen between them, and now they were cuddling in bed as if they'd been together for years. And he couldn't be happier about it.

He would have thought he would be having doubts. This was the first woman he'd been involved with since Imogen had left him at the altar. He had guarded his heart so fiercely, not getting involved with anyone for fear of getting hurt again, and here he was snuggling up to this wonderful woman. And this couldn't possibly have a happy ending. She was leaving in less than two weeks. There was no way she would stay in Sandcastle Bay, she had lived in London her whole life, what could this tiny village offer her in comparison to London? In reality, he should end things now before they got any closer. He knew that if he let things continue, he could easily fall in love with her. But he couldn't walk away from her either. He was enjoying himself way too much spending time with her to put an end to it now. He would just have to make sure he didn't involve his heart in this. This was a fling, nothing more, and he was damned well going to enjoy it now before it ended.

He looked down at her, her eyes still closed, a smile on her face, and he stroked a finger down her cheek. Whatever happened, he needed to make sure that Tori wasn't hurt through this thing between them.

Her breathing was slightly heavy, little warm puffs of air tickling his neck, and he realised she was still half asleep.

'Are you enjoying your time here in Sandcastle Bay?' he asked, softly.

'I can't remember the last time I've been this happy,' she mumbled, her voice barely a whisper.

He smiled at this. He shouldn't feel so protective of her. She was a grown woman who could make her own decisions. They both knew this was a short-term thing and if it made them both happy, then there was nothing to worry about.

She opened her eyes and smiled when she saw him.

'I brought you something,' he said, proffering the lilac paper lily.

Her smile grew and then she leaned up and kissed him. There was something so wonderful about kissing her, it filled him with this glorious feeling of excitement. He felt a connection to her he'd never felt with anyone before. Something pulled him to her. But it wasn't love, it was lust, that's all it was. He needed to keep telling himself that.

Tori pulled back a little. 'What time is it, are we late?'

'We have time.'

She grinned. 'Time to continue doing this?'

'Absolutely.' He bent his head and kissed her again, he didn't know if he could ever stop.

Eventually, Tori pulled back again. 'I need to get a shower before we go out, want to join me?'

He laughed. 'Have you seen the size of that shower? I wouldn't fit in there by myself, let alone with you. Besides, lying here in bed kissing you is hard enough without taking it any further. I don't think us both being wet and naked together is going to help my restraint.'

'Fair point.'

She slipped from the bed and walked into the bathroom, wearing only her knickers and bra, and he quickly averted his eyes. Although it didn't seem she was shy, and he'd already seen her half naked the night before when the bat had attacked her, it didn't seem right to ogle her in that way. He smiled. At least not until they'd slept together.

The shower started running and suddenly her bra came flying out of the bathroom and landed on the bed, followed by her knickers.

He laughed, and she peered round the door, only her face and her bare shoulder showing. She smiled mischievously and then ducked back inside the bathroom.

Maybe they would be together a lot sooner than he thought.

CHAPTER 16

Tori looked out over the sea as Aidan pulled the car into the cliff-top car park. A gazebo had been decorated in fairy lights and Star Wars bunting and Tori smiled. She hadn't been sure what to wear to Matthew's memorial, though Aidan had assured her it was very casual. Judging from the array of jeans and Star Wars t-shirts on display, she could see that she had been right to wear her shorts and t-shirt and sweep her hair up into Princess Leia buns.

They got out and, as they walked along the path towards the gazebo, Aidan took her hand.

It was a lovely gesture of support and solidarity but she suddenly worried what Isla and Melody would make of it. They had only just found out about her and Matthew and now she was turning up to his memorial hand in hand with somebody else. Was it inappropriate or thoughtless? Would they think she didn't really have feelings for Matthew at all if she had started something with Aidan only a few days after they'd met? The very last thing she wanted was to do anything to hurt Melody and Isla, especially not over Matthew.

She let go of Aidan's hand and made a show of checking her hair buns, so it wasn't so obvious. When she put her hand back down, she didn't take his again and made sure that she was slightly further away from him, so he couldn't take hers either. She chanced a glance at him, hoping he hadn't noticed, but from his expression, she guessed that he had definitely noticed and wasn't particularly happy about it.

Before she had the chance to explain, Melody came bouncing down the hill to welcome her. She hugged Tori.

'I'm so glad you're here.'

'I'm glad to be here too. I brought the top of the cake.' Tori held up the tin.

'Oooh, let's see.'

Tori popped off the lid, and presented the large circular cake topper with the Millennium Falcon painted on top. As Melody admired it, Tori noticed Aidan leaving her side and making his way into the party by himself. Crap, she'd hurt him.

'Elliot will love this, come and show him,' Melody said, linking arms with her and escorting Tori into the gazebo.

There were about twenty people there, including Leo, Jamie, Emily and Agatha and several others that Tori didn't know. Everyone was sitting around chatting, drinking and eating. As with most parties, the men were together in one part of the gazebo and the women were together in another. No sign of Melody and Isla's mum though.

'Your mum couldn't make it?' Tori asked delicately.

'She didn't think this kind of celebration was appropriate,' Melody said. '"*I'm* still grieving,"' Melody quoted in a haughty voice. 'The implication being that I'm obviously not. "I'm not ready to *celebrate* the death of my son just yet."'

'It's a celebration of his life, not his death,' Tori said.

Melody shrugged. 'I'm happy she's not here, she would be bitter and angry the whole time and that's not what today is about.'

Melody brought Tori over to the men's section where they were all drinking from bottles of beer and laughing loudly at some joke one of them was telling.

Elliot was sitting on Leo's lap, Leo with one arm around him as he chatted to him about something Elliot was playing with. Tori smiled because this was very much a manly corner but the fact that Leo was there playing with Elliot seemingly wasn't odd for any of the other men.

They both looked up as Tori and Melody approached.

'Hey, I'm glad you're here,' Leo said. 'I'm sure Matthew would be happy too.'

Another punch of guilt kicked her in the stomach. It was Matthew's birthday and she had spent the morning lying in bed kissing another man. Quite honestly, Matthew had barely entered her mind.

She smiled at Leo and then addressed Elliot. 'I have the cake topper.'

'With the Millennium Falcon on it?' Elliot's eyes lit up.

Tori dropped to her knees in front of him and showed him the cake top.

'That's amazing, exactly like the one we had last year. Can we put it on the cake now?'

'Sure we can.'

Elliot climbed down from Leo's lap and took Tori's hand and pulled her over to the cake, which had been decorated haphazardly with several stars around the outside that were definitely Elliot's handiwork.

'So, we need to put a little bit of icing on top of the cake,' Tori explained. 'Then we can stick the Millennium Falcon on the top. I've brought some soft icing with me, do you want to take a spoonful and spread it out over the top of the cake.'

Elliot nodded seriously as he carefully did what Tori asked. She lifted the cake topper out of the tin and passed it to him. Reverentially he placed it on top of the cake.

'Now press down really gently in the middle and around the edges of the topper,' Tori said.

Elliot did as he was told and then stepped back to admire his handiwork.

'I think Dad would have loved this,' he said, quietly.

'I think so too,' Tori said.

Marigold came bouncing over, dragging Aidan behind her. She was a mass of blonde curls, and dressed in a pink glittery top that had a My Little Pony on the front and pink sparkly leggings. She even had My Little Pony trainers.

'Marigold! Look what we did,' Elliot said, proudly.

Marigold studied it for a moment. 'Wow, that Millennium Falcon is even better than the one Han Solo flies.'

Tori laughed. It was so unexpected that this vision in pink knew about the Millennium Falcon.

'Her dad is a big fan,' Aidan explained, dryly. 'He makes her watch it and in return she makes him watch all the Disney films. It's a fair exchange.'

'Daddy says his favourite is *Lion King* but secretly I think it's *Frozen*; he knows all the songs,' Marigold said.

'I love *Frozen*,' Elliot declared. 'Olaf is my favourite, he's so funny.'

'Elliot, I have a secret I'm not allowed to tell anyone. Want to know what it is?' Marigold said.

Elliot nodded.

'Maybe you shouldn't be telling anyone if it's a secret,' Aidan tried.

Marigold rolled her eyes. 'Elliot isn't anyone.'

She grabbed Elliot's hand and ran off with him to the other side of the gazebo and whispered in his ear.

Tori was left with Aidan and for the first time since they'd met it was suddenly awkward.

'Are you angry with me?' she asked, quietly.

He smiled sadly. 'I'm not angry. We both agreed that we didn't want to give the villagers any fuel for their gossip and we didn't want to encourage Agatha either.' He nodded in Agatha's direction and Tori looked over and saw that she was watching them intently. 'It's fine.'

Before she could explain that that wasn't the reason she had dropped his hand, Leo suddenly burst out laughing.

She looked over at him. Elliot was standing next to him looking excited, obviously having just imparted this wonderful secret to his godfather.

Leo looked over at Emily and raised his glass. 'Congratulations, Sis.'

Tori glanced at Emily, who was suddenly blushing. Tori noticed the glass of orange juice in her hand and guessed the secret herself.

'Marigold Breakwater,' Emily admonished, her hands on her hips.

'I only told Elliot that you were pregnant, no one else,' Marigold said and there were cheers from the rest of the people there. Emily looked aghast and then smiled as Aidan moved to hug her.

'It's very early, we're not telling anyone yet,' Emily tried and then laughed as Jamie and a few others moved to hug her as well. She looked at the man next to her for support, presumably her husband Stanley, but he was laughing too.

'I told you not to tell Marigold yet,' Stanley said.

'I wanted her to be a part of it… Oh, bugger it, I don't suppose it matters.'

Tori went over to offer her congratulations as well and there was lots of chatter about how long they'd known and when the baby was due and whether Emily thought it was a boy or a girl.

As everyone returned to their own conversations, Tori moved over to Isla and Melody, still not entirely happy with how things stood with Aidan. She needed to talk to him to explain but as he was chatting with Leo and Jamie, now clearly wasn't the best time.

'How did the first berry-picking go?' Isla asked.

Tori couldn't help blushing as she remembered her first kiss with Aidan, the way he had held her, the way he tasted, his gentle touch, how it had felt more incredible than anything she had ever experienced before. She remembered the kisses on the blanket under the stars when they had taken a break and watching the sunrise together. Were there any words she could use to describe how wonderful the night before had been? And in reality, she couldn't tell them. Not now, anyway. This was a day to remember Matthew, to celebrate his life. She couldn't tell his sisters that her every single thought was occupied with Aidan Jackson.

She realised they were still waiting for an answer.

'It was nice,' Tori said. Although clearly, they were waiting for more. 'Umm, berry-picking is very therapeutic. And working at night is rather beautiful, just you and the stars.'

'You, Aidan and the stars,' Isla said.

'Sounds very romantic,' Melody said, dreamily.

This was a dangerous road to go down.

'A bat attacked me,' Tori blurted out, trying to change the subject.

'What?' Melody said.

'Yes, it got stuck in my hood and then fell down my top, it was very traumatic,' Tori played it up. It was a great anecdote, although it had resulted in Aidan ripping her clothes off. Maybe she'd leave that part out of the story.

'Oh my god, that sounds like my worst nightmare,' Melody shuddered.

'I've always liked bats,' Isla said. 'There's something so fascinating and kind of creepy about them. I love watching shows about them, but that's too up close and personal, even for me.'

'What happened? Did it bite you? Are you going to become a vampire?' Melody teased.

'I don't think it bit me, but I did wake up this morning with a sudden aversion to garlic, so who knows.'

They laughed, and she was relieved that the topic of Aidan and the romance of being together under the stars seemed to have passed.

Agatha came over to join them, a mischievous grin on her face. 'So, did you have a good night last night?'

Her eyebrows waggled, the spark of amusement in her eyes. She couldn't possibly know what they had got up to. Tori knew that small village gossip spread like wildfire, but they had been completely alone when they had kissed. Or she bloody hoped they were. Had there been any stragglers that had seen it? No, they had definitely been alone.

'Yes, the fruit-picking was fine but nothing else happened thanks to your insane tattoo.'

'What do you mean; my tattoo choice for you was inspired.'

'You let Agatha choose a tattoo for you?' Isla asked. 'Are you crazy?'

'I think I must be and I didn't know what it was until Aidan saw it.'

'What was it?' Melody asked.

'Aidan's face inside a heart.'

Isla choked on her drink, Melody stared, her mouth falling open, then they both burst out laughing.

Agatha clapped her hands together in delight. 'I thought it was wonderful.'

'And Aidan saw it?' Isla said, barely able to speak through laughing so much.

Tori's cheeks burned red as she remembered his reaction. 'Yes, he saw.'

Agatha's eyes lit up. 'But how did he see it? The tattoo is in the middle of your back. Was he taking you from behind and then saw his face staring back at him?'

Melody's laughter got louder.

'No. I was attacked by a bat and it got stuck down my hoodie. Aidan…' she paused while she rectified the story, so it didn't sound anything remotely sexy or romantic. 'I pulled my top off and when Aidan came over to see if I was OK, he saw it then. To say he was freaked out was an understatement. What were you thinking?'

'I'm sure he was flattered,' Agatha said.

'No, he wasn't. Do you not know the art of subtlety at all? No man wants to date someone who turns up at their sort of first date with a vibrator stuffed in their bag or has their face tattooed in a heart. Why don't I just go over to him now, get down on one knee and propose to him, scare him off once and for all.'

'You two are soul mates. You're supposed to be together forever. He is never going to run away from you because he loves you. He might not know it yet, but he does. I'm just helping things along a little. I haven't got long on this planet. My bones are creaky, I find it difficult walking around. I think I'm well past my expiry date and I want to see you two get married before I shuffle off this mortal coil. I'm sorry if I want to speed things up a bit. When you get to my age—'

'Stop with the feeble old lady act. We all know you're going to outlive us all,' Tori said. 'I'm getting it covered tomorrow.'

'No, you can't do that. It's a declaration of your love. Why would you want to cover it?' Agatha protested.

'Because it's creepy and embarrassing.'

'Well rumour has it, Aidan went to Rosie's tattoo studio this morning and got his own tattoo.'

Tori stalled in her tirade. 'He did?'

'Yes, on his back apparently. Several people told me about it, it's the talk of the village.'

Tori cringed at being the focus of village gossip. 'What did he get?'

'Rosie isn't saying, but I imagine it was something beautiful and romantic, something just for you.'

'I'm sure that isn't the case at all.'

'Rosie said you would love it.'

Tori had no words at all. What on earth would Aidan get tattooed on his back?

'Ooh, must go and say my congratulations to Emily,' Agatha said, moving away before Tori could tell her off any more.

Elliot came running over and climbed up on Isla's lap.

'Its exciting news, isn't it, about Emily's baby?' Elliot said, playing with a toy tiger.

'It really is,' Isla said, kissing the top of his head as she wrapped her arms around him.

'Marigold said the baby was growing inside Emily's tummy right now.'

'Hmmm,' Isla said, visibly cringing as she waited for the inevitable question.

Elliot played with his tiger, moving the legs and letting it walk up Isla's arm, giving little growling and roaring noises. Maybe the question wasn't coming at all.

'Marigold is going to be a big sister or brother.'

Isla smiled. 'Big sister; it doesn't matter if Emily has a boy or girl, Marigold will be his or her sister.'

'I think I'd like a sister,' Elliot said, simply.

'You would?'

'Yes, then I'd have someone to play with all the time. Girls are fun; Marigold is fun.'

'Yes, she is,' Isla said.

'Do you think I could have a sister one day?'

Isla clearly thought carefully how to answer that question. Because a full sister would be impossible. A half-sister maybe, if his mum, wherever she was, had another child, but as his mum wasn't in his life, he would be unlikely to know or meet her. If Isla was to ever have any children of her own, they would technically be Elliot's cousin.

'I'd like you to have a sister too,' Isla said, carefully.

'You would?' Elliot said.

'Yes. One day, I might have children.'

'You would?'

'Yes. How would you feel about that?'

'I'd love that. And if you had a girl, she'd be my sister?'

'Sort of, yes.'

'Could we have a sister soon?'

Isla hesitated. 'I have to find a man to have a baby with. I can't have a baby on my own.'

Elliot frowned with confusion and Tori exchanged smirks with Melody.

'How did the baby get into Emily's tummy?'

Isla took a deep breath. 'Stanley gave Emily the baby.'

Elliot nodded as if he understood. 'Stanley could give you one too.'

Isla let out a strangled laugh, which she quickly turned into a cough.

'That's not how it works. A man can only give a woman a baby if they both love each other very much.'

Tori smiled at that very sweet, completely untrue statement.

'Stanley loves Emily, he doesn't love me,' Isla says.

'Oh, I see, so you need someone who loves you very much to give you a baby,' Elliot said.

'Yes.'

Elliot thought about this for a moment. 'I love you very much.'

'I love you too, this much,' Isla said, holding out her arms so they were really wide.

Elliot giggled.

'But the man needs to be someone my age.'

'Leo!' Elliot said, triumphantly. 'He loves you very much. I'll go ask him.'

'No, that's…' Isla said, suddenly clearly alarmed at the prospect of that conversation. But before she could stop him, Elliot had climbed down and ran across the gazebo to Leo who was talking to a group of other men. Leo immediately scooped him up and held him on his hip.

Tori didn't hear what Elliot said but she guessed the moment that he had announced his big plans as the whole group burst out laughing.

'Oh God,' Isla said as Melody and Tori barely contained their laughter. 'Please let the ground swallow me up.'

Leo looked over at Isla, a big grin on his face. He whispered something in Elliot's ear and Elliot smiled and nodded.

'What is he saying?' Tori asked.

'I have no idea,' Isla murmured. 'But I don't hold out hope that it's anything good.'

Leo put Elliot down and he came running back over. 'Leo says to tell you, if that's what you want, he'd be very happy to oblige.'

Isla blushed furiously. 'That's nice of him.'

'What does oblige mean?'

Isla swallowed. 'It means… yes.'

'Yayyyy!! I'm going to get a sister. I'm going to go and tell Marigold that I'm going to be a big sister too.'

He ran off before Isla could stop him and she let her head fall into her hands.

'I'll give it half hour before the whole of Sandcastle Bay knows me and Leo are going to have a baby together.'

Tori laughed.

Jamie walked over to Melody looking embarrassed and awkward. Silence fell over their little group and the smile fell off Melody's face.

'Hi Melody,' Jamie said, looking like he'd rather be anywhere else but here.

'Hello,' Melody said, quietly.

Silence.

Tori looked at Isla; it was almost painful.

'Hey Jamie. Why don't you join us?' Tori said, indicating the seat next to Melody.

Jamie cleared his throat, pushed his hand through his hair and sat down.

More silence and Tori cast around for a suitably neutral, easy topic of conversation.

Music started playing on the other side of the gazebo and Tori nearly sighed with relief at the distraction. She looked over at the source of the music. On a white screen, photos of Matthew were suddenly projected. People fell silent as they watched this tribute that had clearly been put together by one of his friends.

'Oh yay, that's my daddy,' Elliot said as he stood in the middle of the gazebo watching the photos.

Different photos flashed up of Matthew on the beach, another drinking a beer at a barbeque. One in fancy dress. There was one of him with Isla and Melody, one with Leo.

As she watched the photos Tori swallowed at the sudden realisation that there wouldn't be a photo of her and Matthew together, unless it was of them when they were children. There would be nothing to mark their sort of relationship, there was no proof it had ever happened, other than the memories in her head. God, she missed him, she missed talking to him, hearing his voice. Emotion clawed at her throat.

A photo of Matthew and Elliot together flashed up.

'Yay! That's me and Daddy,' Elliot said, clapping his hands.

Leo probably saw it before anyone else – maybe he had been waiting for it. The smile on Elliot's face faded, his lip wobbled. As his little chest heaved and Isla stood up, Leo was already hurrying across the gazebo and scooping Elliot into his arms.

Elliot wrapped his arms around Leo's neck, sobbing hard as he buried his face into his shoulder.

Leo moved quickly across to Isla and sat down next to her on the bench, shifting Elliot so he was sitting between them on both their laps. Leo wrapped an arm round Isla's shoulders and kissed her head as she leaned on his shoulder and snuggled into Elliot, whispering words in Elliot's ear that brought the sobbing down to a whimper and a tiny smile appeared on his face.

Tori looked over at Melody who had tears streaming down her cheeks as she alternated between watching her nephew and looking at the photos. Jamie offered out a tissue. Melody smiled gratefully as she took it and after a few seconds Jamie reached out and held her hand.

Tori smiled slightly that they both had someone. Even if they weren't in proper relationships with them, they at least had men who cared about them.

She glanced over at Aidan who was watching her with concern. She wanted him to come over and hold her hand, or wrap an arm around her shoulders as she continued to watch the photos of Matthew, but not only was that weird, him comforting her over the loss of another man, but she'd already made it clear that she didn't want any public displays of affection. He wasn't going to come anywhere near her now, at least not publicly, and that was her fault.

The photos came to an end and there didn't seem to be a dry eye in the house.

Emily stepped forward, wiping her eyes, and Tori realised just how much Matthew's death must have touched everyone. Marigold and Elliot were best friends so of course Matthew, Emily and Stanley would have spent time together.

'It was Marigold and Elliot's idea that we have a balloon release. We have some helium balloons and we're all going to write a message to Matthew on the balloons and release them into the sky.' Emily gestured to the multi-coloured balloons that were all currently weighted down and bobbing gently in the sea breeze. She offered out a pile of felt-tip pens and labels and people came and took one and went back to their chairs to write a message.

Some of the lads started laughing as they showed each other their messages, obviously writing something funny to Matthew, and Tori liked that. People had very happy memories of him, the photos reflected that, and their messages were obviously a reflection of that too.

She took a label and a felt-tip pen and watched as Isla and Leo helped Elliot and each other to write one.

What could she say to Matthew? All the things she never told him, all the things she had wanted to tell him over the last year.

She placed the pen on the label and wrote down one line.

I loved you too.

She stared at the words. Was it enough? It was everything that she ever wanted to say and had always been too afraid to.

She read it again. Loved not love. She would never forget the time she had with Matthew but she knew, in her heart, she had moved on now. And not just because of Aidan, that transition had happened a while ago. The only thing she had to decide now was whether she was strong enough to take a chance on love again, which meant taking a chance at being hurt again.

She looked over at Aidan and smiled at him. There was no choice here. She was already in too deep to walk away.

Everyone moved to tie their labels on the balloons and then gathered together on the cliff top. As they all shuffled together in readiness to release the balloons, she felt a warm hand slip into hers.

She looked round to see that Aidan was standing next to her, holding her hand. Everyone was standing too close together to notice and her heart filled with love for him. She squeezed his hand in return.

The small crowd started a countdown and as they reached 'one', the balloons were released and bobbed in a rainbow of colour into the sky. They watched as the balloons floated out over the sea until they disappeared into the horizon.

People started to move back into the gazebo and Aidan quickly dropped her hand.

'I need to get off and deliver the fruit we picked last night. Jamie is going to take you home whenever you're ready. I'll see you later,' Aidan said.

Before she could say anything, he gave her a half smile and walked off. She returned to her seat with Melody and Isla, feeling an ache in her heart. In trying to prevent hurting Isla and Melody she had hurt Aidan and she knew she needed to talk to him later.

CHAPTER 17

Tori knocked on Aidan's door, still not entirely sure what she was going to say to him. Her brain was overthinking everything again. Had she hurt him by dropping his hand? Was she ready to go public with what they had and be a victim of the gossip of the village and Agatha's crowing that she had got it right the first time she had seen Tori? And spending the day today thinking about Matthew, and remembering how much it had hurt to lose him, would it be better to call time on this thing now so neither of them got hurt again?

Aidan opened the door.

'I just wanted to talk about…' Tori trailed off as she realised that Aidan was standing there in only his jeans. He was barefoot and the jeans weren't even done up properly at the top, revealing the top of tight black shorts and his chest in all its yummy glory. Words failed her as she stared at his body, all smooth and toned and strong. Just below his belly button a thin smattering of hair disappeared into his jeans.

'You ogling my elbows again, Tori Graham?'

'Oh god, sorry, I just wanted to say… today at the memorial…'

'How are you doing with that? It must have been emotional for you. I just wanted to come over and hold you, but I knew you didn't want that.'

'I didn't not want that. I'm sorry I hurt you by dropping your hand. You were being so sweet and supportive, and I basically threw that back in your face, but I was worried about what Isla and Melody would think of us. They've only just found out that I had this sort of relationship with their brother and I wondered whether showing up to his memorial with another man would be insensitive. I didn't want to hurt them and then I hurt you instead.'

His face softened. 'It's OK, you didn't hurt me. It takes a lot more than that to hurt my feelings. And what you did was completely understandable.'

'It was?'

'Yes.'

'It's just… this…' she trailed off. She had no idea how to tell him that she was scared, how to put into words that this felt like something special, something incredible between them, and that made her even more terrified of losing it. She had fallen in love with Matthew and it hurt so much losing him.

'I was just lying down for a nap.' He paused. 'Why don't you join me?'

She stared at him, words getting stuck in her throat as emotions bubbled through her.

'You said a nap was something you did with someone special.'

He shrugged. 'It's just a nap. It can mean whatever you want it to mean. It is just two people sleeping in the same bed after all.'

She hesitated.

He held out his hand and her body betrayed her by automatically stepping forward and taking it. He pulled her gently into the house and shut the door behind her.

She stared up at him and couldn't resist reaching up and stroking his cheek. He placed a kiss on her hand.

'I don't have any pyjamas with me,' she managed to say.

He smiled. 'I don't think we need to worry about that.'

Aidan started to walk upstairs, tugging her behind him. Her heart was thudding inside her chest. Would they not need to worry about pyjamas because they'd both be naked? Oh god, were they really about to have sex? She wasn't sure she was ready for that. But sex with Aidan would be amazing, she had no doubt about that. If he made love half as well as he kissed, she was in for an amazing time.

She eyed his strong, muscular back and realised he had a tattoo in the middle of his back, exactly where hers was. It was dark brown and had obviously been done with henna as well.

She pulled him to a stop and he looked round at her with concern.

'Your tattoo?'

He grinned and turned back so she could see it.

She stepped up and laughed loudly. Right in the middle of his shoulder blades was a heart with her face inside.

'Oh god, that's so funny. And so creepy.'

'I thought it might make you feel better about yours.'

Tori couldn't stop laughing. 'It's certainly done that. I can't believe you've done that. You know people in the village are talking about it.'

'People are talking about yours too, so hopefully mine gives some balance.'

'It's so amazing and not at all stalkery,' she said, dryly.

He laughed as he walked into the bedroom and Tori was relieved – the tension that had been hanging in the air about what was going to happen next had vanished. There was a huge, king-size bed in the middle of the room and a large walk-in shower in an en-suite just off the bedroom, which was all black marble tiles. The shower looked easily big enough for two people and her head was suddenly filled with images of the two of them in the shower together.

'What are you thinking?' Aidan asked.

'That I've never had shower sex before.'

Holy shit, had she just said that out loud? She looked up at him in horror and it was clear that she had. He was smiling.

'I'll bear that in mind.'

'I didn't mean… I just…'

'Let me get you a t-shirt.'

He moved to his chest of drawers and pulled out a black t-shirt, handing it to her. She stared at him for a second and he turned away, moving to the window to pull the curtains. It was ridiculous for him to try to be respectful and not look at her while she changed when they were about to share a bed together. She quickly slipped out of her top and pulled his t-shirt over her head. It was huge and came down past her bum. She slipped out of her shorts too and watched as he pulled his jeans down, so he was just in his tight black boxer shorts.

He got into bed and then held up the duvet for her. There was a reason couples should only do this in stage four of their relationship, when they were completely comfortable with each other. This was so intimate, way too intimate for a couple who had only shared a few kisses.

She slid into bed by the side of him and lay on her back, watching the sunlight that drifted through the crack in the curtains play on the ceiling. He was lying on his side and she knew he was watching her. If her heart beat any faster, it would likely explode out of her chest. How could he make her so nervous, so excited, so desired from just a look? It was almost too much to bear, so she rolled on her side facing away from him. There was a pause from him and then she felt him shuffle closer to her, his warmth surrounding her. He tugged gently on the sleeve of her t-shirt, so it slid off her shoulder, and immediately placed a kiss there and then another on her collar bone where her shoulder met her neck. This was everything, feelings tumbling through her like she was hurtling downhill on a rollercoaster. She closed her eyes as he moved his mouth to her neck.

'Oh god, Aidan,' Tori whispered.

He stilled. 'Do you want me to stop?'

'Christ no. I want you to keep going, and that's what scares me.'

'It's just a nap, I promise. Nothing more.'

She didn't know whether to be relieved or disappointed by that.

He stroked his hand across her belly as he shifted her back slightly against him, so she was hard against his chest. She wanted to turn round and kiss him but she knew if she did that any restraint she was clinging to would go straight out of the window. Although it was very evident that his restraint was at breaking point too.

Would it be the worst thing in the world if they did sleep together? Surely, they were heading in that direction anyway. Was he annoyed that she wasn't quite ready to take this any further? He seemed very chilled out about it just being a nap and nothing more.

He swept the hair off the back of her neck and placed a kiss at the very top of her spine. And then, with a deep contented sigh, and his mouth almost pressed against her, he clearly drifted off to sleep.

She lay there in his arms for the longest time, feeling his hot breath against her skin, her heart thudding against her chest. He had been right that napping with someone was something you did in stage four of the relationship because this was heaven and right then she never wanted it to end.

She closed her eyes and let the heat of his body seep into hers, before slowly drifting off to sleep.

Aidan woke a few hours later and smiled to find a sleeping Tori in his arms. He placed a gentle kiss on her bare shoulder, but she didn't stir. It was hugely tempting to stay there, holding her for the rest of the night, but there were berries to pick and he needed to make them dinner before they went out in the field. Though a few more minutes wouldn't hurt.

He was kidding himself if he thought it was just a nap. He'd known that when he had asked her to join him and he'd tried to play it down, but he hadn't expected for it to be so bloody wonderful. Holding her in his arms, caressing her skin. He'd wanted to forget the nap and just make love to her there and then. She wasn't ready for that though, he'd seen that fear in her eyes when he suggested she join him. He wanted her to want that too and although it was clear that she did, he wanted her to be relaxed about it and not look ready to run away at the prospect of it. Her fear of commitment and relationships was built in deep; every time she had put her trust in someone they had left her – even Melody to an extent had left her, though theirs was a different kind of relationship. He was a fool though, because as he was slowly coaxing her to open up to him, to trust him, he was falling for her too and there was no way this was going to end happily for either of them. She was leaving in less than two weeks, going back to her fast-paced life in London. She wouldn't stay here, no matter how much fun they had.

He sighed.

They were both grown adults and capable of making their own decisions and mistakes and he decided that he would deal with the consequences when they happened. For now, he was going to enjoy what they had because there was no way he could back away from it.

He hugged her closer to him and kissed her neck. He felt her come alive in his arms, stretching against him with a big smile on her face as she woke up.

'Best nap I've ever had,' she said, sleepily. 'I think napping with someone is the only way to nap from now on.'

'Same time tomorrow then?'

'Definitely.'

He smiled and kissed her neck again, feeling her pulse race against his lips. He moved his hand to her bare thigh, stroking slowly upwards as he trailed soft kisses up her neck. She turned her head to look at him, running her fingers through his hair at the back of his neck as he kissed her. Her lips against his was a wonderful feeling.

She rolled onto her back, holding his face as the kiss continued.

He pulled back slightly, needing to stop before he got carried away, but the look of desire in her eyes stalled him.

'I want you so much,' Tori said.

Christ. That was the only nudge he needed.

He shifted his fingers higher, teasing the waistband of her knickers, and he watched her to gauge her reaction. A look passed between them, it was so obvious what she wanted, it was almost as if she had shouted it.

He slid her knickers down her legs and she stroked his face, letting him know it was OK. He toyed with the hem of the t-shirt she was wearing and then gently tugged it off her, lifting it over her head, before kissing her again.

God, he needed her so much right now.

He gently removed her bra and then stared down at her. 'Tori Graham, naked in my bed.'

She smiled, and he bent his head and kissed her as he slid his hand up the inside of her thigh. She gasped against his lips as he touched her. He moved one hand to cup her breast, running his thumb over her nipple, wanting to touch her everywhere at once. She moaned softly, and it made his stomach clench with need.

He felt her orgasm first on his lips, the change in her breath, the needy way she continued to kiss him as her body shook underneath his.

She ran her hands down his back and pushed his shorts down his thighs. He quickly kicked them off and then caressed his hands down her ribs and stomach as he watched her for any sign of fear and doubt in her eyes.

'We don't have to do this, if you're not ready,' Aidan said.

'I have never wanted anything as much as I want this right now,' Tori said, smoothing her hands down his arms.

He leaned over to grab a condom from the bedside drawers and quickly slid it on. He moved so he was on top of her and she wrapped her arms and legs around him, gathering him close to her. He slid carefully inside her.

'Oh god,' she sighed, contentedly, as if this was the thing she had been missing her whole life and she'd suddenly found it. It filled him with so much desire for her. She stared up at him, stroking his face.

He just wanted to stay like this forever, right here, caught in this moment.

He kissed her, moving slowly against her, touching her, caressing her skin, trying to let her know how he felt for her. There was something special between them, surely she felt that too?

She gathered him tighter, arching her back, taking him in deeper.

'Aidan.'

His name on her lips was no more than a whisper. He stared down at her, her eyes closing in pleasure, the pleasure he was giving her.

He kissed her neck and felt the change in her body as he drove her closer, took her higher.

Her eyes opened, locking with his.

'God, Aidan, this is…' she said, breathlessly.

'I know.'

'It's never been like this before.'

'Not for me either.'

She caressed the back of his head. 'I don't want this to ever end.'

'I'm never letting you go,' he said, the words on his lips before he could stop them. Was that too much, too soon? But he knew he meant them. No matter how scared he was of getting hurt again, he couldn't walk away from her.

He felt her go over the edge, her body tightening around his, his name on her lips like a song, as he found his own release. He kissed her hard, held her tighter against him, Tori clinging to him like he was the air she needed to breathe as pleasure racked through his body. Her moans of pleasure against his lips suggested she was loving this as much as he was.

As the feeling passed he buried his face in her neck, trying to catch his breath, feeling her heart thunder against his own. He heard her whisper.

'I want this forever.'

'Well, I'm going to make a start on dinner,' Aidan said after he had kissed her for what felt like an eternity. She didn't think she would ever get tired of kissing Aidan Jackson. He stared down at her with such affection. 'Might have to be my legendary beans on toast, I'm afraid, we're running very late tonight.'

'Beans on toast sounds perfect,' Tori said.

He kissed her again as if he couldn't bear to be parted from her and then he reluctantly climbed out of bed. A naked Aidan was one of the best views she had ever seen. Although sadly he didn't stay naked for long; she watched him get dressed with a big smile on her face.

He turned round and saw her watching. 'See something you like?'

'Very much so.'

'My elbows?'

She laughed. 'That's it, exactly.'

'Well I'll show them to you and any other parts after we've done a few hours of berry-picking, if you want?'

'Are you suggesting a sleepover?'

'That's exactly what I'm suggesting.'

Tori grinned. 'I think I'd like that very much.'

Aidan bent down to pull his socks on and she was treated to a lovely view of his bum. He straightened and shook his head reproachfully when he realised what she had been staring at.

'Agatha's set me up with a right pervert. First you turn up to our first date with a pair of handcuffs and a vibrator and now you can't keep your eyes off me and spent the whole time we were having sex fondling my elbows.'

She burst out laughing.

He grinned. 'It's OK, I like your perverted ways. You can have a shower if you want to.'

'You could join me if you want to,' she said, feeling bold and confident with him. She'd never felt confident in the bedroom before.

'Nothing would make me happier, but then we'd never get out of here tonight.'

'Damn those berries.'

'We can add shower to our list of places we're going to have sex.'

Her eyes widened. 'There's going to be a list?

'Hell yes, there's going to be a list. Bed to start with, then the shower, kitchen table, probably outside in the berry field. Sofa, lounge wall. I'm sure we can think of some more.'

'Sounds like it's going to be a lot more than a one-night stand.'

'It was always going to be a lot more than that with us.'

'I think it might even be… something,' Tori said.

He nodded, clearly knowing exactly what she meant.

'I think it might be a hell of a lot more than that.'

With a final lingering kiss, he left the room. She rolled onto her back, smiling to herself. He was right. This thing between them was so much more than she ever imagined it would be. Things with Luc had never felt like this, she never had banter with him, he never made her laugh and that, she realised, was an important feature in a relationship. She'd never felt so confident around a man before. And the sex, well it had never been like this. Sex with Luc had been nice, at best, something that she kind of felt obliged to do. Sex with Matthew had been lovely, familiar, she'd felt safe with him; he was one of her closest friends after all. But this connection with Aidan was different. The sex had been wonderful, gentle and passionate, and it was as though their bodies knew one another completely while at the same time there was the thrill of everything being so new and exciting.

But what did that mean for them? She was leaving in a few weeks. She could come and visit him in between work and he could visit her but, as Leo had said, long-distance relationships rarely worked.

So, what was the alternative? Move down here to Sandcastle Bay? It was viable that she could do it work-wise, providing she had her laptop, plasticine and a few other essential bits of kits, she could do freelancing animation work from pretty much anywhere in the world. But God, she would miss London. And what would Aidan think of her creepy stalker tendencies if she suddenly suggested that? She shook her head at her foolish heart. They had slept together once, and it had been amazing, but it didn't mean that Aidan was thinking about marriage, five children and happy ever afters. And she was an idiot for thinking that way too. She'd never wanted to fall in love, because that would only lead to hurt. But for the first time in her life, she wanted to follow her heart and see where it took her.

CHAPTER 18

'I better go, I need to get home and have a shower before I meet Melody and Isla at eleven,' Tori said, stroking Aidan's face as they lay in bed together. They had spent another five hours picking fruit the night before. They'd come back to the farmhouse where there was no question of her going home when Aidan had suggested she joined him for a shower. She was pleased to find out that shower sex with Aidan Jackson was just as good as she had imagined it was going to be. They'd ended up sleeping together in Aidan's bed, wrapped in each other's arms, woken early and made love again. She was never going to get tired of this.

'You could have a shower here,' Aidan smirked, before kissing her again.

She grinned. 'You're such a bad influence on me. You'll make me late. And even if I did, I don't have any clean clothes here to get changed into after, so I'd end up going home anyway.'

Aidan sighed theatrically. 'You have a point. You'll come round later for our nap though?'

'Wouldn't miss it.'

She got out of bed before she was tempted to stay there any longer and quickly got dressed.

Aidan got dressed too and then she followed him downstairs.

'When am I going to see this boat that you're sailing on in this weekend's festivities?'

'I can show you now if you like?' Aidan said, grabbing an apple and throwing one to her, before taking one for himself.

'Oh yes, I'd like that.'

He gestured for her to go out the door ahead of him and then she followed him to a nearby barn.

'You should sail with me actually, as you are part of Heartberry Farm, even if it is temporarily.'

'Is that not against the rules? I thought it was supposed to be men only, so they can declare their love to the woman of their dreams by presenting them with a piece of the coveted heartberry cake.'

'It's quite relaxed actually. Plenty of women have sailed in the race and if they got a slice of the cake they've presented it to their men. It's true that men do use this boat race to make their feelings for their object of affection known, but there are many men who take part in the boat race to prove their boat-design skills or boat-handling skills and will just eat the cake themselves if they win it. Leo's boats are more about being elaborate and extravagant and crowd-pleasing than trying to win a woman's hand. He usually gives his winning slice of cake to Emily or Marigold. He's never given it to any other woman. Although this year it might be different.'

'Oh?'

'Well, he might give it to someone else this year.'

'Someone blonde?' Tori asked.

'Maybe,' Aidan grinned.

Her heart filled at the thought of Leo and Isla together. Though as Isla had already turned down multiple wedding proposals from Leo, it might take more than a slice of cake to convince her to give him a chance.

Aidan's hand hovered on the door handle of the barn. 'So, want to be my first mate?'

'Well, I don't know the first thing about sailing.'

'You won't need to.'

'OK then, might be fun.'

Aidan smiled and opened the door. He stepped inside and flicked on a light switch and Tori walked inside.

The room was largely empty apart from a few tools and machines along one wall, but there was nothing in there that remotely resembled a boat.

Her eyes fell on some wood in the middle of the floor, tied together with bits of rope and string. Her eyes widened as she realised this was the boat. It looked like some kind of haphazard raft that Robinson Crusoe might build.

'Is this the boat?' Tori said. What had she just agreed to? This didn't look capable of going even a few feet in the water before it broke up. Aidan was a big man as well, which meant he weighed a lot. In fact, she knew that he did, having had his body pinning her to the mattress quite a few times now. This didn't look strong enough to hold *him*, let alone both of them.

'Yes, I know it doesn't look like much, but it should do the job.'

'Should?'

He laughed. 'That's the point of the race, people build water crafts and only the best boats will get to the island safely. Half of the entrants end up in the water. It really is a bit of fun rather than a serious boat race.'

'I know but I was expecting something a bit more...'

'Professional?'

'Boat-shaped.'

He laughed again.

'How is it going to move anyway? Or are you just hoping it will float in the right direction?'

'No, I have an oar, I figured I would treat this like a giant paddleboard.'

'Any other form of propulsion?'

'Well, that's where you come in. I've adapted these foot pumps. The air pipes are going to be shorter and the end is funnel-shaped, so more air will burst out of them in a kind of V-shaped angle. There'll be three of them attached to the back. You'll jump on them alternately to give it a little burst through the water. If we need to turn the raft then you can jump on one of the side ones, depending on which way we want to go.'

Tori stared at him and then back at the boat. 'You want me to jump up and down on a boat that's made from oversized matchsticks? I don't fancy our chances.'

'There will also be balloons on the sides to help it float.'

'Oh, why didn't you say so? Balloons, of course!' Tori said, dryly.

'Of course, if you're too scared…' Aidan trailed off, clearly knowing she would take the bait.

She was supposed to be trying things outside of her comfort zone after all.

'Oh, what the hell,' Tori said. 'I'm in. But if I fall in, you'll be in big trouble, Aidan Jackson.'

He wrapped his arms around her and kissed her nose. 'If you fall, I will catch you.'

'You're so smooth.'

'And you love it.'

She smiled at him, because she really did.

'So, are either of you making a boat for the boat race this year?' Tori asked Melody and Isla as they wandered around the aquarium. Leo was walking with Elliot a little way ahead as Elliot excitedly pointed out the different animals.

'The boats are made by all the local businesses and, as I don't have a job, I've been let off the hook,' Isla said. 'Leo said I can go on his if I want but then Elliot would want to go as well, and I'd spend the whole time worrying he was going to fall in and drown. So, I think we'll just cheer him on from the bank. Melody, have you made a boat?' Isla asked, obviously knowing that she hadn't.

'No, you know I'm not the least bit practical when it comes to stuff like that. I'll stand and cheer everyone else on,' Melody said.

'And hope that Jamie will give you a piece of his cake,' Isla teased.

'He's not going to do that,' Melody said. 'Though if he offered it to me, I wouldn't say no.'

Isla laughed. 'What about you Tori, will you be hoping that Aidan gives you some of his cake?'

'I'm going to be going on the boat with him actually, representing Heartberry Farm together. It's very unlikely we'll get to the island to get the cake, his boat looks like it's made from matchsticks, but if we do manage to get to the island without drowning, we'll share the cake,' Tori said.

'Oooh, you know what the villagers will make of that, don't you,' Melody teased. 'There's a lot of rumours about you two already, though I imagine a lot of that has to do with Agatha.'

Tori smiled. 'I don't care, they can make of it what they want, and if they want to talk about us, let them.'

'That's a very relaxed attitude from you,' Melody said.

Tori shrugged. Nothing was going to bring down her happiness today.

'And would there be any truth in those rumours?' Isla asked, obviously noticing the huge smile on Tori's face.

Tori hesitated. Would it be right to tell them the truth, when Matthew's memorial had only happened the day before? She didn't want to hurt them. But they already knew that she liked Aidan and she couldn't lie to them. They had seen her hesitate anyway, so they knew that something was going on.

'We slept together,' Tori said, quietly.

There was no judgement or anger from her friends, only happiness and excitement. Melody went one step further and squealed with joy, which made both Leo and Elliot turn around with interest. Isla waved them on and Leo took the hint.

'When was this?' Isla whispered, though their voices seemed to echo around the glass walls of the aquarium.

'Yesterday evening.' Tori cringed over the timing of it happening after Matthew's memorial. 'And late last night after the berry-picking and, umm, this morning too.'

'I'm so happy for you,' Melody said. 'So, you… *like* him?'

Tori smiled at Melody's hope for a happy ending. 'I *really* like him.'

'This is fantastic,' Isla said, linking arms with her. 'You're always so anti-relationships so I'm glad Aidan has found a way to knock your walls down.'

'I don't know if it will amount to anything, I leave in a few weeks,' Tori said. 'And he couldn't live any further away from me. But I'm really happy right now and if there is something worth fighting for when I go home, we'll make it work somehow.'

'This is a big thing for Aidan as well,' Isla said. 'He hasn't been involved with anyone since his fiancée ditched him at the altar a few years ago.'

'Maybe you can help heal each other,' Melody said, dreamily. 'And rather selfishly, if it does work out between the two of you, then you'll be here more often, and I'll get to see you more.'

'I want to come down and see you guys more often anyway. Being involved in that film was fantastic but I've always loved the freelance stuff and if I take on more of those projects I can do that anywhere. Regardless of what happens with Aidan, I promise I'll make more of an effort from now on. But yes, being with him does have the bonus of seeing more of you.'

'So… you slept together three times in less than twenty-four hours. Sounds like it was good sex?' Isla asked, obviously fishing for details.

'I'm not giving you a blow-by-blow account,' Tori laughed. 'No pun intended.'

'Oh, come on,' Melody said, linking her arm through Tori's as well. 'Just a few little morsels.'

'OK.' Tori paused, wondering how on earth she could find the right words to describe what had happened between her and Aidan. It wasn't just sex and they both knew that. 'It was amazing. It was like how sex is supposed to be, like how it is in the movies.'

'What, passionate, urgent, tearing each other's clothes off and sleeping with him on the nearest flat surface?' Isla asked.

'No, tender and sweet and… full of love.'

She saw their looks of surprise.

'I know, I know, I shouldn't be reading into this. It could just be a fling to him. I wasn't looking for anything when I came here. He knows I'm leaving in a few weeks and he told me he's not looking for anything serious. Lord knows that I probably shouldn't be either, I swore off men ages ago. But there's something about him that I just can't walk away from. What we shared was something special, I can't explain it but there was this connection there that I've never felt with anyone before.'

'I can tell you really like him, your eyes are bright with happiness and I can't remember the last time I saw you smile this much,' Melody said.

'I think it's OK to have some fun and enjoy spending time with him without any labels or worrying about where it's going,' Isla said.

'I suppose I'm still wary about getting hurt again. I was so scared of getting hurt when I was seeing Matthew and losing him was so painful. I don't want to get carried away and start thinking it is what it isn't. If I let myself fall in love with him, I know it will hurt even more when it comes to an end,' Tori said, hating her cautious heart which was always there, striving to be heard.

'*If* it comes to an end,' Melody said.

'I'm trying to hold myself back but if I don't give it my all then that's not giving this relationship a chance. I don't know, it's complicated,' Tori sighed.

'Only if you make it complicated,' Melody said.

'I agree, this will either work or it won't,' Isla said. 'You might *not* fall in love with him. If after a few weeks, you realise this isn't for you, then you can walk away relatively unscathed.'

'But I don't want to hurt him either. That's the very last thing I want. I'd rather end things between us now than do anything to hurt him.'

Leo came over then, with Elliot swinging from his hand.

'Elliot wants to go to the shark exhibit next. Well, specifically he wanted you to take him to see the sharks,' Leo said, meaningfully.

Isla obviously took the hint that Leo wanted to speak to Tori without Elliot overhearing. She took Elliot's hand.

'Don't ruin this for her,' Isla whispered in his ear.

Leo shook his head. 'I won't, I promise.'

Isla took Elliot ahead of them, following the signs for the sharks, and Melody went with them. Tori and Leo followed slowly behind.

Tori waited for some kind of warning from Leo to stay away from Aidan or maybe he would make her feel guilty by mentioning Matthew. She wondered idly whether to mention the idea of the prank they wanted to play on Agatha, but it seemed somewhat redundant now that she had slept with Aidan. They were now together, and Agatha was sure to hear anyway.

'I couldn't help but overhear,' Leo said, softly. 'It echoes in here. So, it seems you owe me fifty pounds.'

Tori laughed with relief. 'A price I'd happily pay.'

'Aidan doesn't get involved with women easily. He's not a… fling sort of person. He swore off relationships years ago, same as you, so you are both taking a risk on each other. If he's getting involved with you, it's because he really likes you, because he sees something special in you. So, if your worry over this is that he might not feel the same way as you do, then I would very much doubt that to be true. Give him a chance, see where it goes. And if you think it doesn't have a future, then tell him straight away, don't string him along until the end of your visit. He's a big boy, he can handle himself. Nothing hurts like being jilted at the altar by the woman he loved. If this was to end after a few weeks, I think he'll be OK. It will hurt him obviously, but he will survive it. He chose to get involved with you, knowing you would be leaving, so he knows the risks.'

She thought about this and knew he was right.

'Thank you,' Tori said.

Leo shrugged. 'I want him to be happy and I have a funny feeling you're going to give him that, even if it does only last a few weeks.'

'I'll get you your money.'

Leo laughed. 'Keep it. Besides, if the relationship does end up being a serious one, you'll need the money to pay off Agatha in a year's time.'

'What?' Tori asked in confusion.

'Aidan had a bet with Agatha too. She thinks you'll get married within the year.'

Tori laughed. 'A year? That's optimistic even if things do work out between us.'

'Well keep your fifty pounds, just in case.'

Leo shoved his hand in his pocket and pulled out a folded piece of paper. 'This is the email Matthew wrote to you. Like I said, I have no idea if he intended to send it or not.'

She felt the smile fall from her face as she held it in her hands, feeling the weight of his words before she had even opened the page.

She unfolded it and stopped walking, so she could read. Leo waited for her a little way off.

Tori,

God, you infuriate me so much. Always you run, you push people away, afraid of making connections. And I know why. I was there remember, when your dad walked out of your life. I held your hand when you cried, when your heart broke beyond repair, when you decided that your dad obviously didn't love you. The one man who should have been there for you, the one man you thought you could trust, let you down so badly, you turned away from love for the rest of your life. And not just your relationships with men, your relationship with friends. Me, Melody and Isla have always been there for you and we always will be. There was never any pushing us away, but you've never really made any real friends outside of us. Colleagues, associates, acquaintances yes, but never real kinds of friends because letting people in would require you to trust them and you couldn't do that.

Tori swallowed down the tears clogging in her throat. He was so right. She had no friends beyond Melody and Isla. When Melody had left London, she had been utterly alone.

She'd never realised before that she hadn't wanted to make more friends, that maybe, subconsciously, she was pushing people away.

With Luc, you held yourself back too. I know that you eventually fell in love with him and like the other men in your life he let you down. I'm not saying there was any excuse for what he did, he was an asshole and should have had the balls to talk to you, break up with you if he no longer wanted to be with you, not sleep with someone else behind your back. But maybe it never worked out because of more than him being an unfaithful shit. You held back for so long. Maybe he never felt that connection from you, maybe you always kept that piece of your heart locked away and maybe that was one of the reasons it never worked.

And then there's me, your best friend. You trusted me to be the first person you made love to, and now I need you to trust in me again. I let you go before, let you push me away the first time we made love because I knew you needed that space after we were so intimate together. I knew you were so scared of love and, at eighteen, I didn't see any way past that.

I'm not letting you walk away now.

I love you and, if I'm honest with myself, I think I have always been in love with you.

There are no guarantees in love. There are no guarantees in life. Life is not a rose-tinted happy smiling place, it's a messy, crazy, wonderful thing. There will always be things that will hurt us, physically, mentally, emotionally, no matter how much you try to protect yourself from it. Life is hard but it's so much better when you have someone by your side to enjoy the highs with and navigate the lows. Sometimes you have to take a risk, follow your heart, be brave and stop worrying about the what ifs.

I'm coming to London next weekend and we're going to talk about this properly. No more running away.

I love you.

Matthew xx

Tori was almost sobbing by the time she got to the end of the email. Fear had held her back her entire life and she had let it ruin this wonderful relationship with her best friend, the man she loved. She had missed her chance with him, holding back, just like she'd done with Luc too.

Her dad walking out on her when she was a child, the first and only man she had loved with everything she had, had such huge implications on the rest of her life. But she knew she couldn't let it affect her any more.

'Ah come on, don't cry,' Leo said, awkwardly, as he approached. 'Isla will give me hell thinking it was something I said that upset you. And as you know, Isla is not someone you get on the wrong side of.'

Tori laughed through her tears. 'I'll tell her it's hay fever.'

'She'll see right through that one. Not too many flowers inside an aquarium.'

She laughed again, wiping her tears away. 'I'll put my sunglasses on, she'll never know.'

'Oh, like wearing sunglasses inside isn't obvious,' Leo complained, but it was clear he was only teasing her. He fell in at her side as they made their way slowly towards the sharks. 'Did I do the right thing showing you that email?' he asked, quietly.

She nodded.

'And has it made any difference to how you feel about your relationship with Aidan?'

'Actually, it has.'

Leo cringed. 'That's the last thing I wanted.'

'No, Matthew was right, it's time to stop running away and be brave for once.'

Leo let out a sigh of relief.

CHAPTER 19

Aidan knocked on the door of Blossom Cottage the next day and smiled when Tori came practically bouncing to the door, a huge smile filling her face, her beautiful red curls swinging about her cheeks. It was crazy, it had only been a few hours since she'd left his bed but he had missed being around her.

'I'm so glad you're here. You get to see your advert being made, well a tiny part of it. Not many clients get to come on set and see it, so it's exciting that you're here,' Tori said, visibly buzzing with happiness. He wanted to reach out and kiss her.

'I'm excited to see it too,' Aidan said, though it was seeing Tori at work that he was most looking forward to. It was clear she was in her element; she obviously loved her job and it was wonderful to see.

She took his hand and pulled him inside. He saw that there was a green screen set up against the wall in the back of the lounge and the coffee table had been pulled into the corner. There was lighting, a laptop, a camera hooked up to the laptop, and there was Max centre stage, ready for his starring role.

Before she got there, Aidan snagged her and pulled her back to him, wrapping his arms around her waist.

'Hello.' He bent his head and kissed her, and felt her smile against his lips.

'Hello you.'

She reached up and kissed him again, running her hands round the back of his neck. He pulled her closer, wanting to stroke everywhere at once. He felt her tongue against his and then she moaned softly against his lips, before she pulled away.

'Now that's a proper welcome,' he said.

'Sorry, I'll make sure all welcomes are like that in the future.'

He grinned. God, he hoped so.

'Did you hear the latest about Hurricane Imogen?' Tori asked, rubbing his shoulders, soothingly. 'Apparently now it's been downgraded to just a bad storm, but they are still predicting extreme high winds and large waves hitting this part of the country.'

'I know,' Aidan said. He'd been making a point of listening to the news every day to hear progress of Hurricane Imogen. He was trying hard not to get anxious about the storm, it could blow itself out completely before it reached these shores. Sandcastle Bay had endured bad storms before and Heartberry Farm had survived so he shouldn't get too worried, though he knew he would need to keep an eye on it. He looked at Tori's face, creased with concern, and he wanted to take that away and for her to smile again. 'Que sera, sera, remember?'

She forced a smile on her face and nodded.

He slipped his hand into his pocket and presented her with the paper rose he had made that morning, watching her face genuinely light up with a big smile this time.

'This is so sweet, I love that this has become our thing,' Tori said.

'I like that we have a thing.'

'I do too. And look, you've inspired me actually. I have a commission for an advert for a zoo and I thought I would do it with origami animals. I have to discuss it with them, but this morning I made an origami tortoise, a penguin, a giraffe and I'm halfway through making a fruit bat. I'll take some photos of these later and send them over as part of my concept, so I wanted to thank you for inspiring me. And I have something for you too actually,' Tori said. 'Though I feel bad that it's not anything origami.'

She pulled out of his arms and walked over to the mantelpiece. Picking up a white envelope, she held it out to him, excitedly.

He took it and slid it open. Inside was a voucher and small brightly coloured brochure.

He read the voucher and his heart filled with love for her. It was a voucher for a three-day cookery course at the nearby college focussing on making various cakes, pies and desserts.

'I passed the college the other day and couldn't help popping in,' Tori said, excitedly. 'This sounds right up your street. I've bought this voucher for you, so you can book yourself on a course at a time that suits you. I know you're always busy with the fruit but maybe later in the year you might be free to do it. They run the course twice a month and it's only three days.'

'This is perfect,' Aidan said, softly.

'It is?'

He nodded. 'You bought this for me?'

'Yes. I know opening your own dessert business and distributing pies and cakes across the UK is a lot easier said than done, but even if you don't want to do that or haven't got the time, I still thought this would be fun for you to spend a few days indulging in your passion, even if it's just for you.'

'This is…' he swallowed. 'Nobody has ever asked about what I wanted to do with my life. You were right, it was expected that I would take over the farm and I just accepted that. This is so thoughtful. Thank you.'

Tori smiled. 'Ah, I'm so happy you like it, I wasn't sure if you would think I was interfering. I'm already pushing you into doing this advert and now…'

He pulled her back into his arms. 'I've told you, you never have to worry about what you do or say around me. This is really kind, thank you.'

Tori reached up and kissed him again.

'By the way, I meant to say, I haven't seen Beast for a few days. Is it normal that he just disappears?'

Aidan nodded. 'Yes, he always turns up.'

'The food is still getting eaten but that could be foxes or badgers or something else. The bowls are going missing too.'

'If the bowls are going missing, it's likely to be Beast. I shouldn't worry too much. I'll ask around and see if anyone has seen him, but he sometimes wanders off with his girl-friend, so he's probably fine.'

Tori nodded before she turned back to her little make-shift set.

'OK, are you ready for a thrilling few hours? This anima-tion malarkey is very fast-paced.'

Aidan laughed, having guessed from her previous brief descriptions that it was anything but.

She pulled him over to the set and he could see that Max looked ready for action, flat cap, twinkle in his eye, cheeky smile, and…

'Green wellies?'

'Jenny will be wearing purple,' Tori explained. 'It seemed more fitting this way.'

He smiled. 'I really like that.'

'So, we are about ready to do the first shot. Do you want to do the honours?' Tori said.

'What? No, I don't know anything about animation or—'

'You don't have to. Just look at the laptop and decide if you're happy with the shot and if you are, just press Enter.'

'That's it?'

'Yes, there's nothing fandangled at this stage, it's just taking photos. We can edit stuff out later if it goes wrong. I'm going to put in a countryside background later so we're just focussing on Max for now. Are you happy with this shot?'

He looked at the laptop. Max looked shiny and juicy, just like a real berry, and he had his cheeky smile at the ready. It was perfect.

'Looks good to me.'

Tori gestured to the Enter button and Aidan reached over and pressed it.

'Congratulations, you're now my assistant animator,' Tori said.

'That's the way to do it!'

Tori smiled slightly as all the children sitting on the sand burst out laughing at Punch's antics up in the red and white stripy booth. She was sitting in one of the rows of deckchairs where all the parents were taking a much-needed break while the kids were entertained for half an hour. Now Judy had come back on and was berating Punch for his terrible baby-minding skills. The kids thought it was hilarious. The week before she had come to Sandcastle Bay, Tori had got a last-minute ticket to see *Wicked* in the West End. Because she had been alone, she had managed to get a seat three rows from the stage and it had been amazing. Now she was here, watching Punch and Judy.

The puppeteer had already dropped the plate he was supposed to be spinning. Judy's voice, which had started off high-pitched and feminine, was now distinctly gruff, as if he couldn't be bothered to put on the voice any longer. The crocodile had appeared and, as it had fought with Punch, one of its eyes had fallen out and Tori didn't think that was scripted. The whole thing looked tired and shabby and the booth was shaking so much it looked like it was going to collapse at any second. Life really was different down here if this passed for high-quality entertainment.

'This is shite,' Isla sighed, and Tori laughed with relief that she wasn't the only one thinking that.

Tori leaned forward and looked at Elliot, holding hands with Marigold, Emily's daughter, as they both laughed their heads off. 'The kids seem to like it.'

Emily, sitting in front, turned round to talk to them. 'Part of me knows this is just silly harmless children's entertainment, and living at the seaside, this is our heritage. Marigold wanted to come and see it and I didn't want to say no. But the other part of me wants to shout out to Judy that she can do so much better than Punch, he's a sexist, misogynistic bully who has no place looking after children. Judy would be better off being a single mum than staying with this git and I don't want Marigold growing up thinking this kind of behaviour is acceptable or funny.'

Agatha, sitting next to Emily, nodded. 'Quite right, dear, you need to raise my great-niece to have the highest of standards when it comes to men. I don't want her settling for any old rabble.'

A young mum in front of Emily and Agatha turned round in her seat. 'For goodness sake, Punch is a puppet, not a candidate for the next Prime Minister, get off your high horse.'

She turned back around to carry on watching the show and Tori could see Agatha bristling in her seat, clearly getting ready for a good argument.

Emily placed a hand on her arm and shook her head. 'Leave it, Agatha. Just because I want the best for my child, doesn't mean that everyone else thinks that way about how they raise their children.'

Tori suppressed a smile. She liked this fiery side to Emily.

Melody giggled next to Tori and turned to Isla. 'School-gate politics. You've got all this to look forward to when he's older.'

'It started in Nursery,' Isla said. 'And now he's in Reception it gets worse. I try to keep out of it as much as possible, but Emily has a point.'

As Punch forced Judy to kiss him up on the makeshift stage, Isla booed loudly. The young mum who had challenged Emily turned round and gave Isla the stink eye. It was quite obvious Isla didn't care.

Agatha turned round completely in her chair to talk to Isla, giving up on watching the show. 'You see, you could do a lot worse than marrying Leo Jackson. You could end up with someone like that Mr Punch.'

Tori felt her eyebrows shoot up at the meddling. It wasn't remotely subtle.

Isla shook her head. 'Emily's right, I'd rather be on my own for the rest of my life if the only other option was Mr Punch. Elliot doesn't need a father like that. And don't make it sound like I think I would be scraping the barrel by marrying Leo, or that I think I'm too good for him. I don't think that at all. He would make a wonderful father to Elliot.'

'Then what's the problem?' Agatha said.

'The problem is, he doesn't love me. He cares about me, he adores Elliot, but he doesn't love me.'

'I notice you didn't say that the problem was you don't love him.'

Isla sighed with exasperation. Agatha just didn't give up. Tori looked at Melody, wondering if she should step in and tell Agatha to butt out. Melody cringed at the question. But it was quite likely that now Agatha's attention had been swayed from the high-quality entertainment, they were all going to be in for the Spanish Inquisition.

'The boy asked you to marry him for goodness sake,' Agatha said. 'Of course he loves you.'

Isla looked aghast. 'How did you know that?'

'If you want a private conversation, do it in your own home,' Agatha said, bluntly. 'I have spies everywhere. He's proposed numerous occasions apparently.'

'Wait, Leo proposed to you?' Emily said, turning round and giving the conversation her fullest attention.

'Because he wants to take care of me, because Matthew made him promise at Elliot's christening that if anything was to happen to him, Leo would take care of me and Elliot. That's all this is, a promise to his best friend,' Isla said.

'That boy is crazy in love with you. You mark my words, he'll be giving you his slice of the famous heartberry cake on Saturday as a token of his love for you.'

'Aidan said that Leo has never given his heartberry cake to a woman before, outside of his family, that is,' Tori nodded to indicate Emily. 'Might be a bit optimistic to hope that Leo will suddenly change that.'

'It's not going to happen,' Isla laughed. 'I tell you what, if he does give me his cake on Saturday, I might even say yes to one of his crazy proposals in the future. That will scare the crap out of him if I actually said yes.'

'I just think that if Leo and Isla are going to get together they are better left alone to do it by themselves rather than pushing them to do it,' Melody said, bravely.

'And what about you and young Jamie?' Agatha said, giving Melody her attention now. 'When are you going to ask him out?'

'Agatha, have you asked out Stefano yet?' Tori said, pointedly, in a desperate attempt to rescue Melody.

'I told him I expect to get a slice of his heartberry cake on Saturday, so we'll see what happens. Melody, what about you? In my experience if you want a man like Jamie Jackson, you have to go and get him yourself. He's not like his brothers, he doesn't have that confidence, isn't that right Emily?'

'No, bless him, he's always been a bit shy when it comes to women,' Emily said.

'I can't ask him out,' Melody said.

'Why? Because he might say no? Because then it would be awkward between you? No more awkward than it is now. It's painful being anywhere near the two of you when you're together. Asking him out couldn't possibly make it worse.'

Melody clearly had no words to reply to that. 'But...'

'But if he says no it will hurt?' Agatha said. 'Yes, I know it will honey, but it won't kill you. You pull your big-girl pants up and move on with someone smart enough to snap you up and realise how wonderful you are while I'll give Jamie a clip round the ear for being so stupid.'

Melody smiled slightly at this, despite the interfering.

'OK, I'll try,' she said, which surprised Tori. She was not exactly forthcoming when it came to men herself. 'But it won't be straight away. You have to give me some time to pluck up the courage, to come up with a plan, not keep harassing me about it all the time.'

'At my stage of life, time is the one thing I don't have. I'll give you three months or I'm staging an intervention.'

'What does that mean?' Melody asked.

'Trust me, you don't want to find out,' Emily said. 'How do you think me and Stanley ended up together?'

'Fine, three months, but don't blame me if asking him out makes him run for the hills,' Melody said.

'I don't think that will happen.' Agatha now turned her attention on Tori. 'And how are things between you and young Aidan? You seemed to be cosy at Matthew's memorial the other day. I saw him holding your hand when you were releasing the balloons.'

Tori smiled; this woman really was omniscient. 'We're fine.'

'Having lots of hot sex from what I hear?'

'Unless you have spies in Aidan's farmhouse, there's no way you could know that,' Tori said, then regretted it immediately.

'I didn't know, but I do now,' Agatha said, triumphantly. 'Well, well, well. Now I have fifty pounds riding on you two getting married within the year so if you could hurry things along, I'd be grateful.'

'I'm not getting married just so you can win fifty pounds,' Tori said.

'No, you're right,' Agatha said. 'Marriage is to be taken seriously. But if you want those five children, you better get a shift on, you're not getting any younger.'

Tori's mouth fell open.

'Well, now I've sorted out the lives of my nephews, I'll be on my way. I'm certainly not hanging around to watch this dated crap any more,' Agatha said as she got up out of her deckchair and then walked across the beach.

Tori stared after her in shock.

'Is she always like this?' she asked Emily.

'Yes, sadly, she's been like it all my life. It's easier just to do what she says than try to argue against it, she always wins,' Emily said.

Tori sighed and shook her head. 'Looks like we'll be having a triple wedding then next year.'

Melody and Isla laughed.

The show was still going on: the baby had been stolen by the crocodile and the police were there, although Mr Punch wasn't taking it remotely seriously.

Marigold came over to Emily and Elliot followed her.

'Mummy, I don't like Mr Punch,' Marigold said as Elliot climbed up onto Isla's lap.

Emily turned to give Tori a smug grin. 'No honey, I don't like him either. Men should never treat women like that, not ever,' she said loud enough for the mum in front of her to hear.

Marigold nodded solemnly.

'Shall we go and get some ice cream?'

'Yayyy!'

Emily stood up and took Marigold's hand, waving goodbye to Tori, Isla and Melody.

'What do you think of Mr Punch?' Isla said, kissing Elliot's cheek.

'He's an asshole,' Elliot said, succinctly.

Melody snorted that he had picked up that word from their conversation in the pub the other night.

'Yes he is,' Isla said, proudly.

Tori pulled her t-shirt over her head and moved to Aidan's bedroom window. It was set back from the room in a small bay window and looked out over the fields and hills, and in the distance, the glittering Orchard Cove.

She had never stood half naked at a window before, but it was Aidan's land as far as the eye could see. No one would see her here.

She finished undressing and stretched her arms above her head, feeling bold and confident. Aidan had laid one of his t-shirts on the bed for her, so she would have something to nap in, but as he had already made it clear that he didn't intend to nap until he'd had his wicked way with her, there didn't seem much point in covering up now. He'd already seen her naked several times.

She smiled. God, he made her feel so alive.

Sex with Luc had always been done in darkened rooms. She had never been sure if that was Luc not wanting her to see his body or him not wanting to see hers, but she always felt so shy showing herself to him. Of course, he had seen her naked, but it made her feel uncomfortable and she didn't know why. With Aidan, there was never any of that. She didn't feel shy or embarrassed by him seeing her, she loved the look in his eyes when he devoured her body.

They had spent a few hours that day animating Aidan's advert and, so far, Max had moved a few millimetres. She had been sure that Aidan would grow bored at the seeming lack of progress, but in fact he had loved every minute of it.

She loved spending time with him, chatting and laughing with him, and it didn't matter if they were watching a sunrise, picking fruit or having dinner together, he made her feel so happy. Every moment she spent with him made her fears and doubts slowly ebb away.

There was a noise behind her and she turned around.

Aidan was standing in the bedroom door, dressed only in those gorgeous tight black shorts she loved so much. He had the most impeccable body and her hands itched to touch him.

She lifted her eyes to his face and realised he was staring at her as if she was some rare and beautiful treasure that he wanted to hold.

He walked towards her slowly, his eyes drinking her in, stopping only briefly to grab a condom from the bedside drawer.

'You look incredible,' Aidan breathed as he closed the final gap between them. He stroked his hand across her shoulder and down her arm so gently he was barely touching her. 'The way the sunlight caresses your skin, you look magical. I want to kiss you everywhere the sun touches.'

He placed the condom on the windowsill and Tori looked down and realised her whole body was bathed in the golden sunlight. She smiled at the thought of him kissing her everywhere.

'I think I'd be OK with that.'

He smiled and placed a gentle kiss on her collar bone and then on her shoulder, caressing his hands across her body as his mouth followed her arm down to her wrist, her palm and then each one of her fingers. He got down on his knees and placed gentle kisses on her hip, then trailed his hot mouth across her stomach. He licked across her belly button and she found her fingers in his hair. He was barely touching her, but it was so sexy.

He looked up at her as he kissed across to the other hip and his eyes were so filled with adoration that it nearly brought her to her knees.

He stroked his hand across her ribs as he moved his mouth up over her stomach and then around her breast. Everything about his actions was about giving her pleasure, not him, and she could see how much he was enjoying that.

As he slid his tongue over her nipple, he moved his fingers between her legs and any other coherent thought went clean out of her head.

'I don't think the sunlight is touching down there,' Tori breathed, her whole body coiling with a delicious need. She felt him smile against her breast and then she was spiralling out of control, throwing her head back and shouting out his name. Her body was so responsive to him. She was almost embarrassed how quickly he could make her come, whereas Luc would often try unsuccessfully for a few minutes and then skip ahead to the main event.

He moved his mouth up over her chest, slowly trailing up her throat as he stood back up, and then he kissed her hard, his hands going to her waist.

She snaked her hands up his naked back, feeling the muscles in his shoulders, feeling the tattoo he'd had done just for her, before she let her hands slide down his spine, pushing his shorts off his bum.

He stepped back from her briefly to kick his shorts off completely and then stepped back, kissing her, cupping her face in his hands again.

She pulled away slightly, running her fingers across his chest, and he stared down at her with adoration.

'I've never been touched or kissed with such… reverence before.'

She ran her hand down his chest, down his stomach and then held him firmly, causing him to take a deep breath in. He was already so turned on by her, and she relished in the feel of his rock-hard body against hers. She stroked her hand over him and he grabbed the condom from the windowsill. He quickly handed it to her.

She ripped it open and slid it on and he groaned softly. He lifted her, and she wrapped her legs around him as he pinned her to the wall.

He kissed her as he slid inside her and she breathed against his lips, he shifted her higher, taking her deeper. She clung to him tighter, kissing him, tasting him, feeling his heart beating against hers as he moved inside her, harder and with an urgency she'd not felt from him before.

He pulled back enough to whisper against her lips.

'I'll kiss you like this forever, if you'll let me.'

It was the thought of him doing just that that sent her orgasm roaring through her.

CHAPTER 20

Tori let herself back into Blossom Cottage the following morning after spending several hours berry-picking and another wonderful night in Aidan's bed. She could have stayed there all day with him, but she wanted to get back to Max. Aidan had stuff to do around the farm and he needed to finish off the boat before the big race the following day. She was meeting Melody, Isla and Elliot later so she had a few hours to work with Max.

She looked over at Max, poised waiting for her, and smiled. She walked into the kitchen and started boiling the kettle to make a cup of tea while she worked. A bark drew her attention outside of the window and she saw Beast standing guard over the shed door and Dobby the turkey flapping his wings around. It was almost as if they were having some kind of argument.

She hurried outside and immediately they both turned their attention on her, Beast barking at her, though not leaving his space in the door of the shed, and Dobby running towards her, making his weird gobbling, barking noise and flapping his wings.

She stood her ground this time, refusing to be intimidated by a bird. But as she tried to sidestep him to see if Beast was OK, Dobby blocked her path at every turn, not letting her get anywhere near the shed. Beast was still barking, and she decided to go get some food and see if that would help to calm the crazy dog down.

She returned to the kitchen, poured out a bowl of dried food and topped it off with half a can of wet stuff, which he seemed to like, and went back outside with that and a bowl of water.

The arrival of food at least had the effect of stopping Beast barking, but he still didn't seem to want to leave the doorway of the shed, at least not while she was there.

She went back inside and closed the kitchen door, watching as Beast ran out, took a few mouthfuls of food and then dragged the bowl back into the shed.

What was going on? Whatever was happening, Jamie would probably be looking for Dobby.

Tori texted Aidan and asked for Jamie's number. A few moments later, the number arrived on her phone followed by another text from him:

Moving on to a different Jackson brother?

She laughed and texted back.

He has better elbows than you.

So true. You OK?

Just Beast and Dobby causing some kind of disturbance. Nothing to worry about.

She dialled Jamie's number and he answered almost immediately.

'Hello?'

'Jamie, it's Tori.'

'Hey Tori, how you doing?' Jamie asked, easily, and again Tori was struck with how laid-back he was, the complete opposite to the way he was when it came to Melody.

'I'm fine. I'm just letting you know Dobby has come round for a play-date with Beast, although Beast doesn't seem too happy to see him.'

'That's odd.'

'That your turkey has escaped again and, not content to chase me down the hill, he has now turned up at my house to haunt me even more?'

He laughed. 'No, that Beast has taken exception to him, they're normally best friends. Beast often turns up at my house to see Dobby, although I haven't seen him for several days. I'll pop by, see what's going on.'

'And take your turkey back home?'

Jamie laughed again. 'That too. I'll be there in five minutes.'

'I'll put the kettle on.'

'I take my coffee with lots of milk and three sugars, please,' Jamie said, cheekily.

Tori smiled. 'It'll be waiting for you.'

She hung up and made herself a camomile tea and Jamie's coffee exactly how he wanted it. Before she had taken her first sip, there was a knock on the door. Sandcastle Bay really was very tiny.

She opened the door and Jamie was standing on her doorstep grinning at her. She handed him his mug and moved back to let him in.

He stepped inside and took a big sip, seemingly in no hurry to sort out the turkey problem. His eyes fell on Max and he hurried over.

'Don't touch him,' Tori quickly said. 'Sorry, I didn't mean that to sound so harsh, but we're between takes and if you touch Max, you could ruin the shot.'

'Oh, I have no intention of touching him. I would freak out if someone touched one of my sculptures before it was finished,' Jamie said, squatting down to have a look. 'Aidan said you were an animator, how fascinating. What do you use?'

'This is newplast plasticine mainly. There's a few other things mixed in to get the right colours and to stop it fading under the bright hot lights.'

'I see. I've had to do that with some of my sculptures.'

'What medium do you use?' Tori asked.

'Everything really. Clay mainly. I love porcelain but that's expensive, but I've also used plasticine, Play-Doh, Fimo, anything that's soft and malleable, and then added other ingredients to some of the things to preserve it.'

'I would love to keep some of my characters, but they are not in any fit state by the end of shoots. But once you've made your sculptures, you sell them on; I think that's got to be hard too.'

'Some I keep. I've just started one that I don't think I'll ever sell.'

'Oh, what's that?'

Jamie took a big slug of his coffee, turning to look back at Max. 'Will you use the same model for the whole of this project?'

Tori noted the quick subject change away from his own work. Some artists, she knew, wouldn't talk about or share their work until it was finished.

'No, I will probably make between five or ten different models, some for close-ups, some smaller ones for long-distance shots. I normally make moulds for something like this, so each of the models are the same, but I didn't bring that gear with me. Max here isn't too hard to do though and as he will be walking and moving it won't look too obvious if he looks slightly different – well, I will notice but I doubt anyone else will.'

'So, you're doing an advert for Heartberry Farm? Aidan mentioned that too.'

'Yes, it's for social media so I can have a bit more fun with it.'

He stood back up, taking another swig of coffee. 'I can't imagine making a sculpture and then spending several days moving it out of its original shape. Please tell me Max here doesn't get squashed at the end of the advert. I don't think I could take it.'

Tori laughed. 'No, he falls in love.'

He turned to face her, a mischievous smile on his lips. 'Ah, and how are things going with my brother?'

She smiled at the tenuous link and then decided to tease him. 'Well he's amazing in bed, he can do things with his tongue—'

'Whoa, I don't want to know that,' Jamie said, looking horrified.

'Well then, don't ask.'

He laughed. 'Fair point. It's good to see him having a bit of fun. He hasn't been with anyone since Imogen left him and I was worried he would never find anyone again. Now he's with you and I couldn't be happier for him.' He must have seen something in her face because he quickly seemed to backpedal. 'I mean, of course it's not anything serious, I didn't mean that. Of course, it's never going to end with marriage and babies. It's not love for him, you don't need to worry about that. I just meant a casual, meaningless fling is exactly what he needs to get him back in the saddle again.'

Tori felt the smile fall off her face. The last few days she had pushed away her doubts, just like Matthew had told her she should, and embraced the possibilities of a serious relationship, but Jamie didn't see it going that way at all. Surely Aidan still didn't think it was a casual fling as well?

'Oh god, I didn't mean that, that sounded awful, didn't it? Not meaningless. I know he likes you, I just meant that it's never going to be anything more than just sex. I know that Agatha would love to see the two of you get married but that's not going to happen, is it?'

Tori swallowed. 'I'm not sure what will happen between us.'

'But you go back to London in a few weeks,' Jamie said.

'Yes, I do but we might...' she trailed off. What would they do when her time here came to an end? Travel back and forth between here and London to visit each other? She worked during the week and Aidan would be busy with people coming to the farm at weekends to pick their own fruit. Could they really make this work? Would Aidan even want to, or was this really a casual, meaningless fling to him?

'Oh crap, I've upset you. What the hell do I know about what you and Aidan have? He could be planning to propose to you at the festival of love this weekend. Don't pay any attention to me. I never say the right thing.' He finished off his coffee. 'Let's go get this turkey.'

He walked past her, but she caught his arm. 'Why do you think this isn't anything serious for him?'

'I don't think that, I just thought this was just something casual for both of you, just a bit of fun. I didn't realise it had become something more. Imogen was from London and they met while she was working down here for a few months. He fell in love with her very quickly and he said after they'd broken up that he would never fall in love like that again. He would take his time to get to know someone, work out if he could trust them before letting himself fall in love again. He knew that Imogen would never stay in Sandcastle Bay, he never felt like he had anything to offer her, and in the end, she left him because a life with him wasn't enough for her. He said he'd never fall in love with someone like her again.'

'You think I'm like Imogen?'

'Oh god no, you're nothing like her. I didn't like her at all. I just meant that Aidan knows you're going back to London in a few weeks and I thought he would be more cautious with his heart after what happened with Imogen. Look, please don't pay any attention to my ramblings. We haven't really spoken about your relationship at all, so what would I know?'

Aidan and Jamie hadn't spoken about her. Was that a good thing or bad? It had been a long time before Luc had introduced her to any of his friends, most of them hadn't even known she existed. Luc had said that he wanted to keep their relationship special and just between them, but had it been because it didn't really mean anything to him at all, or so he could just keep playing the field? Had Aidan not talked about it with Jamie because he didn't see it going anywhere? And why was she suddenly second-guessing this thing between them? She was happy, why not just enjoy it now and stop worrying about the future?

'Let's go and get Dobby before I say anything else to upset you,' Jamie said.

He moved into the kitchen and she followed, hating the ache in her heart that this conversation had given her.

She needed to talk to Aidan, she hadn't discussed any kind of future with him. As far as he was concerned, she could just want something casual.

Urgh! Relationships were so complicated and tricky to navigate. One or both parties invariably got hurt and that was why she had avoided them for so long.

Beast had returned to his spot near the door of the shed and Dobby was patrolling the garden as if he was on guard too.

Jamie stepped outside and immediately Beast started barking at him. Dobby charged towards Jamie and she wondered how he would deal with the turkey but, to Tori's surprise, Jamie immediately bent down and hugged the bird, actually hugged him, Dobby wrapping his wings around Jamie's back. It was the sweetest thing she'd ever seen.

'Hey you,' Jamie said, softly.

It was no wonder that Melody had fallen head over heels in love with this man. Apart from his ability to put his foot in it every time he opened his mouth, he was really very likeable.

Beast was continuing to bark as Jamie scooped the turkey up in his arms and walked back towards the house.

'I'll just put Dobby back in the car and I'll be back in a second to see what's wrong with Beast.'

'OK.'

He disappeared inside the house and Tori heard the front door close as he went out to the car. He reappeared a few moments later and dug into his pocket, fishing out a bag of chicken.

'Let's see what's got Beast so upset, though I have a fair idea.' Jamie walked towards the shed and Beast continued to bark, though Tori could tell he was interested in the chicken, as he licked his lips.

She followed Jamie. 'You do?'

'Hmm, when he roams the streets of Sandcastle Bay, he is often seen in the company of another dog called Beauty. No idea where she came from, she might have escaped from one of the tourists that came down here. Beauty is skittish and nervous and won't let anyone near her and Beast kind of takes care of her.'

'You think Beauty is in the shed?'

'Yes, Beast is guarding something, and I haven't seen Beauty for several days.' He offered out the chicken and Beast stopped barking and wolfed it down. Jamie peered into the shed. 'Ah, yes. Seems I was right. I thought Beauty was getting a bit fat, although hard to tell under all that fur.'

Tori looked round the door and saw a large scraggy grey dog lying on the mattress. Next to her was a whole bundle of black curly-haired puppies.

'Oh, Beast is a daddy.'

Jamie grinned at her. 'Seems that way. No wonder he was so protective. I wonder if he'll let us in to check on them, though Beauty might not be too happy.'

'I'll get some more food and drink for her. If she's feeding that many puppies, she must be starving.'

Jamie nodded. 'Good idea.'

She rushed back into the cottage, filled two bowls with food and then carried them back out to the shed.

Jamie squatted down, so he was face to face with Beast, offering out some chicken. 'Hey Beastie, can we come in and see your puppies?'

Beast took a piece of chicken and moved back inside, dropping it in front of Beauty. It was so sweet the way he was looking out for her.

Jamie inched into the shed and Tori followed him. He crouched down slowly in front of Beauty, offering out the chicken. The dog hesitated, and Beast snuffled against the side of her head. It was as if reassuring her it was OK because, after that, she took the chicken from Jamie. Whether she was too tired from the constant demands of the puppies or she sensed that Jamie wasn't a threat to her, she didn't get up or try to get away. Tori moved forward and squatted down next to him, holding out her hand so Beauty could sniff her.

'OK, let's see what we've got,' Jamie said softly, and he moved round and picked up one of the tiny black bundles of fur. 'This one's a boy.' The puppy snuffled and yawned in his hand and Jamie handed it to Tori to hold. She cradled it in her hands, feeling the warmth from the puppy seep into her. 'These two are girls,' he said, putting them down softly on the mattress as he moved on to the others.

Tori continued to hold and stroke the tiny bundle of fur, all her fears and worries about Aidan drifting away. She smiled at the power of the puppy.

'OK, we have five boys and six girls,' Jamie said, a note of concern in his voice.

'God that's a lot.'

'Yes, it is. Normally dogs Beauty's size have a litter of between six and eight. It's not unheard of to have ten or twelve but it doesn't happen very often.' He looked at Beauty who still had barely moved since their arrival. 'I don't think they're getting enough milk. I estimate they are three or four days old and I think they should be bigger than this. Some of them are really small. I think she might be malnourished. If she's not been able to get out and get any food, relying solely on what Beast is bringing her, she'll be hungry herself and, with eleven hungry mouths to feed, that lack of food means a lack of milk.'

'Oh no, I feel awful. If I'd known she was in here, I would have put out more food.'

'Well now you know, it will mean that we can get more food inside her over the next few days and she'll probably get better. But I think she might need a hand with these puppies. She can't feed them all. I don't know enough about this though, I'm not sure if normal milk from the shops is good enough.'

A thought occurred to her.

'You know who would know. Melody.'

At the mention of her friend's name, Jamie blushed. 'I'm not sure…' he started awkwardly. It was almost painful to watch.

'No, she would. Her mum used to breed Labrador puppies. Quite often there would be one or two puppies that weren't taking the milk or would get pushed out the way of the stronger puppies and Melody and Isla would help their mum to hand-wean them. She would know exactly what to do. Let me give her a call.'

Jamie nodded as he watched Beauty eating the food that Tori had put down for her. 'Well that's a good sign, at least she's strong enough to feed herself. Why don't I go and get more chicken? I'll give the vet a call as well, have them all checked over, if the dogs will let the vet anywhere near them. If you can talk to Melody, I can pick up supplies, depending on what she wants.'

'If you're going to the shop to get supplies, why don't you give Melody a call yourself rather than me relaying what she says to you? Do you want her number?' Tori said, cringing a little inside that she was interfering. But it was only a little and really it was for the good of the puppies.

'I have her number,' Jamie said. 'I'll, umm... give her a call. I'll be back here shortly.'

He moved off towards the house, obviously thoroughly despondent at the thought of calling Melody, and Tori couldn't help a little smile spreading on her lips. She put the puppy down next to Beauty and went off into the cottage to look for any other meat she could give Beauty and Beast until Jamie came back.

She had just finished making sure the dogs had fresh water and dishing up two big plates of all the ham and pork slices she'd bought for her sandwiches when there was a knock at the door.

She went to answer it, expecting to see Jamie, but Aidan was there instead.

'Oh, hello.' Warmth flooded through her as soon as she saw him.

He leaned down and kissed her on the cheek and then, when he went to pull back, he changed his mind and kissed her gently on the mouth and all those wonderful feelings for him bubbled to the surface. It had to be more than just sex for him, she had to believe that.

'I believe you have an animal problem,' he said.

'Multiple animal problems actually.'

He frowned in confusion as she let him into the cottage.

'We have puppies,' Tori said, leading him out the back towards the shed.

'Beast had puppies? With Beauty?'

'It sure seems that way.'

She peered round the shed door and Aidan did the same and there was Beast, playing the doting father perfectly as he lay next to Beauty, admiring his children.

'Oh wow,' Aidan said, softly.

'There's eleven of them. Jamie thinks that Beauty might struggle to feed them, even if we keep her well-fed. He's going to call the vet and Melody, who might be able to help us – she used to help breed puppies.'

Aidan moved slowly into the shed, letting Beast and Beauty sniff him before he crouched down to look at the puppies.

'Wow, Beastie, look what you did,' Aidan said, stroking Beast behind the ears. Tori placed the plates of meat down near their heads and Beauty and Beast gobbled them up.

'Should we bring them into the cottage?' Tori asked.

'We can, if you're happy with that?'

'I'm happy with it. I'm spending every night with you anyway. We're practically married already,' Tori teased, and then wondered if she should talk to him about their relationship. Was it too soon to ask about their future?

'Yes, apart from the wedding ring and the happy ending,' Aidan said.

Tori didn't know what to say to that. There was a tone to his voice that she just couldn't pick up. Anger, disappointment? Or was it something else?

'And you don't want that, do you?' Tori asked, quietly. 'When we first met you said you didn't want any kind of relationship.'

He turned to face her. 'So did you. Or have you changed your mind?'

Oh god, she couldn't tell him that she was thinking of marriage and happy ever afters with him already, it had only been a few days.

She swallowed. 'Do you see it going that way?'

He focussed his attention on one of the puppies, picking it up gently in his large hands. 'I have no idea where this is going. I think we probably want very different things.'

'What is it that you want?' Tori asked.

She watched him cradle the puppy in his arms and she suddenly wondered what he would look like cradling his own baby in his arms. A stab of longing flashed through her as she thought about a tiny dark-haired baby that was half hers and half his. She quickly pushed that thought away. What was wrong with her? She'd never been particularly broody before but that was because she had been so anti-relationships. Closing herself off to any relationship meant closing herself off to the possibility of having a family of her own too. But now, staring at this wonderful man, she suddenly wanted all of that: marriage, children, the happy ever after with him.

He looked over at her, staring at her as he tried to form the words in his mouth.

'I want…' He reached out to touch her face. 'I want to carry on exactly as we are now, having lots of fun and lots of great sex, and not ruin this with talks of the future. Because if we talk about this now, one of us will end up getting hurt and then it will be over before it's even begun.'

She swallowed down the huge sense of disappointment flooding through her.

'So just keep things casual?' she said, trying to keep the emotion out of her voice.

'Yes,' he said, almost urgently.

'Meaningless?' she asked.

He flinched. 'Whatever this is between us, I've never thought it was meaningless. Is that what you think? Because if you do, I think we better end this right now.'

There was a noise at the door and Tori looked round to see Jamie arrive.

'I've brought reinforcements,' Jamie said, grinning hugely, clearly with no idea what he had just walked in on. A few seconds later, Melody arrived, a big smile on her face too.

Tori smiled slightly at the sight of the two of them together.

'Ohh, look at the puppies,' Melody said, moving slowly into the shed, stroking Beauty and Beast and then picking up one of the puppies. Beauty still seemed too tired to care. 'God, this one is so small.'

'Can you help them?' Tori said.

'Yes, absolutely. We can hand-feed the three smallest ones and supplement the others with what Beauty is giving them until she is back on her feet. We've already been to the vets and they've given us special puppy milk and bottles and syringes just in case the bottle teats are too big. The vet's going to come round later to check on them all. We've got some special puppy sheets too for when they need to go to the toilet, we have loads so enough to keep us going for a while. Jamie bought it all,' Melody said, looking at Jamie adoringly.

'We're going to move them into the cottage, so we can keep an eye on them more easily,' Tori said.

Aidan put his puppy down. 'I have some tarpaulin in the back of the car. I'll put that down in the lounge and cover it with some old sheets and blankets. We'll have to build some kind of makeshift pen once the puppies get a bit older, or they'll be getting everywhere, but they don't seem very mobile at the moment.'

He left the shed, and for a moment Tori wondered whether she should go after him, but she wanted to talk to him alone, without any chance of Jamie or Melody overhearing. She turned back to Jamie and Melody and watched them for a moment as they held the puppies. Maybe a tiny bit more meddling wouldn't go amiss.

'Is there any chance you two could stay here tonight to help feed the puppies and keep an eye on Beauty? I have to help Aidan with the heartberries, I know he's worried about the storms that will probably be here in the next day or so. He thinks there's a possibility the heartberry field will flood early and we'd lose half the crop, so we're trying to get as much as possible done at night. I probably won't be back until nine or ten tomorrow morning and I can take over the day shift.' Tori laid down the bait, hoping they would take it.

'I can stay here,' Melody said.

'I can too, we can take it in turns to do different shifts,' Jamie said.

'You can sleep in my bed,' Tori said, suppressing a smile when they both blushed. Clearly that was taking the meddling a step too far. 'I mean, take it in turns to sleep in my bed.'

They both nodded, and Tori nearly cheered with joy that her plan had worked. Nothing might come of it, but it couldn't hurt to force them to spend a night together, even if it was strictly platonic.

She just needed to sort out her own love life now.

CHAPTER 21

Tori walked up the drive to Aidan's farmhouse later that afternoon.

Between her, Aidan, Jamie and Melody, they had carefully relocated Beauty and the puppies to the lounge of Blossom Cottage. Beast had gone backwards and forwards to the shed making sure all the puppies had been brought into the house before settling down next to Beauty. But as soon as the dogs were comfortable, Aidan had left, citing that he had work to do. Tori knew that was true, but she still sensed that it had more to do with their conversation earlier in the shed.

Instead of meeting on the beach as planned, Isla and Elliot had come round and Elliot couldn't have been happier, playing with and hugging all the puppies. She had spent a few hours with them, all the time thinking about Aidan and what she wanted to say to him. She still had no clue.

She knocked on his door and a few moments later he answered. His face softened as soon as he saw her, and he reached out for her briefly before he let his hand fall at his side.

'I never said I thought what we had was meaningless, I was asking if *you* thought it was meaningless,' Tori said, quickly.

He stared at her. 'Oh.'

'Look, I have no idea what is going to happen when I leave here, and I understand you don't want to talk about it. But you have made me ridiculously happy these last few days, there is definitely nothing meaningless about this.'

He reached out and took her hand. 'I'm sorry.'

'Don't be,' she said.

'This is something special, and I know this will probably never end in marriage and two kids—'

'Five,' Tori interrupted.

'Five kids?'

'That's what Agatha has predicted,' Tori said, wanting to lighten the mood, though she knew she was just trying to cover over the tension rather than deal with it.

Aidan laughed. 'OK, it probably won't end in marriage and five kids, but no matter what happens, you need to know that this is… something,' he said.

'I know.'

She looked down at his hand in hers and sighed with relief. She looked up and noticed he had a red blobby stain on his chest.

'You have jam on your shirt,' Tori said and reached out to wipe it off but just ended up smearing it over his shirt.

He watched her intently as her hand moved across his chest. He was so hard and strong and suddenly all thoughts of removing the jam scattered from her brain. She smoothed her hand over his muscles and slowly down his belly towards the top of his jeans. She brought her other hand to join the first, caressing and stroking him through his shirt.

He cleared his throat. 'What are you doing?'

'I have no idea but I'm enjoying myself,' Tori said.

As she continued to stroke him, tracing his muscles through his shirt, Aidan pulled her inside and closed the door.

'What are you doing?' Tori asked.

'I'm going to enjoy myself too,' Aidan said. Bending, he threw her over his shoulder.

She squealed as he carried her up the stairs to his bedroom. He threw her down on the bed.

She laughed as he bent over her and kissed her hard. 'What are you doing? Do you think you can just throw me over your shoulder, carry me to your bedroom and make love to me?'

'That's exactly what I think.' He placed a soft kiss on her neck, sending goosebumps right across her body.

'I'm not sleeping with you,' Tori said, undoing the buttons on his shirt. 'Urgh, I don't find you attractive at all. Your elbows are too lumpy and don't even get me started on your knees.' She ran her hands across his wonderful warm chest and wrestled the shirt from him completely. God, he was magnificent.

'If we're not sleeping together, why are you undressing me?' Aidan said, kissing at the very base of her neck, seemingly not perturbed at all by her slur on his looks.

'You have jam on your shirt, I'm just helping you out of it. Don't want to get jam on your nice clean sheets.'

'No, of course not,' Aidan said, popping the button of her shorts and then pulling down the zip. 'You have jam on your shorts too.'

'I do? How careless of me,' Tori said, lifting her bum so he could tug down her shorts. It seemed she had jam on her knickers as well as they were quickly removed along with the shorts. 'I'm pretty sure I have jam on my bra as well.'

'Let me check,' Aidan said, tugging her t-shirt over her head and throwing it across the room as she undid his jeans and pushed them down his thighs. 'Ah yes, you do.' He quickly divested her of her bra, so she was naked underneath him. 'And jam on your breasts.'

He bent his head and kissed her breast, licking across her nipple, sending sensations of pleasure shooting through her body. She cried out, grasping the back of his head as she arched against him. He moved his hand between her legs, stroking at the very top of her thighs. Her orgasm came so fast and hard, it left her breathless, and he kissed her, catching her gasps on his lips.

He pulled back and wrestled himself out of his jeans and tight black shorts.

'Condoms,' she breathed.

'Top drawer.'

She quickly leaned over and yanked the drawer open, grabbing a handful and tossing them back on the bed.

'Though I have to ask, if we're not sleeping together, why we need condoms?' Aidan said, picking one up.

'Well, better to be safe, now we're both naked. I wouldn't want you accidentally falling inside me.'

Aidan chuckled. 'That would be very careless. And seven condoms?'

'Just in case you're feeling particularly clumsy. It might happen again and again.'

'That would be terrible.'

'God yes, awful.'

She watched him slide the condom on and her eyes widened as she realised how ready he was for this.

She quickly sat up, pushing him on his back and straddling him. A second later he was deep inside her.

He groaned, and moved his hands to her hips. 'Careless.'

'Oops,' Tori said, resting her hands on his chest as she stared down at him. He felt so amazing. She started to move but he caught her hips and held her steady.

'Just wait a moment, let me look at you,' Aidan said. He moved his hands across her ribs, trailing his thumbs across her stomach. He slid his hands over her breasts, caressing her hair through his fingers. 'Whatever happens between us, I want to remember you like this, sitting on top of me, looking like an absolute goddess. I want to remember the sunlight in your hair, every beautiful freckle on your skin, your cheeks flushed from the orgasm I gave you and the look in your eyes that says you never want to be any place but here. Whatever happens, I want to remember this moment forever.'

'Oh,' Tori said, quietly. Right then the humour and silliness faded away and there was just the two of them, caught in this moment. And it was true, there was nowhere else she wanted to be. In her heart, she knew she could never walk away from him.

He stroked his hands back down to her hips, gently urging her to move, but she was frozen there. She had fallen in love with this wonderful, kind and funny man. And what the hell was she going to do about it? That thought was terrifying and wonderful all at once. She had to put the brakes on, lighten the mood somehow, while she digested this.

'When we get married, when my snoring keeps you awake every night, when I wake up with morning breath and my hair sticking out in every direction like a bush, when my singing in the shower sets your teeth on edge and my tidiness and my ability to burn the simplest meal drives you mad, you can remember this moment.'

She expected him to laugh it off, or at the very least to stop looking at her like she was a queen. But he sat up and cupped her face, kissing her gently.

'I'm looking forward to it,' he whispered against her lips. He moved against her, taking control, which she was glad for as she was suddenly incapable of doing anything. 'You don't scare me, Tori Graham.'

'I'll just be scared for the both of us,' Tori said.

'You worry about tomorrow and I'll take care of today,' Aidan said.

Emotions bubbled through her, this need for him, this fear of what would happen, sensations of pleasure spiking through her body – it was an overload of so many feelings all at once. Her body started to move, falling in rhythm with him, and for a while she was able to push aside her worries and doubts, and just enjoy the moment.

He wrapped his arms around her, gathering her close so he was deep inside her, and then kissed her sweetly on the forehead.

'I'll take care of you,' he whispered, and it was this tenderness towards her, this feeling of being safe, that sent her over the edge.

The day of the boat race arrived with high winds and occasional showers. As Tori and Aidan walked down the drive towards Blossom Cottage, her hair whipped around her face. The storm was due to hit later that night, getting worse in the early hours of the following morning. Because of the supermoon, the tides were at their highest at this time of year and she knew that Aidan was worried, no matter what he said.

They had decided that, as soon as the sun set that day, they would start picking the fruit and work through the night to get as many heartberries as possible. Over half the field had already been harvested but that meant that they still had half the field to lose if the storm turned really bad that night.

It would sadly mean they would miss a lot of the festivities that night. Aidan had suggested she could go to the festival instead, but the heartberries were very important to him and the villagers and she couldn't let him pick them alone just so she could enjoy some fireworks.

She glanced over at him and saw the frown on his face. There was nothing they really could do now. She had suggested they started picking the fruit that day instead of going to the boat race, but Aidan had insisted they needed to be picked at night. So, she would just have to keep his mind off things until they could get back to the heartberry field later that evening.

'I wonder how the puppy-sitting went last night for Jamie and Melody,' Tori said. 'Melody said the puppies would need feeding every two to three hours, so I don't imagine they got a lot of sleep.'

Aidan looked at her and smiled. 'Are you trying to set Jamie and Melody up by getting them to look after the puppies together?'

Tori smiled. 'Maybe.'

'You can't push two people together, it will either happen or it won't. Interfering might be more of a hindrance than a help,' Aidan said.

'I don't know, a little bit of a nudge didn't seem to do us any harm,' Tori said, squeezing his hand. Would they have got together if his aunt hadn't been so insistent? Maybe she owed Agatha a bit more gratitude. 'You know your brother better than I do, does he have feelings for Melody?'

Aidan was silent for a moment. 'I think I'd better plead the fifth on that one.'

Tori laughed.

'Does Melody have feelings for Jamie?' Aidan asked.

'Oh, look, a squirrel,' Tori pointed wildly into the trees and he laughed.

'Nice change of subject.'

'Well, let's see how well they got on last night,' she said.

She opened the door quietly, not wanting to frighten Beauty or the puppies and just in case Jamie or Melody were asleep.

She stepped into the lounge and Aidan followed her. She smiled.

Jamie and Melody were fast asleep on the sofa, his arm around her shoulder, her head on his chest and three tiny bundles of fur on their laps.

'It seems they had a very good night together,' Tori whispered, unable to keep the smile from her face. Maybe this would be just the nudge they needed to get them together or at least start the ball rolling.

'Maybe we should take over the morning feed, let them sleep a little while,' Aidan whispered.

Tori nodded.

She looked over at Beauty and saw she looked a lot more awake today. All the puppies were currently sleeping, and Beast was dozing, keeping one eye on his children.

Tori gently picked up the empty bottles and Aidan followed her into the kitchen. He set about getting bowls of food ready for Beauty and Beast while she made the milk bottles up for the three smallest puppies.

She walked back into the lounge and scooped up one of the tiny puppies. Aidan put the bowls of food and water on the floor and then picked up another puppy.

As Jamie and Melody had the sofa, Tori and Aidan sat down on the floor and started feeding the puppies. There was something undeniably sweet and achingly endearing about feeding newborn puppies, their tiny bellies getting fat with warm milk.

Melody shifted slightly in her sleep and Jamie instinctively pulled her closer to him as he carried on sleeping himself. Tori couldn't help grinning and Aidan smiled too.

'OK, maybe a tiny bit of meddling doesn't hurt,' Aidan whispered.

Melody stirred and opened her eyes sleepily. She looked up at Jamie just as he woke and looked down at her. For just a moment, they were aware only of each other and the look of adoration that passed between them was unmistakable before they suddenly realised where they were and that they had an audience.

Jamie straightened, realised his arm was around Melody's shoulders and quickly removed it.

Melody looked embarrassed as she stood up.

Tori passed her the third bottle to try to cover up the embarrassing moment.

'We've only fed these two. Little Spike over there still needs a bottle,' Tori said, pointing to the tiny puppy whose fur was sticking up around its ears.

Melody quickly scooped it up and focussed all her attention on feeding it and Jamie went to check on the other puppies.

Tori sighed as she watched the two of them almost pretend the other didn't exist. Maybe an afternoon at the Heartberry Love Festival would be just what they needed.

CHAPTER 22

Tori looked around as everybody loaded their boats into the water, lining the shore. There were about thirty to forty boats of all different shapes, sizes and colours. Over on the opposite banks of the river, there were another thirty odd boats in different shapes too. Some had wings or fish scales painted on the sides or, in the case of one, hundreds of rubber ducks strapped to the edges. She smiled when she saw Mark and Mindy's boat in high-vis green with 'Mindy's Seaweed Shakes' emblazoned on the side. Some people had just used giant inflatable sharks or crocodiles as their water crafts, which somehow seemed to Tori that they were cheating not actually building the boats themselves. However, knowing how hard it would be to direct those inflatables across the water with any kind of speed, she decided to let it go.

Some of the vessels were fairly impressive, while others didn't look like they would stay together for any length of time. And then there was Leo's, a great big water dragon that had scales that glistened and sparkled in the midday sun, eyes that moved and even breathed fire. Aidan had mentioned that his brother always tried to better himself every year and the villagers now expected some kind of extravaganza from Leo.

Aidan set about making sure the balloons were tied to the sides of his boat securely and Tori helped him.

'So, we have to get to the island and back?' Tori asked, looking at the island in the middle of the wide river. It was probably no more than twenty or thirty metres away but, to Tori, it could have been an ocean on their little boat of matchsticks.

'In theory, we just have to get to the island to win a slice of the heartberry cake, though of course we have to get back once we've won it. But it doesn't really matter so much if our boat breaks up and we don't make it back.'

'Except that we would get wet,' Tori said.

'Well, yes, there is that.'

The wind raced up the river, making the boats bob and bump into each other.

'And we have the wind to contend with as well,' she said, still not entirely convinced that this boat race was a good idea.

Aidan looked out to where the river met the sea and the white caps that were clearly visible as the sea swelled and surged towards the village. He frowned with worry and she knew it wasn't over the boat race but what would happen to the heartberry field later that day.

'So, we need to beat Leo and his ridiculous dragon,' Tori said, trying to get his mind off the storm. 'Show him that bigger isn't always better.'

Leo, who was taking care of last-minute preparations next to them, turned around. 'Not a chance.'

'Hey, my little boat might not look like much, but it's got weight and size on its side. It's small and nippy – your boat is too big to go anywhere fast,' Aidan said.

'Nippy might be a huge overstatement,' Tori muttered.

'I don't need speed, when I have style,' Leo said.

Tori had to admit he had that, the boat was stunning.

'Besides, I have a secret weapon,' Leo said.

'If you tell me you have an outboard motor underneath the dragon's tail, there's going to be big trouble,' Tori said, knowing that the only rule when it came to the boats was that they weren't allowed to have any kind of motor engine attached. Propulsion had to come from hard work and a hell of a lot of luck.

'You'll have to wait and see,' Leo said, cryptically. 'But obviously my boat is going to beat yours.'

'How do you know my boat won't win?' Jamie called across.

Tori looked over at his boat. It was an impressive sight. Made mainly from reclaimed driftwood, it looked beautiful and like something that should be on display in a museum or a giant art exhibit. But attached to the sides were what appeared to be clay waves, in beautiful metallic hues of greens and blues. There was even a small mermaid attached to the front, which looked like it was made from sea glass. But the boat didn't seem like it was made for the river. It was definitely sitting very low in the water with the heavy weight. It looked like the only thing keeping it from sinking right now was Jamie's business partner Klaus, who was a giant of a man, holding onto a rope at the back of the boat as he stood on the banks. He looked like a Viking with his long red beard and leather headband wrapped around his forehead. Tori only hoped that Klaus had inherited some of that boat-building blood from his ancestors because she fancied her chances of getting to the island safely a lot more than Jamie's right now.

Melody came over to Jamie and he gave her all his attention as she presumably wished him good luck.

'Well, that's progress,' Leo said, softly.

The four of them had spent the morning making sure all the puppies and Beauty and Beast were well-fed before they left for the boat race. Despite the slightly embarrassing way the two of them had woken up, Jamie and Melody had whiled away the morning chatting and sitting next to each other as they fed the puppies. It was huge progress from the longing looks and awkward silences they had apparently endured for the last year.

The Mayor stepped up on a podium on the island and started thanking everyone for coming, before outlining the rules. Basically there weren't any, and then he started explaining the legend of the heartberry boat race, presumably for any tourists or newcomers who didn't know.

'Hundreds of years ago, Alfred Jackson would row out to this island with his crop of the full moon heartberries and Matilda Loveheart would row out from her little cottage on the other side of the river in Meadow Bay to collect them. A week later she would return with the coveted heartberry cake and they would share it under the stars. Now even then, they knew the legend of the heartberries, how by sharing the cake, their love would last for all of eternity. And boy would they need that luck of the berries. As many of you know, there was a great feud between the families in Meadow Bay and Sandcastle Bay and no trade was allowed to happen between the two villages, and definitely not any kind of romantic shenanigans. Which is why our lovers would meet under the light of the moon, here on the island, which was considered to be neutral territory. It was here they first consummated their love, conceived their first child and later, when the forthcoming arrival of the child was discovered, where they wed, ending the feud between the families once and for all. We celebrate this every year with a boat race from Sandcastle Bay and Meadow Bay to the island, where the people from both villages can enjoy the heartberry cake together. Now legend has it that if any of the winners share that cake with their beloved, they will be together forever.'

The crowd predictably ooohed and ahhhed.

'So, without further ado, let's start this race.'

The crowd cheered and clapped.

'Ten, nine…'

There was suddenly a mad rush as everyone with a boat started frantically preparing their crafts for take-off. Aidan untied the rope holding his boat to the shore and grabbed his paddle. Tori moved to the back, ready to start jumping up and down on the foot pumps.

'…Two, one. *GO!*'

Aidan pushed their boat off from the bank and started paddling frantically on the side, before moving over to the other side and doing the same. Tori held her breath as the boat bobbed around on the water, drifting out from the bank so they were soon in deep water. Miraculously the boat seemed to float. She jumped on one of the foot pumps, which seemed to make no difference to the speed and propulsion of their boat.

She laughed as two men on the back of an inflatable crocodile and shark drifted past, downstream, heading out to sea rather than towards the island. Thankfully there were two rescue boats at the mouth of the river, ready to scoop up any stragglers who would end up floating out to the sea. The two men seemed to think the whole thing was hilarious as they desperately tried to propel themselves back to the island with only their hands to help them.

There was a very small pirate ship, complete with a sail and a Jolly Roger flag, filled with pirates. As they bumped against Mark and Mindy's boat, the pirates stepped aboard, waving their swords and shouting about commandeering the other vessel, much to Mindy's annoyance. Tori glanced across at Leo's sea dragon which was powering ahead towards the island, cutting through the water easily. Jamie's boat was clearly struggling and seemed to be taking on water at the back, but Jamie and Klaus were taking it in their stride, laughing as they tried to bail the water out and paddle towards the island too.

'Keep jumping,' Aidan said.

Tori leapt on the foot pumps again, doing a jump on each of the pumps for good measure.

As Leo's boat inched ahead, the wings lifted, and two water cannons moved out from underneath, squirting gallons of water on any of the nearby boats. Aidan got it full in the chest before he managed to stagger out of the way, laughing at the sneaky tactics. Another boat was getting wet too but Jamie's boat, which was struggling behind, ended up with a jet of water right in the prow and started to list dangerously.

Tori laughed as they struggled to keep the boat afloat, but it tipped over throwing both Jamie and Klaus into the water.

Leo cheered, and she looked round at him as he did a little victory dance. Aidan was still paddling frantically, and she looked back over at Jamie and Klaus. The boat had flipped upside down and Klaus was wading ashore but there was no sign of Jamie.

Her heart stopped. Was he underneath the boat?

She looked around frantically, but he was nowhere to be seen. And nobody else seemed to have noticed.

Without thinking she dived into the water, the icy cold hitting her hard as she surfaced and swam towards the boat. Something crashed into the water behind her and she glanced around to see Leo and Aidan powering through the water towards the boat, clearly having spotted the problem too.

Something moved on the shore side of the boat and Tori saw Melody wading out to Jamie's boat, getting there before Tori, Aidan and Leo could. With seemingly superhuman strength, Melody ripped the boat away and Jamie staggered to his feet in the water, coughing and spluttering.

Tori watched as Melody wrapped an arm around Jamie's shoulders and helped him ashore as he leaned heavily on her. Paramedics came running down to help him onto the bank and check him over but Jamie didn't seem to be any worse off for his ordeal.

'That's definitely progress,' Leo said, as he trod water next to her.

'Looks like Melody is taking very good care of him,' Tori said, watching her friend stay by his side.

Aidan clipped Leo round the back of the head. 'Dick,' he said.

Leo nodded. 'Yep, totally deserve that.'

'Well, I guess none of us are going to have everlasting love now,' Tori said, as she looked round and saw Aidan's matchstick boat had impaled itself on some rocks.

Leo looked round too and smiled. Tori glanced over at what he was looking at and saw that his spectacular dragon had beached itself miraculously on the island.

'Speak for yourself,' Leo said. He swam across the river towards his boat, climbed aboard and then stepped ashore to claim his piece of cake, accompanied by a few others who had successfully made it to the island from both sides of the river.

She turned back to Aidan, who put his hands around her waist as they both trod water to keep themselves afloat.

'We've already eaten the magical berries,' Aidan said.

'That's true and we both know how accurate Agatha's predictions are.'

'So, who needs some stupid cake,' Aidan said, moving to the shore and then helping her up the bank.

'Exactly,' Tori said, though she couldn't help feeling a tiny bit disappointed. She noticed Aidan looking wistfully over at the island where they were doling out the cake. It seemed he was a bit disappointed too.

The storm hit early that evening.

Dark clouds had been racing across the sky all day and the festivities of the Heartberry Love Festival had to be accommodated around several heavy rain showers.

The celebrations were well underway in the village hall, with dancing, singing, eating and various games throughout the night. Although rain was predicted to continue for most of the night, Leo had insisted that wouldn't stop him delivering the firework extravaganza later that evening and everyone in the village was really looking forward to it. Aidan felt bad that Tori wouldn't get to see it all – the love festival was always a good night.

After Jamie's soggy ordeal at the river earlier, he and Melody had decided a quiet night in looking after the puppies was just what they needed, so Aidan and Tori were free to start picking the fruit whenever they wanted.

The weather forecasts were not good. The news was reporting that over a foot of rain would be dumped on the south-west corner of England overnight and Aidan was even starting to worry that the river would flood on the far side of the heartberry field.

Aidan looked out the window of the farmhouse at the trees bent at odd angles as the wind ripped across his land. Rain lashed against the window. The sky was a deep purply grey, making it almost as dark as night out there even though the sun wasn't due to set for a few more hours yet.

Tori wrapped her arms round his stomach as she stood behind him, pressing a kiss into his shoulder blades.

He wrapped his hand around hers, holding it against his heart. He was glad she was here. And not just because of the help he needed with picking the berries, but also for emotional support too. Hell, it wasn't that he wanted her for that, he just wanted her close. She had this glow about her that spread warmth and happiness wherever she went, and he wanted to hold onto her forever. But he knew that wasn't going to happen. He knew she liked him a lot but there was a big difference between liking someone and giving up your whole way of life to spend the rest of your days with them. There was no way she would leave London to live here, there was nothing in Sandcastle Bay for her, and he had nothing to offer her either. A life on a fruit farm was not exactly exciting or fast-paced. Imogen had hated it here and Tori would grow to hate it too and then she'd start to hate him as well.

Could he move to London to be with her? Life would be so different there, fast, loud and congested. What would he do for work? And what would happen to the fruit farm if he were to sell it? He couldn't see any of his brothers wanting to take on that responsibility, and Emily was busy with her café. He couldn't sell it on to someone outside the family. Developers were clamouring for land to build houses and flats in seaside locations and his land offered so much opportunity for that. River and sea views plus all the fields and hills. He had been offered large sums of money on many occasions to buy his land and he had always turned them down. He couldn't do that to his family's legacy or to the people of Sandcastle Bay. The heartberries were too important for that.

And none of this mattered anyway. They both agreed this was going to be something casual. Tori would probably be horrified that he was thinking of selling everything he owned to move to London to be with her.

No, this was simply a bit of fun and he was totally OK with that. She was leaving in a week and that was just fine. He hadn't fallen in love with her, not at all. Definitely not.

He turned round and took her in his arms, kissing her sweetly, and his heart ached inside his chest. He could say it a hundred times, but he couldn't persuade his heart that he didn't have feelings for her.

He sighed. He had been telling her not to worry about the future, but he was now doing exactly the same thing. When things had first started between them, he had been very laid-back about it all but now, as his feelings for her deepened, so had the fear and doubt.

She reached up and stroked his cheek as she kissed him, and he was hugely tempted to strip her naked and make love to her here on the floor of the lounge. Not just for sex, but because he needed to be connected to her in every way that he could. He could easily lose himself in her for hours and then the heartberries could be ruined under a sea of water.

He pulled back just as she was reaching for more.

'I think we better go and check on the heartberry field. We are about two hours from high tide, so it will give us a good indication of how this storm is going to affect us,' Aidan said.

'You say the most romantic things,' Tori said.

He cursed to himself. She had been kissing him, stroking his face, and he was talking about bloody berries. He wasn't a romantic sort. That was what she wanted, what she deserved. But she wouldn't get that from him. He thought back to when she'd thought he had planned a romantic picnic for their first night of berry-picking and how disappointed she'd been when she'd found out it was just some snacks he always packed for late-night fruit-picking. She really was in for a lifetime of disappointment if she was with him. Imogen used to berate him for his lack of romance too. Sure, if he really thought about it, he could arrange a sunset walk or remember to give her a bunch of flowers from time to time but that kind of thing never came naturally to him.

'I'm sorry,' Aidan said.

She frowned. 'Don't be. I know you're worried. I'm ready to go whenever you are.'

'I promise you a night of romance when we get back.'

'Ha, by romance you mean hot sex? I'm totally on board for that.'

Was that really all he had to offer her? A great night in the sack?

'Well, I can definitely deliver on that,' Aidan said, trying to keep the emotion out of his voice.

'You always do.' She trailed her hand over his chest down to his belly. He caught it and kissed each one of her fingers and then turned her hand over and kissed her wrist, feeling her pulse race against his lips.

'Come on you, let's go,' Tori said, reluctantly. 'You keep kissing me like that and we're never getting out of here.'

He let her go and handed her a raincoat, then grabbed his and they walked out to the jeep.

They started the drive down to the heartberry field.

'Did you see that Leo shared his piece of cake with Isla and Elliot?' Tori said and he knew she was trying to distract him.

'I didn't see it but I certainly heard about it.'

'There was practically a collective gasp from the villagers when he did it,' Tori laughed.

'He's never given his cake to anyone before, it's a big thing. In the eyes of the villagers, he is publicly declaring his love for her and she accepted it and ate it. I'm not sure if she knows the significance of that but I imagine the villagers will be taking polls over when they'll get married now.'

'I think it will take a bit more than a slice of cake to get her to walk down the aisle with him.'

He frowned. 'She doesn't have feelings for him?'

'Oh, I'm pretty sure she's crazy about him but if he really does love her, he needs to tell her with more than a piece of cake. The actual words will probably do it.'

'That's not Leo's style.'

'Well he needs to change his style,' Tori said.

Aidan thought about this. Leo knew exactly what he was doing and for him to share the cake with Isla he must have real feelings for her. Maybe he needed to have a word with him about being a bit more explicit. Although knowing Leo, he would tell Aidan where to stick his helpful advice.

Tori sighed contentedly. He looked across and saw her smiling as she looked out the windscreen.

'You OK?'

'This view, I could look at it forever.'

He tried to see it through her eyes. The sky was charcoal grey with clouds of damson purple, the sea below them a churning swell of inky blue and white-capped waves. There was no sun at all.

She must have seen his scepticism.

'I know you don't see it because you see it every day, but this view over the fruit fields and the sea beyond is beautiful. The sea changes every day, different colours, different conditions. It really is incredible. My view from my flat in London stays the same day in and day out. Yes, the weather changes, but it's the same buildings, the same traffic that rushes past every day. This is amazing.'

Could this view really be enough to make her want to stay? He shook his head. He was not naïve enough to think it could be as simple as that.

'I'm loving this holiday,' Tori went on. 'The beaches, the berry-picking, your wonderful crazy family. You.'

He reached across and put a hand on her thigh. 'We've had fun, haven't we?'

She looked over at him with uncertainty in her eyes. 'We have. Are you OK, you seem distant?'

He hesitated and then decided to share some of his feelings at least. 'I'm just worried.'

'About the berries?'

'Well yes, that, but about us. The future.'

'I thought that was my job,' Tori teased.

He smiled as he rounded a bend in the driveway.

'The way you talk sometimes, it's like you see a future here that's beyond just a few weeks' stay. I worry that…' he trailed off. He worried that he was seeing things that weren't really there, that he was getting his hopes up and then he would be bitterly disappointed when she left with not so much as a backwards glance. But he couldn't say any of those things to her.

'You worry that I'm getting the wrong impression of what this is,' Tori finished for him, completely inaccurately. 'You don't need to worry that I'm going to turn into a weird stalker, that I'll turn up at the farmhouse with all my suitcases at the end of my stay and declare that I'm moving in. You said you wanted to keep this casual, I get that.'

He cringed. He regretted that conversation, he'd handled it badly. She had wanted to talk, and he had closed her out.

'Well actually I don't,' Tori said. 'The way you hold me when we make love, the way you kiss me and look at me says this is way more than casual, but you say you don't want anything serious and I just can't reconcile the two. I leave in a few days, is that going to be it? We're both just going to walk away from this and never see each other again?'

'Well you'll be back to visit Melody and Isla, we'll see each other then,' Aidan said. He realised he was terrified of losing her but probably more scared of trying to keep her, of falling in love with her and then losing her in a few months' time when it came to an end.

'So that's it?' Tori rounded on him. 'Casual sex every time I swing into town?'

'What else can I offer you? Did you really see this working? You would never give up your life in London and move here. There's nothing for you here, no cinemas, no glamorous clubs or parties, no big department stores or designer shops. Life in Sandcastle Bay would never have been enough for you. It never would have worked,' Aidan said.

'You're laying the ghosts of your past at my feet,' Tori said. 'Imogen might have wanted all of that but that isn't me. You clearly don't know me at all if you think those things matter to me. I might live in London but that doesn't define me.'

'So, you'd really move here? You'd end up resenting me because of it.'

'Why would I resent you? If I moved here, it would be my choice.'

'Because I'm not enough for you. I'd never be enough. When Imogen left she texted me to say that she deserved more than this. And she's right. I can never give you everything you deserve. I'm a farmer in some tiny little village in the middle of nowhere. You've been to Hollywood. You're jetting off to New York in a few months. You have this big glamorous life in London. I can't compete with that.'

'I've never been interested in a glamorous life and it makes
me sad that you would think that of me. In fact, my life of
sitting in my pyjamas in my flat, reading my books, making
stupid origami animals, and eating a takeaway most nights
is as far away from glamorous as humanly possible. I love
being an animator but it's not a glamorous life, working
with plasticine models every day, and I can do my job from
anywhere in the world – it doesn't have to be London. What
Imogen said to you was horrible, you're a wonderful and kind
man and any woman would be incredibly lucky to have you
by their side for the rest of their life. I'm so sorry that your
heart has been bruised and hurt in this way, but my heart has
been damaged too. The difference is I'm prepared to take a
risk again, to give us a chance and maybe we can heal each
other. There are no guarantees in love and I can't promise we
will be together forever, fate has a nasty way of interfering
just when you think everything is going OK, but surely, it's
worth a shot. We deserve to be happy, you make me happy
and that's all I'd ever want from you. You are enough for me.
You. Not Sandcastle Bay.'

'What are you suggesting? We get married, you move in
here? I barely know you.'

He recoiled from the lie. He knew her well enough to know
he wanted forever with her. He shook his head at that thought.

'I fell in love with Imogen so quickly, got caught up in the
moment. We were due to marry six months after we first met.
I never took the time to get to know her properly. I swore I
would never do that again.'

'I'm not expecting a proposal of marriage here. That's not
what I'm asking. If we have something special, we can make

this work. I can visit you, you can visit me. I can rent a house here in Sandcastle Bay for six months, give us a proper chance to see if we really do have something. I'm just asking if you think we have a chance here?'

He stared out of the window. God, he wanted that, to make a life with her here. He would be lying if he said this was anything but casual for him. But could he really trust in what they had? Could he take a risk with his heart?

'I'm not worth the risk, am I?' Tori said, quietly. She groaned and let her head fall into her hands. 'This was never anything serious for you. I've done it again, haven't I? I've let myself think this was something more, listened to my heart. I'm such a fool. Every single time I think I can trust someone I get it thrown back in my face.'

It was his turn to get angry now. 'I'm not like Luc or your dad. But you've been carrying this fear that I would let you down since we first met, just waiting for it to happen. You never trusted me and how can I let myself believe in our relationship if you wouldn't believe in it either?'

'You gave me nothing to trust,' Tori said.

'How can you say that? I got a bloody tattoo with your face on my back just so you wouldn't feel bad about your own ridiculous tattoo. This relationship has always been way more than just casual, you know that. We had something special. The connection we share when we made love, I've never had that with anyone before.'

'But you're not willing to take that final step with me.'

He returned his attention back to the window and didn't speak for the longest time as he tormented himself with the ifs and buts. When he eventually spoke, his voice was thick.

'If we carry on with this, one or both of us will get hurt. Neither of us wanted to risk that again. Love doesn't endure, we know that.'

He rounded the corner and saw the heartberry field below them and his heart dropped into his stomach. The far corner, where the river flowed down by the side of the field, had completely flooded. It wasn't much, maybe twenty or thirty feet had been lost, but that was hundreds of berries and he knew it was going to get a lot worse later when it was high tide.

He glanced across to Orchard Cove and could see the waves crashing right against the boundary of the field. Once it was high tide large parts of that area of the field would be lost too.

'Shit.'

'Oh no,' Tori gasped, as she stared down at the field too.

He quickly drove down the last part of the drive, parked his jeep at the back of the field and got out. Tori was already hurrying out too. The rain lashed against them, soaking their hair to their heads in a matter of seconds. They would need to start picking the fruit now. They should have come down earlier rather than waiting for sunset, now they'd left it too late.

They hurried into the field, getting soaked. Now they were closer to the sea the wind was roaring around them. They moved quickly to the coastal side of the field that bordered Orchard Cove. The waves were crashing furiously on the very edge of the field, biting at the leaves of the furthest bushes, and it was only a matter of time before the tide brought the sea straight into the field. Aidan knew it would spread quite some way amongst the berries.

His heart sank. Before the sun set later that night, most of the field would be lost underneath the sea.

'We need to start picking the berries now,' Tori said, realising the severity of the situation.

He stared at her, stunned that she would push aside their argument for the sake of the berries.

'We have two hours before most of this field will be underwater,' Aidan said. 'We can't get them all.'

'We can pick some berries – we will lose some, but we can save some too.'

'There isn't time,' he said, hopelessly.

'So, what, we just give up?' Tori said. 'That's not who I am. I fight for the things that matter, and this is important, this matters.'

He looked at her, caring so much for these damned berries, and he knew she was right.

He turned away to look at the field. If they were quick, they might be able to do one or two rows before they had to abandon their attempts. It wasn't enough.

He turned back to face her. 'We're going to need some help.'

She nodded. 'Start picking, I'll see if I can round up a few hands.'

'They'll be in the village hall, celebrating the love festival.'

'Don't worry, it will be fine, I promise.'

He couldn't believe that, but if they got one or two people to help, they could save a few more berries.

She turned and ran towards the gate at the far end of the field that would take her down a little road towards the main part of the village.

In all the hundreds of years the fruit farm had been in his family they had never lost a harvest yet and he wasn't about to give up now. He turned to the nearest bushes and started picking the berries. He had to trust that she would bring help.

CHAPTER 23

Tori ran as fast as she could to the village hall, the noise of laughter and merriment ringing out loud and clear above the sound of the storm. She just needed to get a few people to help. But who would leave the warmth and fun of the village hall to go out in the wind and rain and pick some berries?

She opened the door and the noise got louder. The whole village was here, laughing, chatting, eating and drinking. This was one of the biggest nights in the Sandcastle Bay social calendar and people were enjoying it to the max. The dance floor was heaving, the villagers doing their best moves as the band played some great seventies song that everyone knew the words to. Families, couples, friends, all dancing together.

Tori looked around desperately for anyone she might recognise, but she didn't really know anyone from Sandcastle Bay. Leo was probably here somewhere with Isla, but he might be outside getting ready for the big fireworks display later. Jamie and Melody were with the puppies at Blossom Cottage. Emily was here somewhere but she was pregnant, Tori couldn't ask her to come out in the rain and cold to pick the berries. Who else could she ask?

But she couldn't let Aidan down.

She hurried towards the stage, pushing her way through the throngs, and quickly climbed the steps, waving to the band to stop, which they did. The crowd fell silent and Tori stared out at the sea of faces. Oh god, what was she doing? No one was going to care.

One of the band handed her a microphone and she put it to her mouth with shaky hands.

'Hello, um, I'm Tori Graham, I'm helping Aidan with the fruit-picking at Heartberry Farm and—'

'We know who you are, love,' an elderly man said from near the front.

'You're Aidan's girlfriend,' a voice piped up from the back and the crowd giggled slightly.

'What's wrong, love?' the first man said.

'The storm has flooded part of the heartberry field and it's going to get worse in the next few hours, and we haven't reached high tide yet. We're going to lose the rest of the heartberry crop tonight.'

She stared at the faces. No one moved, no one said anything.

'We need your help,' Tori said.

They all started talking between themselves and then they all turned away from her. They were just going to carry on with their party and ignore it. No one was going to help, not one person. Emotion clawed at her throat. She had let Aidan down. She had wasted time coming down to get help when she could have stayed to help him pick more berries.

She watched them and as they moved she realised they were making for the door. Her mouth fell open as everyone, every single person, young and old, walked out. Even the band were quickly putting down their instruments and hurrying out into the rain too. They were all going to help. She nearly wept with relief. She quickly put the microphone down and hurried out the door after the departing crowds.

Aidan threw another handful of berries into his punnet and spotted movement at the gate. He saw a few people walking into the field and sighed with relief that Tori had managed to round up a few stragglers to help. They still wouldn't be able to save all the fruit but at least they could pick a bit more now.

He moved back to his jeep to grab a few more boxes but when he turned back he was stunned to see what was clearly the whole village walking into the field. Some were already starting to pick the berries and put them in the boxes or containers they had brought with them. Others were moving towards him to collect a box or punnet from him.

He couldn't help but smile. He might have known that the whole village would come out and help. The heartberries were important to them, but it was more than that. He lived in a part of the world where people cared about each other and wanted to help. He loved it here and, try as he might, he could never imagine living anywhere else.

He handed out baskets and boxes to people, thanking them for coming, and then Tori approached.

'Can you believe this?' she said, looking around in awe as the villagers moved steadily through the rows, clearing the bushes of fruit.

'Actually, I can,' Aidan said. 'Thank you for doing this.'

'We're not out of the woods yet,' Tori said, taking a box from him.

As the wind whipped around them and the rain impossibly seemed to get heavier, Aidan knew she was right. It was going to be a long night.

Tori rested her head against the car window as the jeep bumped along back to the farmhouse after dropping all the berries off in the cold store in one of the barns. She could barely keep her eyes open.

It had been a race against time as every minute that passed the waves had crept over the westerly corner of the field near Orchard Cove and the water had flooded in from the river in the northern corner too. By the end of the night over half the field had disappeared under the water. But although it had taken several hours they had cleared every single berry from every bush.

She was soaked through to the skin, her body was aching, and she felt exhausted from the adrenaline that had coursed through her over the urgency of the night. She just wanted to climb into bed and sleep.

The jeep came to a stop outside the farmhouse and Aidan got out. She tried to summon up enough energy to get out too, but she couldn't even do that.

He opened her car door and, to her surprise, he lifted her into his arms and carried her into the farmhouse. She wrapped her arms around his neck as he kicked the farmhouse door closed behind him and carried her upstairs. He sat her down on the bed and then removed her wellies and socks, which were soaked through. He quickly undressed her and then started undressing himself.

'Let's take a shower,' he offered out his hand.

She eyed the bed; it looked so warm and inviting.

'We need to get you warm first,' Aidan said.

She nodded. He was right, she was cold.

She took his hand and he led her into the bathroom, turning the shower on. When it was hot enough, he tugged her under the spray with him, wrapping his arms around her and holding her tightly against his chest, leaning his head on top of hers as the hot water poured over them.

He held her there in his arms for the longest time. God, she was going to miss him so much.

As she had been picking the berries that night, she had decided she had to bring this to a close now before she fell even further in love with him. But hell, if it was going to come to an end, she was damned well going to enjoy being with him one more time.

Aidan leaned round her and turned the water off. He grabbed a towel and wrapped it round her, quickly towelled himself dry and then sweetly scooped her up and carried her back to the bed.

'I'm going to go home tomorrow,' Tori said, quietly. 'All the berries are picked now, there's no reason for me to stay.'

He stared at her for a moment then leaned over and kissed her.

She closed her eyes and kissed him back. He rolled her onto her back, kissing her softly and gently. His hands stroked across her body, caressing her, adoring her. She couldn't help tears escaping her eyes. He leaned back slightly and kissed the tears from her cheeks.

He leaned over to the drawers and grabbed a condom and a few moments later he was inside her. He lay down on top of her, his arms either side of her head, trapping her in that wonderful moment, so it was just the two of them, the world fading away. She wrapped her arms and legs around him, holding him close. He was moving slowly, staring down at her.

She moved her hand to his face. 'I love you.'

He paused for a moment, his eyes clouding with concern.

She ran her fingers over his lips and he kissed the tips. 'I know you don't feel the same way and it's OK, but I do love you.'

He kissed her hard, and they found their high together.

He collapsed on top of her, his head buried against her neck as he tried to catch his breath. She stroked the back of his neck and closed her eyes, safe in his arms, at least for now, then drifted off to sleep.

CHAPTER 24

Tori looked down at a sleeping Aidan as she buttoned up her shirt. It was still early but she wanted to be out of there before he woke. They'd had fun and she would never regret that. She couldn't be angry at him just because he didn't feel the same way. But it was better to walk away now, there was no point in prolonging the agony. Although she didn't think this pain in her chest could get any worse.

She noticed the sheets of coloured paper on top of the drawers that he had obviously been using to make the paper flowers for her.

She picked up a red sheet and quickly folded it to make a paper heart, she laid it on the pillow next to him, then placed a gentle kiss on his cheek. He smiled in his sleep and her heart ached.

She looked around the room to make sure she had everything and then, giving one last look at Aidan, she left the room. She'd only made it to the front door before the tears spilled over her cheeks.

Tori walked back down the drive and into Blossom Cottage. Melody and Jamie were sitting together on the sofa, feeding the puppies and laughing and chatting. She really didn't want to talk to anyone right now, but she needed to pack and leave, and she would need to explain to Melody why she was leaving early.

Melody looked up at her as she walked in, a huge smile on her face, which quickly fell from her lips.

'Oh god, what's wrong?' she said.

Tori gestured helplessly over her shoulder, trying to find the words. 'It's over between me and Aidan.'

The words made her choke and tears filled her eyes again.

Melody leapt up, handing her puppy to Jamie and quickly enveloping Tori in a giant hug.

Tori wrapped her arms around her and cried into her shoulder.

Melody brought her to the sofa and sat Tori down between her and Jamie.

'What happened?' Jamie said.

'He's scared of getting hurt again,' Tori said, wiping the tears away only for them to be replaced with more. 'He cares about me, but he's not willing to take a risk.'

They were silent for a moment and Jamie, clearly not knowing what to do or say to make the situation better, handed her a puppy which in some small way helped. Tori snuggled it against her chest, burying her face into its warm fur.

'Was this to do with what I said?' Jamie said.

'No, we are totally capable of screwing this up on our own, we don't need any help,' Tori said.

'He's crazy about you, anyone can see that. I was wrong about that. There is nothing casual about the way he looks at you,' Jamie said.

'It's not enough though.'

'Do you like him?' Melody asked.

Tori nodded. 'I've fallen in love with him.'

Melody took a little intake of breath, and despite everything let out a tiny squeal of excitement. She really couldn't help herself.

'And did you tell him that?'

'Yes, he didn't say it back.'

'Perhaps he just needs more time, you guys haven't known each other long,' Jamie said.

'I'm not expecting marriage and happy ever afters. I thought I might rent a house here for a few months, see if we actually have something. He didn't even want to do that.'

God, saying it out loud was completely heartbreaking. Aidan didn't want anything more from her than sex. That's what it had been all along.

They fell into silence. There really wasn't anything to say.

'The man's an idiot,' Jamie said, and Tori smiled despite everything. 'You have made him happier over the last few days than I've ever seen him. I can't believe he would throw that away.'

'I get it, he's scared. I've been there. Love hurts and he's trying to protect himself. I'm not worth the risk.'

'Idiot,' Jamie muttered, loyally.

Tori sighed and turned to Melody. 'I need to go, I'm sorry. I know I was due to stay for another week, but I just can't stay here and see him every day, it hurts too much.'

To her surprise, Melody nodded with understanding. 'I know, it's OK.'

'Why don't we arrange for a week's holiday somewhere soon? We could get a cottage, maybe in the Cotswolds, just me, you, Isla and Elliot.'

'I'd really like that.'

Tori hugged her and then went upstairs to pack.

She had just lifted the suitcase onto the bed when there was a big crash downstairs, which sounded like the front door had been slammed open.

There were raised voices and feet thundering on the stairs and then suddenly Aidan was standing in her bedroom, staring at her.

His eyes fell on the suitcase.

'You're really leaving?'

'Yes.'

He looked pained. 'Why?'

She looked at him incredulously. 'You know why.'

'You said you loved me.'

'Yes, you never said it back,' Tori said, tears choking her voice.

'I did. I told you I loved you, straight after we made love, I said I loved you and that I had never felt this way about anyone before which was what made it so scary, because I knew if I lost you it would hurt even more.'

She stared at him, her heart thundering in her chest. 'Wait, what? You never said those things.'

'I did. You fell asleep. I didn't realise when I was giving my big speech, I was too busy kissing you all over. I was hopeful you had heard some of it, you went to sleep with this big smile on your face. And then I wake up this morning and you'd gone, leaving only your heart behind.' He had the paper heart in his hand.

'I…' Tori had no words, tears filling her eyes again. 'You love me?'

He sighed and moved closer, cupping her face with his large gentle hands.

'I love you. I've fallen head over heels in love with you, your kindness, your passion, the way you make me laugh. I love all those things. I want to make a future with you.'

'Oh,' Tori said lamely, tears coursing down her cheeks.

'I'm sorry I was an ass, I was scared, and I know how hard it was for you to put your heart out there like that and even harder that it was rejected.' He handed her the paper heart and as she took it she realised it had plasters over it. She laughed. 'I want to take care of your heart from now on, I want to heal it of all its cuts and bruises.'

'And I want to help heal yours,' Tori said, leaning forward and placing a kiss over his heart. 'And we'll go slowly. I can get a cottage down here. We don't have to rush anything.'

He smiled. 'I love you, I want you with me at Heartberry Farm, that's where you belong. I realised that last night, watching you work so damned hard to save the berries in the pouring rain, running backwards and forwards, taking the full baskets from people, replacing them with empty ones, working so well with the people of the village. You belong here, and I was an idiot to doubt that.'

Her heart soared. 'I belong with you, I love you. Wherever you are, that's where I belong.'

He kissed her, wrapping his arms around her and lifting her against him. She couldn't help but smile as she kissed him back.

He lowered her to the bed, the kiss continuing.

'Um, Aidan, Tori. We're going to go,' Jamie called up the stairs, awkwardly. Tori laughed against Aidan's lips as Aidan sighed. They'd both forgotten that Jamie and Melody were there.

'OK,' Aidan said.

He kissed her again.

'We've fed the puppies,' Jamie said, and Tori heard Melody giggle.

'OK, thanks,' Aidan said, kissing her again.

'And, umm, they'll need feeding again in two hours, so, um, don't be too long, umm… doing what you're doing,' Jamie said, and Melody's giggles got louder.

'OK!' Aidan said, his voice getting louder, laced with irritation.

'And Beauty and Beast have already been fed too,' Jamie said, and Tori got the impression he was now doing this deliberately.

'Get out,' Aidan said, and Tori laughed.

They heard the door close below them and Aidan sighed with relief.

'I hate my brother.'

'I love him. I love all your crazy family.'

'Good job too, because they'll be your family soon enough.'

She smiled at that thought. 'When we get married, we can have Dobby as the ring bearer.'

He laughed. 'Agatha got it right for once, she saw our fate even before we saw it.'

'I might have to thank her for the nudge,' Tori said.

'Oh, don't do that, she'll be smug enough when we tell her we're together.'

Tori laughed, and he kissed her. She wrapped her arms around him and kissed him back.

As he moved his mouth to her neck, she glanced out the window at the glittering sea of Sandcastle Bay.

It was funny how fate worked. It might look like it was against her sometimes but also it had a canny knack of giving her exactly what she needed. Fate had given her Matthew, who had gifted her strength and courage to give love a chance after her heart had been bruised so badly. It had led her to Leo who had encouraged her to take the fun path, to take a risk. And those roads had led her to Aidan, the man she loved with everything she had. Right then, she couldn't be happier with fate. Following the fun path was definitely the way forward from now on and it looked like she would have some gorgeous company on her journey.

The End

A LETTER FROM HOLLY

Thank you so much for reading *The Holiday Cottage by the Sea*, I had so much fun creating this story and I hope you enjoyed reading it as much as I enjoyed writing it.

One of the best parts of writing comes from seeing the reaction from readers. Did it make you smile or laugh, did it make you cry, hopefully happy tears? Did you fall in love with Tori and Aidan as much as I did? Did you like the beautiful Sandcastle Bay? If you enjoyed the story, I would absolutely love it if you could leave a short review. Getting feedback from readers is amazing and it also helps to persuade other readers to pick up one of my books for the first time.

If you loved the other characters in this story, Jamie and Melody's story can be found in *The Cottage on Sunshine Beach*.

Thank you for reading and I hope you all have a wonderful, sparkly summer.

Love Holly x

HollyMartinAuthor

@HollyMAuthor

hollymartinwriter.wordpress.com

ACKNOWLEDGEMENTS

To my family, my mom, my biggest fan, who reads every word I have written a hundred times over and loves it every single time, my dad, my brother Lee and my sister-in-law Julie, for your support, love, encouragement and endless excitement for my stories.

For my twinnie, the gorgeous Aven Ellis for just being my wonderful friend, for your endless support, for cheering me on, for reading my stories and telling me what works and what doesn't and for keeping me entertained with wonderful stories and pictures of hot men. I love you dearly.

To my friends Gareth, Mandie, Angie, Jac, Verity and Jodie who listen to me talk about my books endlessly and get excited about it every single time.

For Sharon Sant for just being there always and your wonderful friendship.

To my wonderful agent Madeleine Milburn and Hayley Steed for just being amazing and fighting my corner and for your unending patience with my constant questions.

To my lovely editor Natasha Harding for being so supportive and being a pleasure to work with. To my structural editor Celine Kelly for helping to make this book so much better, my copy editor Rhian for doing such a good job at spotting any issues or typos and Loma for giving it a final read through. Thank you to Kim Nash for the tireless promoting, tweeting and general cheerleading. Thank you to all the other wonderful people at Bookouture; Oliver Rhodes, the editing team and the wonderful designers who created this absolutely gorgeous cover.

To the CASG, the best writing group in the world, you wonderful talented supportive bunch of authors, I feel very blessed to know you all, you guys are the very best.

To the wonderful Bookouture authors for all your encouragement and support.

To all the wonderful bloggers for your tweets, retweets, facebook posts, tireless promotions, support, encouragement and endless enthusiasm. You guys are amazing and I couldn't do this journey without you.

To Andy Symanowski who gave me loads of advice about animation and patiently answered all of my questions.

To the lovely Tori Graham who won a character named after her in a charity auction after paying a huge and generous sum. I hope you like your namesake.

To anyone who has read my book and taken the time to tell me you've enjoyed it or wrote a review, thank you so much.

Thank you, I love you all.

Read on for the beginning of Holly's novel,
The Summer at Buttercup Beach

CHAPTER 1

Freya Greene stared in wonder at the glorious sight of Rome Lancaster naked from the waist up. They were experiencing the first really hot day of the year with temperatures apparently hotter than Miami. Freya spent quite a bit of time working outside during the course of her job, and she loved it, but even she hadn't been looking forward to working outside in such sweltering conditions today. Now, however, she had changed her mind.

Freya and Rome had been working alongside each other all morning on the roof of a three-storey townhouse overlooking Buttercup Beach. They were replacing the old skylight with one of Rome's beautiful stained glass creations. They had chatted, laughed as they always did, and then suddenly Rome had wiped the sweat off his head and stripped off his t-shirt without any kind of warning. After almost two years of working alongside him, she had seen him topless before, but not as many times as she would like. And as winter had dragged on into a relatively cool spring, his wonderful body had been well and truly kept under wraps. Now it was out for her to enjoy.

He was so broad and muscular, but not from working out in a gym, just years of hard labour instead. His stomach was toned and showed the faint lines of a six-pack. His chest was smooth and hairless though there was a thin trail of dark hair leading from his belly button that disappeared into his shorts. His arms were so strong. Safe. With his dark, curly hair, soft grey eyes and dark stubble that covered his jaw, he was beautiful.

She felt a bit bad ogling her best friend like this, but if his fifty-six thousand followers on Instagram could enjoy his body then it didn't hurt to look for a few seconds surely.

Except it had been a good minute, maybe two, and to her horror she realised that Rome had noticed her staring.

Embarrassed, she took a step back, and toppled straight off the roof.

She plummeted head first down the side of the building and let out an ear-piercing scream, but she fell only a few feet before the safety harness she was wearing kicked in and she was jerked to a halt. Rome had made a big fuss about her wearing one and though at the time she hadn't thought it was necessary, right now she had never been so grateful for his overprotectiveness.

She swung like a pendulum for a few seconds, her heart racing in her chest as she tried to grab onto the scaffolding to pull herself back up, but it was just out of her reach and the swinging motion of her body made it even more difficult.

Rome was suddenly there, leaping onto the scaffolding from the roof, and as she swung back towards him he wrapped his arms round her back and dragged her up. She reached out to grab him too, wrapping her arms round him, which made it even more awkward for him, and as he pulled her to safety, he stumbled back himself and hit the platform with her lying on his chest, his arms tight around her.

For a few seconds, Freya felt only relief, her body roaring with adrenaline as she clung to him, but then she realised her cheek was resting on his warm bare chest; how fantastic he smelt, that gorgeous tang of the ocean, coupled with that wonderful clean sandalwood smell. For a brief moment, she closed her eyes and relished in the feel of lying on his chest, feeling his heart hammering against her cheek and how utterly right it felt to have his arms wrapped round her.

'Jesus Christ, you scared the crap out of me,' Rome said, shattering her moment of bliss. 'What the hell were you doing just staring into space? You should have been paying more attention.'

He slid his hand up her back to cup her neck and all words she had wanted to say to defend herself stalled in her throat. It was such an unconscious gesture, but for her it meant the world.

'It was just the heat,' Freya said, lamely, and then winced. She was not a girl who fainted in the heat and telling Rome that the hot weather had made her feel funny made her cringe.

'It is getting hot up here,' Rome admitted, begrudgingly. 'Maybe we should take a break for a little while. Get some lunch, come back to it this afternoon when it gets a bit cooler.'

'Sounds good,' Freya said, though she made no attempt to move and Rome didn't relinquish his hold on her either. She wondered, not for the first time, whether he was starting to have feelings for her too. There had been many such gestures over the last few months and more frequently over the last few weeks: little looks, comments, touches. She was so confused by it all. One minute she was convinced he had feelings for her and the very next it seemed those feelings weren't there at all, almost as if he had simply flicked a switch and turned them off. If only she had that luxury of turning off her inappropriate feelings for her best friend.

In an attempt to distract herself from how wonderful it felt to be lying on Rome's chest, she shifted her attention to the view. From up here she could see almost the whole of Hope Island, the tiny town with its cute little shops, cafés and windy lanes and almost all of the seven hundred and eighty nine houses. She smiled to herself at that little factoid Rome had told her and the fact that she had remembered it. Stretching out almost the entire length of the island was Buttercup Beach with its golden sands and crystal blue waters and beyond that, out in the sea were the shadows of the other Scilly Isles. Hope Island was the hilliest of all the islands and even though it was the most westerly, on a clear day you could even see the cliffs and hills of Land's End. She squinted at the horizon which was a smudge of purple haze and tried really hard not to focus on the feel of Rome's fingers at the back of her neck.

Eventually, when her heart had slowed and she had probably laid on him for a lot longer than was socially acceptable in these circumstances, Freya lifted her head to look at him.

'Thank you for saving me.'

'Well the harness did that, I just made a fumbled attempt to grab you and ended up falling on my arse. Let's go get something to eat.'

Freya nodded and carefully climbed off him and then stood up. He stood up too, towering over her.

'Are you OK? Are you hurt?' he asked, his hand on her shoulder, his touch searing against her skin.

'No, I'm fine. A little shaken but I'm OK.'

'A little shaken? I don't think my heart will stop pounding for several hours yet.' He leaned forward and detached her harness from the roof, reattaching it to the scaffolding so she could climb down. It was something she was perfectly capable of doing herself but she sensed he was in protective mode now and probably wouldn't even allow her back on the roof later that afternoon, or at least not unless she was attached to two or three safety ropes just in case.

He swung himself over the side of the scaffolding to the ladder, moved down a few steps and then waited for her, clearly wanting to make sure she could manage the ladder without hurtling to her death. She smiled at him, wanting to take care of her. Even though she hated to play the damsel in distress, there was something wonderful about him looking out for her like this.

She climbed onto the ladder with ease and, with him close behind her, they both made their way down the ladder.

Once down on the ground she turned to face him and saw his eyes were still shadowed with concern.

'See, I didn't die.'

'Not from lack of trying,' Rome grumbled, unhooking them both from the scaffolding.

She watched as he pulled his t-shirt back on and then wandered over to the van to put away their tools and lock it up. Not that anything would go missing parked in the private driveway of the house. It was very unlikely that anything would go missing if the van was left wide open in the middle of the town. Hope Island just wasn't that sort of place. There really was no crime on the island, beyond the occasional teenager getting a bit drunk and disorderly, the crime rate was almost non-existent. Everyone looked out for each other here. It was one of the things that Freya loved about the place.

Once the van was secured, Freya and Rome walked down the drive and headed towards the high street, through the tiny lanes, past the whitewashed cottages with blue shutters or houses painted in bright colours, the little shops that sold cute seaside paraphernalia and Rosa's where they'd end up two or three times a week for coffee, great food and wonderful chat with her friends.

'What were you thinking about up there?' Rome gestured back to the roof. 'You were standing there with this big smile on your face. You looked so happy there for a while, before you tried to kill yourself. I thought that whatever it was that had made you so happy, I wanted some of it too.'

But that was the problem. He *didn't* want it. Freya was in love with her best friend and it was that feeling that made her so happy. Sometimes it was hell, but a lot of the time, working with Rome, talking to him, spending time with him, was complete heaven. But despite what he'd just said, he didn't want that kind of happiness, he wasn't looking for love.

After his fiancée had died six years before, he had shut himself off from ever finding love again.

That didn't stop him dating though. There had been too many women to count over the years. And after his mini brush with fame the year before, the queue of women wanting a piece of him had got even longer. But not once had anything ever happened between Freya and him. Though if he wasn't attracted to her, why did she keep catching him staring at her in ways that went far beyond anything that could be classed as friendly?

She knew she wasn't a typical girly girl. She rarely wore a dress, preferring jeans and shirts. She lived in her Timberland boots. Her blonde hair was short, cut in an elfin style and streaked with blue, and she had a tiny nose piercing. If Rome's type was girly and feminine then she didn't stand a chance.

She realised he was still waiting for an answer. 'Just... excited to see the window when it's in. You've worked so hard on this one and I can't wait to see the owners' faces when they see it.'

He smiled, swinging his arm round her shoulders in a way that was more brotherly than anything else. 'I love how passionate you are about our company. You've always been my little cheerleader. The company wouldn't be anywhere near as successful if it wasn't for you.'

'You have no idea how crazy talented you are, the success is down to you, not me,' Freya protested.

'The work you've been doing over the last few months has been outstanding,' Rome insisted. 'I've been so impressed with how quickly you've picked it all up. You really do have a natural talent for this stuff. The success is ours; don't doubt yourself.'

'Does that mean you've forgiven me for posting that video on Twitter?'

He laughed and shook his head. 'I'm never forgiving you for that.'

When she'd started working for him, she'd wanted to increase his social media presence. He'd had no interest in it so she had taken care of it. Every day she would post a picture of one of his stained glass pieces or a work in progress on Instagram, Twitter or Facebook and after a while it started to have an impact. The tweets would get retweeted, the Facebook posts would be shared and they'd started to see a real increase in the number of enquiries and sales. And then, the year before, she had posted a mini video of Rome working on a piece. It had been a hot day and he'd been working topless but Freya had mainly wanted people to see a different side to the company, to see how a piece was made. She hadn't expected the reaction that it got. Within twenty-four hours, it had been retweeted over four thousand times. The comments hadn't been about the piece he had been working on or the beauty of the stained glass as was usually the case, they'd all been about him and most of them were really X-rated. Freya had been horrified and knew that Rome would be furious so she hadn't told him. But the sales over the next few days went through the roof and in the end she'd had to admit the truth.

He'd found it hard to believe that one fifteen-second video of him half-naked would have such an impact on sales. So to prove it to him she took a photo of him, topless, holding one of his stained glass panels. The piece had sold within minutes of her posting it on Instagram and by the end of the day they had received orders for fifty more. In the next six months, profits for Through the Looking Glass had gone up by over a hundred percent.

Rome had become an mini internet sensation and, while he thought the whole thing was ridiculous and insisted that most of the time she stick to posting pictures of the pieces and not him, she had compromised that she'd post pictures or videos of him once a week under the hashtag, 'Feel Good Friday'. She had to give the fans what they wanted.

They walked into Pots and Paints, the little pottery painting café owned by Eden, Rome's sister and Freya's best friend. They seemed to end up there for lunch most days. Eden would quite often join them if she wasn't too busy but as the long summer school holidays had just started, she had been rushed off her feet the last few days.

Eden waved at them as they came in and then turned her attention back to some children as she showed them how to use the templates on the side of the mugs they were painting.

Rome walked behind the counter, served two people who were waiting for coffees and then turned his attention to Freya. 'What would you like to eat?'

She smiled at how easily he switched from working on a roof, to patiently teaching her how to work with stained glass, to serving behind the counter at his sister's café. Rome was solid, dependable and generous with his time and money. Some of the many things she loved about him.

'That salmon sandwich looks good.'

Rome nodded and slipped it onto a plate for her before grabbing a bacon and brie sandwich for himself and putting it into the sandwich toaster. He proceeded to make a strawberry milkshake for her and a mango smoothie for himself and then pulled out a twenty-pound note from his pocket and put it in the till, even though Freya knew that was way too much to cover the cost of the lunch, especially when Eden insisted on feeding them for free.

Eden joined him behind the counter. 'Did you just pay for that?'

'Of course not; I know you don't like me paying for my lunch.'

'You bought this place for me, that gives you free lunch and cakes for the rest of your life.'

'I know, which is why I always come in here. I'm not going to turn down free food. Is Clare still on holiday?'

Freya smiled at how quickly he had changed the subject.

'Yes, but she's back next week,' Eden sighed. 'Mum is going to help me for a few days, though I know she doesn't really have time.'

'Maybe Dougie can give you a hand,' Rome said, nonchalantly, though Freya knew there was nothing casual about that remark. Eden had fallen in love with Dougie, who had been her childhood best friend when they were teenagers. And then he'd emigrated to America with his parents. Despite being thousands of miles apart, they'd stayed in touch and he visited regularly and that love Eden had felt for him had never gone away. He was supposed to be moving back to the island in the next few months, something that Eden didn't know whether to be delighted or upset about. 'When does he get here?' Rome asked.

'The weekend.' Eden couldn't hide her grin at the prospect of him coming. 'But he won't have time to help me. He's only here for two weeks and he'll be out looking at houses every day. Anyway, I'm doing OK. How are you getting on at Oakwood House?'

'Fine, we'll be done today. That's if Freya doesn't kill herself first,' Rome said, pointedly. Clearly he wasn't going to let it go.

Freya rolled her eyes and took her sandwich and milkshake and went and sat down in the window while Rome served up his toastie and gave Eden a rundown of how Freya had thrown herself off the roof. He came and joined her a few minutes later.

He took a bite of his sandwich and glanced out the window at the little town square and the multi-coloured bunting that fluttered in the gentle sea breeze.

'So tomorrow is two years since you came to work for me,' Rome said and took another bite of his sandwich.

She watched him in surprise. She hadn't expected him to remember the date. She knew it was exactly two years. The date had been etched on her memory as it was the day she had been supposed to get married to Jake.

After finding her fiancé in the throes of passion with Lizzie, his best friend, two days before the wedding, Freya had fled the little village she had lived in with her fiancé and ended up going on her honeymoon alone, heading to the Scilly Isles where she had spent many weeks on childhood holidays.

On the day that was supposed to be her wedding day, she had headed over to Hope Island on a day trip, wondering what she was going to do with her life. She had no home to return to, no job as she had worked with her fiancé, no friends because all her friends were his friends and no idea what she was going to do next. All she did know was that she was never going to let herself get into that situation again, where her whole life had centred around the man she loved.

She had wandered into Rome's shop and been struck by the complete beauty of his stained glass panels, pictures, mirrors, lamps and boxes. She remembered the sun glinting off the coloured glass in a way that seemed ethereal and magical, as if she had stepped into a different land. She had also been struck with what a state the studio was in, mirrors stacked behind lamps, panels upside down, all the stock in some kind of higgledy-piggledy mess. Rome hadn't even noticed she was there, so intent on his work at the back of the shop that she had quietly wandered deeper between the shelves, admiring each piece.

Then he'd got up and left the studio, unwittingly locking her inside. When he came back several hours later, he'd found the shop had been completely reorganised, with definite sections for each of the products, which were now all displayed beautifully in the best places to catch the light. He had jokingly offered her a job and she had taken it, even though it wasn't really on offer. Unable to backtrack, Rome had offered her a few hours a week, which had quickly extended to a full-time job. She spent the night in the empty flat above the shop since she'd already missed the last ferry off the island and never left. She quickly fell in love with the beauty of the island, the friendliness of the islanders and just how peaceful the place was. Since then, not only had Rome become her boss, he had taught her everything he knew about stained glass. But more than that, he'd become her best friend. He had saved her in more ways than one.

'*I* knew it was two years, I just didn't expect you to remember our anniversary,' Freya teased.

'I first met you on the fourth anniversary of Paige's death. Sadly, I don't think I'll ever forget that date.'

Freya's smile fell from her face. 'Oh God, Rome, I'm so sorry. I never knew that date was so significant to you.'

He shook his head. 'Don't be sorry. It's fine. We were only together eighteen months, she passed away six years ago. I will always miss her and I think I will always carry a piece of her in here but I promise I'm not about to break down in tears because the anniversary of her death is tomorrow. I remember the day me and you met because Paige and I once had a jokey conversation about what we would do if the other died. Paige told me that she would expect me to grieve for her for a certain amount of time and then I had to move on, find someone else, fall in love again. I asked her how long would she expect me to grieve over her and she told me that as she was so brilliant and sexy and funny then four years should do it.'

Freya smiled. She'd never met Paige but, from what she'd heard, she'd been sweet, kind and had a brilliant sense of humour.

'That day you walked into my shop, I'd been down at the graveyard and I told her that even though it had been four years, I still wasn't over her. That nothing had changed, that it still hurt. Every day I'd wake up in our bed and I'd miss her. I'd go to work alone and sit in my studio and I couldn't seem to snap out of it. I… slept with far too many women in an attempt to move on but none of it made any difference. I told her something needed to change and I couldn't see what to do about it. Then I got back to my studio and my whole life changed. There you were, dusting my shelves, rearranging my shop and eating my sandwich.'

Freya laughed. 'I was hungry.'

'I didn't realise it at the time, but you were the change I needed. I looked forward to coming to work, the nights that you came round to my house for dinner made me feel alive again. You've turned my business around, made it a huge success, and I will forever be grateful that I locked you in my studio that day. You make me laugh so much and for four years I never laughed at all. You literally saved me.'

Freya swallowed the lump in her throat, not wanting to tell him that she felt the same way. Was this his way of finally telling her he had feelings for her too? She thought back to the way he had held her after she had fallen off the roof. She remembered when he had cancelled a date the week before so he could look after her when she was ill. In fact, the number of women he dated had been getting fewer and fewer lately; he seemingly preferred to spend time with her instead. Was he finally falling in love with her too? Freya had never imagined that he would feel the same way before but now... Was he trying to tell her he loved her?

'I think we should go out tomorrow to celebrate,' Rome said. 'I have a question I want to ask you and I'd like to do it over a nice meal and a bottle of wine. Will you join me at Envy tomorrow?'

Envy was her favourite restaurant on the island; the food was amazing, the atmosphere was cool, all black and silver and chic, and she always felt like she was at some exclusive restaurant in London every time she went there, instead of the furthest corner of the Scilly Isles.

'I'd love to,' Freya said, unable to keep the excited tremor from her voice.

He smiled. 'Good.'

CHAPTER 2

'So I hear you nearly died today?' Bella, Rome's youngest sister, said as she came back from the kitchen with bowls of ice cream for the three of them. She passed one each to Eden and Freya and sat back down on the sofa.

Freya laughed. 'I did not nearly die.'

She took a big spoonful and let the creamy flavour melt on her tongue.

'The way I heard it was that Rome saved your life,' Bella giggled.

Freya knew what the islanders were like. If there was any kind of gossip floating about, it had already been discussed, dissected, embellished and exaggerated by the time you heard about it. A twenty-inch fish that had been caught in the harbour in the morning had already tripled in size by the time the fishermen had left the pub that same night. It was something that Freya would never get used to. She loved it here on Hope Island and never wanted to leave, but the fact that everyone knew each other's business and felt they were entitled to an opinion on it was something that Freya was not entirely comfortable with.

They were sitting in Eden's tiny cottage having spent the evening chatting and eating pizza. She adored Bella and Eden and she loved how easily the Lancaster family had adopted her as their own. Rome had given her so much more than a job the day they'd first met, he had given her a home, friendship and a family.

'I also heard that Rome is taking you out for dinner tomorrow night,' Eden said, her eyes lighting up with happiness.

Freya choked on her ice cream. 'How on earth did you hear that?'

'Barbara Copperthwaite was sitting at the next table to you two at lunch and she heard him say he wanted to take you to Envy. She said it sounded very romantic.'

Freya sighed. Bella and Eden knew about her inappropriate crush on their brother. She didn't think they knew quite how deeply her feelings ran but she knew they would like nothing more than to see them together.

'It's not like that. Well honestly, I don't know what to think. He said the sweetest things to me over lunch, said how I had changed his life and how grateful he was for me and I got the sense he was talking about more than just work. And I got all excited and thought that perhaps he had feelings for me too, but then we spent the rest of the afternoon as normal, just chatting and laughing and he showed no signs at all of being head over heels in love with me.'

'He adores you,' Eden said. 'And you did change his life. He spent the four years after Paige died barely existing. He moved on autopilot. You changed all that.'

Bella nodded, swallowing a spoonful of ice cream. 'He doesn't have what he has with you with anyone else. He didn't even have that with Paige.'

'He didn't? It sounds like they were very much in love.'

'Maybe they were. But they didn't have that friendship as a base. They had passion and lust. Theirs was a whirlwind affair and I don't honestly know if it would have lasted. They met, fell in love, he proposed after one month,' Eden said.

'A *month*?' Freya was stunned. She knew that things had moved quickly for Rome and Paige but proposing after a month was crazy. But was it? She had fallen in love with Rome within the first few days of meeting him. Maybe for some people you just know. Rome clearly did.

'He was young and they had that crazy, can't keep their hands off each other kind of love,' Bella said.

'You mean like you and Isaac,' Freya teased.

Bella blushed and Freya laughed, knowing that Bella could hardly deny it. They had been together only for a few months but to say their relationship was passionate was an understatement.

'Yes, I guess they were like me and Isaac in the beginning. They had one month together where they saw each other every day, that wonderful honeymoon period where everything is perfect, and then she went off to work in London supposedly for one year but it ended up being a bit longer. So he proposed to her before she left. I think he was scared that she would go off to London and forget all about him. Credit to them both, they kept the relationship going. He'd go up there, she'd come back here on a regular basis. But whenever they'd meet up they would just spend the weekend having sex before returning back to their respective jobs and homes on Monday morning. This kept going for eighteen months before she sadly died in that terrible accident. They never had a proper relationship, never really had the time to get to know each other properly. Never became friends like you and Rome. What you two have is really special. You work with each other, you spend all your spare time together, maybe this could be the start of something more for you two. What better way to start a relationship than two years of being friends?'

Freya stared at her bowl, at the puddle of ice cream as it slowly melted. There was nothing she wanted more than for Rome to fall in love with her too. She had a great job, brilliant friends and lived in the most beautiful place in the world, but her life was missing love and it wasn't just love with anyone she wanted, it was Rome. He was the missing piece that didn't seem like it would ever be filled.

'But he has to want that too and I really don't think he is looking for love,' Freya said.

'I think he is,' Eden said, finishing off the last of her ice cream. 'A few months ago we were talking about love and relationships and he said that, although he preferred to only have casual relationships with women because then he could never get hurt, he said he missed the companionship and intimacy of being in a real relationship. You know what he listed as things that he wanted in a real relationship? Those long, stay-up-late-into-the-night conversations, laughing hard with someone, being with someone you know inside and out. You have all those things and my guess is he's starting to realise that.'

Freya's heart bloomed with hope. Was that really what tomorrow night was going to be about? Could it be the start of a beautiful relationship? She allowed herself to dream for a moment. She imagined him holding her hand and telling her he was in love with her, that he'd always been in love with her. And then they'd kiss. Their first kiss. Would that happen at the restaurant or would they wait until they went back to his place or hers? What would it be like to kiss Rome? Would it be hard and passionate or slow and gentle? Would the kiss lead to something more? The thought of making love to him filled her with so much joy and nerves and excited anticipation all at once. She could be making love to Rome Lancaster this time tomorrow night. OK, maybe that was moving a bit too quickly. If he wanted to date then he might want to take things slowly. But at least they might share a kiss.

Bella took her hand. 'I think Eden's right. This time last year he was going out with a different woman every week. These last few months I could probably count the women he has dated on one hand. And I think it's because no one fulfils what he is looking for like you do. No one makes him laugh like you do. He can't talk for hours with anyone like he does with you. You are everything he needs and wants. My heart says he is in love with you but he just doesn't realise it yet. So if he does ask you out tomorrow night, then take things slowly. He hasn't been in a proper relationship with someone for years and I don't honestly think you could call what he had with Paige a proper relationship either so... be patient with him.'

Freya nodded. She could do that. If he asked her out, she was happy to give him all the time in the world to get used to the idea of being in a relationship again. She would go as slow as he needed.

'You're staying in the same room as him at the Under the Sea carnival next week, aren't you?' Eden asked.

Freya nodded. The Under the Sea carnival happened every year in Penzance with a float to represent every town or village in Cornwall. This year's float from Hope Island had been decked out with dolphins and waves made entirely from her and Rome's glass work so they were going along to help oversee their float in the parade. They had both worked so hard to get the decorations for the float ready. Rome had given her free rein over how she wanted to design the dolphins and she had utilised all the skills he had taught her over the last few years to showcase what she could do. She was so proud of how it had turned out. The carnival was something she was really excited to be a part of.

'Maybe something might happen between you then,' Eden said, her eyebrows wiggling mischievously.

'It was the only room left, and it's a twin. Hardly romantic,' Freya protested, not wanting her heart to get too carried away. She had been looking forward to the Under the Sea carnival for weeks and going away together felt very romantic, even if it wasn't like that. She'd been looking forward to it even more since she'd found out she'd be sharing a room with him. Even though she'd repeatedly told herself it was just work and that they were just friends, it didn't seem to be sinking in.

'The fireworks after the carnival, the sea views from the hotel window, both of you walking around in your pyjamas, or the lack of them. It could be very romantic,' Eden said, dreamily.

'Take protection, just in case,' Bella said, practically. 'You don't want to get pregnant the first time you make love to him.'

Freya cursed the sudden wonderful image of her holding a tiny baby with black curly hair and grey eyes. Talk about not getting too carried away.

'I'm on the pill anyway, so no babies happening here,' Freya said as the image dissolved in her mind.

Just then there was a knock on the door and Bella shot up as if she'd been electrocuted.

'That will be Isaac,' Bella said excitedly, rushing to the door. She answered it and threw her arms around him as if it had been weeks since she had last seen him, not just a few hours. He kissed her briefly, wrapping his arms around her and hugging her tight.

'Hello, beautiful. Did you have a good night?' he said, quietly, staring down at Bella with complete adoration in his eyes.

Bella nodded. 'Always do with these two lovely ladies.'

Isaac tore his eyes away from Bella and smiled at Eden and Freya. 'Evening, ladies.'

Freya waved and Eden got up to give him a hug. Bella was already pulling her jacket on as she came over and gave Freya a kiss on the cheek. 'Let me know how it goes tomorrow.'

Freya nodded.

Bella hugged Eden and then she and Isaac left.

Eden came and sat down on the sofa next to Freya as they watched Isaac and Bella outside. Isaac said something to make Bella laugh and then he kissed her as if she was the air he needed to breathe.

Freya couldn't take her eyes off them. She had never seen two people so completely and utterly in love as Bella and Isaac.

When they parted, he placed a kiss on her forehead and then took her hand and led her off home.

'God, I want what they have,' Freya said.

Eden sighed next to her. 'Me too.'

Join us at

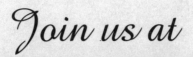

The Little Book Café

For competitions galore,
exclusive interviews with our lovely
Sphere authors, chat about
all the latest books
and much, much more.

Follow us on Twitter at
@littlebookcafe

Subscribe to our newsletter and
Like us at /thelittlebookcafe

Read. Love. Share.